More Praise for

"[Wood] is able to employ her gi
ing to probe not only what make
also focus on details that bring th

—*Amarillo Globe News*

"Poignant . . . The story will bring laughter and tears . . . Put *Roseborough* on the must-read list."

—*Today Lancaster* (Duncanville, Texas)

Praise for Jane Roberts Wood's *Grace*

"Wood's novel is an absolute charmer. Sometimes it's poignant, sometimes it is funny. With a palpable languid Southern air, *Grace* moves calmly toward an ending that is not just happy, but also satisfying." —*Fort Worth Star-Telegram*

"*Grace* is a rare novel: intelligent, lyrical, devoid of coyness and manipulative plot turns, a book for old and young."

—*Austin American-Statesman*

"Jane Roberts Wood's *Grace* is as gentle and lovely as the name suggests." —*Houston Chronicle*

"An uplifting and encouraging story that shows without a doubt the resiliency of the human spirit." —*The Anniston Star*

"Wood's narrative is as compelling as a brilliantly executed history, the vivid details of wartime Texas rendered fresh . . . This novel is a great read by a fine Texas writer."

—*The Austin Chronicle*

Jane Roberts Wood is the award-winning author of *Grace* (available from Plume). A recipient of the Texas Institute of Letters Award, and fellowships from the National Endowment for the Humanities and the National Endowment for the Arts, she is a member of TIL and PEN. Ms. Wood lives with her husband in Dallas, Texas.

Visit www.janerobertswood.com

By Jane Roberts Wood

The Train to Estelline
A Place Called Sweet Shrub
Dance a Little Longer
Grace

Roseborough

JANE ROBERTS WOOD

A PLUME BOOK

PLUME
Published by the Penguin Group
Penguin Group (USA) Inc., 375 Hudson Street, New York, New York 10014, U.S.A.
Penguin Books Ltd, 80 Strand, London WC2R 0RL, England
Penguin Books Australia Ltd, 250 Camberwell Road,
Camberwell, Victoria 3124, Australia
Penguin Books Canada Ltd, 10 Alcorn Avenue,
Toronto, Ontario, Canada M4V 3B2
Penguin Books India (P) Ltd, 11 Community Centre, Panchsheel Park,
New Delhi – 110 017, India
Penguin Books (NZ), cnr Airborne and Rosedale Roads,
Albany, Auckland 1310, New Zealand
Penguin Books (South Africa) (Pty) Ltd, 24 Sturdee Avenue,
Rosebank, Johannesburg 2196, South Africa

Penguin Books Ltd, Registered Offices: 80 Strand, London WC2R 0RL, England

Published by Plume, a member of Penguin Group (USA) Inc.
Previously published in a Dutton edition.

First Plume Printing, June 2004
10 9 8 7 6 5 4 3 2 1

The Library of Congress has catalogued the Dutton edition as follows:
Wood, Jane Roberts, 1929–
Roseborough : a novel / by Jane Roberts Wood.
p. cm.
ISBN 0-525-94715-9 (hc.)
ISBN 0-452-28549-6 (pbk.)
1. Mothers and daughters—Fiction. 2. Runaway teenagers—Fiction.
3. Teenage girls—Fiction. 4. Widows—Fiction. I. Title.
PS3573.O5945R67 2003
813'.54—dc21 2002155236

Printed in the United States of America
Original hardcover design by Eve L. Kirch

PUBLISHER'S NOTE
This is a work of fiction. Names, characters, places, and incidents are either the product of the author's imagination or are used fictitiously, and any resemblance to actual persons, living or dead, business establishments, events, or locales is entirely coincidental.

To Carole Baron, a warm friend and superb editor.

Acknowledgments

I am deeply grateful to my daughter, Melinda A. Roberts of the College of New Jersey, for her sustained encouragement and advice in her fields of philosophy and law. And I especially wish to thank C.W. Smith of Southern Methodist University. His excellent and detailed criticism helped me get *Roseborough* off high center and into its proper orbit. Bettie Tully, of El Centro College, provided valuable information in her field of psychology. My thanks go to Erin Sinesky who shepherded both *Grace* and *Roseborough* into public readership. I also thank Barbara Stanley, a computer genius, who always came when I called.

Finally, my warmest thanks to Ellen Temple and Fran Vick, first publishers, now warm friends. Their belief in my writing has provided encouragement when sorely needed and celebration when there was cause.

Roseborough

It is night after a long day.
What has been done has been done.
What has not been done has not been done.
Let it be.

—A Welsh prayer

Chapter One

1

MARY LOU works at the Dairy Queen. Maudie is the manager and she said it was a computer course that made her marketable. She took it on Monday and Wednesday nights at the Lone Oak Community College right here in Lone Oak, Texas. Well, what with Gundren dead and Echo run away, Mary Lou is just about crazy, but the way Maudie talks about college makes it seem like something to hold to. So on her next day off (she has Mondays), Mary Lou takes the pickup, stained with the blood of the horse that killed Gundren, out to the Lone Oak Community College to sign up for CIS-I.

The Lone Oak Community College is big. All of it's in two huge buildings that are separated by a creek. Mary Lou parks on the wrong side of the creek, and she has to walk through a glass-enclosed walkway over the creek to get to the right building. It's a nice walk because the middle of August is hot. The registration is in a big gymnasium with basketball hoops at each end. There are tables all around and people behind the tables and lines in front of the tables and people moving around like they're lost. There are all kinds of people, like everybody at the Lone Oak Mall just picked up and decided to go to college—fat and thin, high school students and grandmothers, and some not even speaking English—all looking lost. *Somebody needs to get it organized.* This is what Mary Lou thinks.

She finds a registration line, A through G, and gets in it. While she is in the line she reads the fall schedule. She has always loved to read, and she reads all the courses they have there, courses in stress management and family relationships, and then she sees Single Parenting and she says to herself, "Well, now. Here's the answer for Echo and me," and she writes it down. When she stops at the table marked Counseling a lady asks, "Are you a single parent?"

Mary Lou says, "Yes, since Gundren is dead." A slight frown appears on her forehead. "Well, most of the time he doesn't seem dead. It just seems like he's off somewhere, driving his truck," she adds.

The lady—thick glasses, a purple swatch of hair on one side, eyes like a grasshopper's—laces her fingers together and stares at Mary Lou. Then she glances at the table next to hers, which has a longer line in front of it than her table has.

"I'm not a counselor," she says and blinks. She blinks, maybe ten or twenty times. Then she says, "Are you aware that this is a noncredit course?"

"I don't need credit," Mary Lou says. "I've got the money for it."

The lady frowns down at the card in her hand, looks at Mary Lou, and blinks. Then the lady coughs and takes a tissue from her green purse and dabs at her nose and puts the tissue back. She snaps her purse shut.

Taking Single Parenting is not going to be easy. Mary Lou can see that. Maybe she's already failed some kind of a test.

"Is your husband dead or not?"

Mary Lou leans forward. "Dead," she whispers.

"Well, I'm just filling in here," the lady says. "But I guess you know what you're doing." Then she puts initials by Mary Lou's name and nods toward the table that is registering the single parents. A man signs her up quick and easy.

So on a Monday evening in late August here she is in a classroom with three windows and a green chalkboard and six single parents, not looking at anything or anybody. Despite her blue jeans and yellow shirt, Mary Lou has the look of an old-fashioned girl. The cloud of hair pulled loosely up on top of her head is reminiscent, perhaps, of a Gibson girl, and, too, there are those green eyes, their gaze direct yet dreamy, like a cat's. She sits straight, her hands carefully folded on the desk. Her hair is gold or brown or russet, a blend so fine that at any given moment the color depends on the light. At this moment her hair is a fiery russet. A wash of freckles over her nose and a mouth inclined toward a smile give the impression she has known joy.

Now the teacher strides into the room bringing with her the sharp sweet scent of mint. She puts her books on her desk and stands in front of the room and smiles. "Good evening!" she says. Her voice has a throaty lilt. She is tall, her body unfashionably generous. Sensing her energy (or is it the scent of mint?), the single parents move restlessly in their seats, uncrossing their legs or crossing them, before settling back into their former positions. The teacher is wearing a short black skirt and opaque black stockings. She has long legs and a soft mouth and shiny black hair swirled carelessly on top of her head. Her eyes are tilted at the outside corners. Her eyebrows are dark, the left a little higher than the right, giving her a perpetual look of inquiry. Her blue eyes that suggest fields of bluebonnets are fringed by short black eyelashes. Her skin is good, a creamy ivory. Because of her smile and her voice she is most often described by casual acquaintances as "happy" or "carefree." In fact she is notoriously neurotic, given to impulse and vivid fantasy.

Today she wears no makeup. No rings. No earrings. Nothing. *And that's a real shame,* Mary Lou tells herself. *But even dressed so plain, if she came in the Dairy Queen, you'd notice her.*

"I'm glad you're here," she says and smiles so widely the braces on her teeth glisten. Mary Lou has never seen anyone that old, maybe forty, wearing braces. The students silently, tentatively, smile back at her. When she turns and writes *Single Parenting, 5162* on the green blackboard, the movement of her arm jingles two thin silver bracelets. Without turning around she says, "This is the text we'll be using," and writes *Fisher, Barnes and Bean, Eds., Single Parenting.*

Now, while the teacher is writing with her right hand, with her left hand she checks to be sure her black and white silk blouse is tucked into her black skirt, scratches the same place, and then she puts that hand on her hip, still writing.

Mary Lou knows she feels the class watching. She looks out the window. The mesquite down along the creek and the coolness in the classroom make it seem like spring. *Spring.* She says it again, feels nothing. The word has lost its meaning.

The teacher puts down the chalk, turns around and smiles again. Leaning against the desk, she crosses her ankles. "I'm pleased you decided to take the course. This is the first semester it's been offered, and I'm excited about teaching it. Oh, by the way, call me whatever you're comfortable with," she says. "I'm comfortable with Anne."

Mary Lou thinks about that. But before she can decide whether she'd be comfortable calling a lady knowing that much *Anne*, she—Anne—is asking them to put their chairs in a circle.

And then a heavyset lady comes in smiling and saying how sorry she is to be late, but she's just heard about the class and, since she is not in a traditional marriage, she would really like to take it. "Can I just squeeze in here?" she asks and a man wearing fancy boots widens the circle and puts a chair for the lady right next to his.

"My name's Rosie," she says, "short for Rosemary," and smiles around the circle.

The lady doesn't look fat. She just looks solid and sure with her soft brown hair and dimples in her arms.

Then the teacher, Anne, tells them to say one thing about themselves following two rules: Whatever they say has to be positive and it has to be true. Mary Lou thinks of a million things to say. She can say Gundren took Plumb Easy to Mineral Wells for a free breeding. But then if she goes ahead with it and says he was killed on the way it would ruin it. Or she can say she has a fourteen-year-old daughter she loves more than anything else in the whole world. But then she would have to tell that she has run away. So now it is getting close to her turn. A woman with black hair streaked with gray and a round face and a dimple in her chin says she has already done her Christmas shopping. Everybody but Mary Lou laughs. Then the woman, Maggie, next to her says she has invited her ex-mother-in-law over for Sunday dinner. More laughing. Now it is her turn and she doesn't know what she is going to say. She takes a deep breath and opens her mouth. "I love the Lord," she says, wondering as soon as she'd said it, why she said it.

Everybody just looks at her, everybody but Anne, who just nods and goes right on to a man with dark circles under his eyes. After a minute he says softly, "When the circus comes to town, I'm going to take my little boy. He wants an elephant for Christmas," he says, shaking his head in wonderment. The man's face is thin, but when he grins it fills out some.

"I make the best yeast rolls in Lone Oak, and I'll bring you all some," says Rosie.

"All right!" Maggie says.

Well, now if they're talking about cooking, Mary Lou can brag some, too. She is a good cook. Even Gundren says so. She almost hopes they go round again. But they don't.

Driving home that day she begins to worry. What will Anne ask the next time? What if she asks, "What does your husband do?" Lots of people come right out and ask that. Or on forms, it is "Spouse's Occupation." Same thing. Suppose she asks that. In Single Parenting, would she? And if she did, would Mary Lou say, "Deceased?" But that's not an occupation. Or she could say, "He was king of the road." That is true. That's what he was. She loved to see Gundren, wearing his starched blue jeans and wide-brimmed hat and boots, walk out the door. He'd swing into his truck and start it, and then, just before he pulled away, he'd look at her and wink and touch the brim of his hat with his first two fingers. Watching him drive off always reminded her of that old movie where John Wayne sits up high in his saddle and says, "Move 'em out!" But if Anne asks the question, what she'd really like to say is, "He was a Gypsy and he loved horses. Only horses."

Quite honestly Gundren was fair about it. He told her before they got married, "I'm a Gypsy."

"What does that mean?" she'd asked.

He was silent, thinking about it, and then he said, "I don't know." And she was sure he didn't. But then Echo was born, and the Family came, *the Family,* filling up the halls of the Lone Oak Hospital and its nursery windows and, with their trucks and campers, the hospital parking lot so that the doctor sent her home the next day. But the Family stayed on, cooking on fires in the backyard (ruining her hollyhock bed!) and drinking blackberry wine and smoking. The women, wearing black dresses in the daytime and colored shawls over their shoulders at night and with diamonds and blue eye shadow, were something to see. She could hardly keep from staring. Even their hands—tipped by long red fingernails and constantly moving, smoking, or riffling through decks of cards—were like a magician's. There's not much card playing in Lone Oak. The men, quiet and sad, leaned over the fence or hunkered down on the ground beside the fire, rocking back and forth on the toes of their boots. They were noticeable, too. Walking light across the backyard into the barn to whittle and talk in deep guttural voices, they were restless as a herd of horses, easy-spooked. The men, they just waited to be gone, and where didn't matter. Except for babies coming and weddings and funerals, they stayed on the road—driving trucks, working one-ring circuses, doing odd jobs, anything to keep moving. And they swapped. Whether Gundren was home or on the road he was swapping. Usually it was horses, but Gundren would swap anything. She'd come home from the Dairy Queen to find a gold sofa in the kitchen or a broken water pump. And he'd be just as proud as if they needed a sofa in the kitchen or a broken water pump.

On the day Echo got her name the Family left, and that wasn't soon enough for her. They had been there three days having such a fit over Echo that Mary Lou never knew where she'd find her. Sometimes she'd be in a dresser drawer in the house or in an old toolbox in the barn, the men whistling tunes for her and braiding ropes and whittling. She was about to scream when a storm blew up. The women, running in their high-heeled black sandals, hurried out to grab the clothes off the line and run back onto the screened-in porch, chattering and smiling their wide white smiles and wringing the water from the hems of their skirts. Then the rain stopped almost as soon as it started, and just when the women started out back again, a heavy clap of thunder rumbled across the sky, so loud that they all stopped for a minute to listen. Then it thundered again, but this time it was like an imitation of the first, a small polite rumble. The women, going out again to hang up the diapers and towels and sheets, laughed. Mary Lou had to laugh, too. Nature is funny. Gundren's Aunt Labelle (she has this parrot, bright green and blue with a yellow beak, and it was pecking at nothing around her feet) had the baby in her lap, a tiny sweet thing with hair as black as the fur of a kitten and as thick. And she stood up with the baby in the crook of her arm and said, "Her name's Echo," thrusting the word at Mary Lou on the tip of her long red fingernail. "Mary Lou, you call her what you want, but her name's Echo."

She liked the name and Gundren never questioned it, so it's on her birth certificate. Echo. Echo Burgandy.

The next day they swarmed off taking Gran Gran's gold

ring, the only keepsake Mary Lou had of hers. Stealing from kinfolks! That is why she locked up all her valuables in a trunk when they came to Gundren's funeral.

But in just one week the Family left its mark on Echo. Maybe naming her did it. Maybe if she'd named her Betty or Cindy. But it probably wouldn't have mattered.

From the time she could toddle around, Echo practically lived outside. "Come in out of the snow," Mary Lou would call to her, or "Come in out of the heat," or "the rain," or "it's dark," or she'd entice her: "Echo, come have a cup of hot chocolate with your mama." Echo would and she'd smile and say, "Thank you, Mama. I love you," just as sweet as when Gundren said it, but then she'd be right out again.

And in the evening, all up and down our block, you could hear the neighbors herding her home. "Echo, Doreen has to come in now. You run along," and "Echo, better go on home. It's getting late," and "Your mama's calling. Now run on home before she worries."

And when she got a little older she was in and out of her bedroom window all the time, day or night. At night Mary Lou would wake up feeling uneasy, and she'd go out in the backyard and call softly, so as not to wake the neighbors. "Echo?"

"Here, Mama," she'd answer. "Here, Mama. I'm right here." And there she'd be up in a tree or sitting on the back steps, holding one of Sugar's new kittens. "Isn't this kitten the sweetest thing?" she'd say, or "Mama, isn't the moon pretty?" Echo was always, you might say, nocturnal.

And Gundren in all this. Where is he? "Let her alone," he'd say. "She's not hurting a soul." Let her alone was his favorite thing to say.

Well. Now Gundren's been dead thirty-two days and Echo's gone, leaving a note that said, "Mama, don't worry," and Mary Lou hears Gundren saying, "Let her alone. She's not hurting a soul." And on the way to the Dairy Queen or on the way home, she answers, "Me, Gundren. Me. She's hurting me."

The next Monday, Mary Lou, not letting herself think that some of it could be Gundren's, hoses Plumb Easy's blood off the pickup, puts on her good jeans, and takes off for Single Parenting again. Anne is there already, writing on the board. She turns her head and smiles when Mary Lou walks in. Anne is wearing a sweater the color of wheat and a long green skirt and green hose and clogs. Her hair is in a short braid. She looks younger, more noticeable.

"Hello, Mary Lou!" she says. Another single parent comes in. She is pretty and very, very dark. An Iranian? African-American? Maybe an Armenian. Who knows? Last week Anne told the class that fifty-nine languages and dialects are spoken at the Lone Oak Community College.

"Hello, Maggie," Anne says. "Would you and Mary Lou get the chairs in a circle?"

They get the chairs (there are eight) in a circle and Mary Lou watches Anne write the words *fact*, *fear*, and *fantasy* on the board.

By the time she finishes writing, three or four others come in. Then Ed (there are three of them, three men, in the class), walks in wearing shiny black boots with "Ed" on one and "Texas" on the other stitched in blue and winks at her. She just looks right back at him, thinking, *Idiot, oh, you are such an idiot!* until he drops his eyes. The thought of Gundren in the circle at Single Parenting wearing fancy boots makes her smile.

Ed frowns but he does not look up. One thing for sure: Gundren wouldn't have worn boots like that to pull a cow out of quicksand. *Oh Gundren!* she sighs, and it's like he might be there, smiling at her. But he's not. He's gone. And the sorrow rises like a tide and sweeps over her, and she's drowning in sorrow. She shifts in her seat and thinks about Echo. And thinking of Echo, thinking of how quick she is, how she smiles when Sugar purrs, of how she ducks her head when she laughs—thinking of this girl she loves more than anything else in the world—this, this is what saves her.

While Anne goes over the course outline or "syllabus" (she writes this word on the board), Mary Lou worries about Echo. *Where is she right this minute?* she whispers to Gundren, and at the same time she worries about what to tell the class about the "fact," "fear," or "fantasy" Anne has written on the board. But this gets a lot easier when Anne says they don't have to say it. Instead she says she is simply asking them to write it all down. She wants a fact, a fear (Gundren isn't, wasn't, afraid of a thing), and a fantasy.

Maggie leans forward and smiles. Her plaid shirt is starched so stiff it rustles. She looks nice, like a TV commercial for off-road vehicles. Anne raises her eyebrows, waiting.

"By fantasy," Maggie asks, "do you mean something that's not true?"

Anne says, "By fantasy I mean what's not true but what you'd like to make true. When you finish, put your writing on my desk. What you write will be held in confidence unless you wish to share it. We will talk about the exercise, its purpose, next week. Please read the first chapter of the text. We'll discuss that, too."

Mary Lou knows her fantasy. It is there waiting. So she

writes out her "fear" very fast because she does not want anyone to notice that she might feel one little bit like crying. She writes: "I'm afraid Echo will never come home." For "fact" she writes: "Once a Gypsy, always a Gypsy." Then she begins to write her fantasy, and she knows she will like writing it best because this is what puts her to sleep every single night. She writes:

> *Well somebody tells me or maybe I just know it but anyhow there Gundren is! He's on the other side of the ocean waiting for me. He's smiling and his arms are open wide. To get to him all I have to do is swim across the ocean. Easy. Nothing. I am happy. I run across the beach. The sand is hot underneath my feet but close to the water it gets cooler, then damp. I run into the water. The waves splash my ankles, my knees, and when they get up to my waist, I dive into a wave and I begin to swim. I swim past the second sandbar out into the ocean. Way out, the sea is real calm and peaceful. I swim and swim and then, just about always, I fall asleep.*

2

Anne Hamilton has decided to change her life. And the single parenting course is one of her changes. For one thing it's a new course so her teaching load is lighter. She proposed the course last fall. Even after her proposal had been met with enthusiasm by her chairperson, her colleagues, the dean, and the vice-president of instruction, she had almost lost it. She had known she was in danger of losing it when the dean asked her to "drop by for a chat." He had taken off his reading glasses, angled his chair toward hers, and said, "Anne, this idea is great. We need this course. But don't you think that Claude or Roger, someone more grounded by the experience of teaching psychology, would be more . . . ," struggling to finish his thought without leaving the smallest wound, "would be more at ease?" he finished.

"Bill, I can teach this course. I designed it. I have a minor in psychology. And I can teach it. I'm sure of it."

After a minute, "Well, let's give it a try," he had said. "We'll see how the semester goes, and there's always the counseling staff if you need them."

Now looking at their intense faces as they write, Anne knows she was right. She does have a wealth of common sense. She often gives sound advice when it's needed, to her friends, for example, concerning their problems with their children. Claude had suggested the exercise she is using today. "It will warm up the class. Relax them right away," he had said.

She picks up a pen and draws circles. *If I had been asked to write my fantasy, what would I write?* The musical ring of a cell phone breaks the silence of the classroom. Frowning she looks up. Ed, of the cowboy boots and the swagger, turns it off, gestures an apology. Anne raises an eyebrow, nods. Still doodling, she sketches a cell phone and x's it out. Then she draws a Garry Trudeau cowboy hat. Not knowing what she is going to write, she begins:

There's music. Happy. Sing-song. A boy holds my hand. He's little, maybe six or seven. We are going to ride the Ferris wheel and he skips along, holding my hand very tightly.

Carter (his name is Carter, a family name) and I step onto the Ferris wheel; a young man puts a bar across at waist level and secures it. Carter sits close, the carnival music plays, and we rise, rise, up into the sky. Carter holds the bar tightly and grins at me. I put my arm around him. At the very top the wheel stops and we look out over the world. I am not afraid.

She reads what she has written. She likes the name "Carter." It's a great name for a boy. The surprise of it is the "I am not afraid." Looking up, she sees that most of the class has finished. She picks up a paper, sees the name Mary Lou Burgandy written in strong clear handwriting. She reads the "fear" and the "fact." Then she reads the fantasy: *Well somebody tells me or maybe I just know it but there Gundren is. . . .* Startled she reads the passage again, words that seem a bright weave on the gray fabric of the day. She wonders if there is implicit in the passage a death wish, however innocently expressed. No. This passage is not suicidal. It's hopeful; it's like imagining you can fly. Or ride a Ferris wheel without becoming paralyzed with fear. Taking up another paper, she glances at the young woman and is surprised by the intensity of her gaze and by her absurd earrings (a red apple in one ear and a green worm in the other), swinging happily in sharp contrast to her expression, which is as solemn as on that first day when she blurted out her love for God.

Obviously Mary Lou has suffered a loss. Deserted by her husband? An unhappy divorce? But Anne knows that students usually lead messy lives. Her intent is not to rush into the middle of any disorderly life. Her obligation is to make students aware of what it means to be good steady parents. However,

Anne tells herself, if at some point she feels that Mary Lou needs additional help, she will ask her to come by her office and give her the names of two or three experienced staff psychologists.

"I'll see you next Monday," she tells the last two students as she prepares to leave. Before Anne reaches her car she has put all thoughts of Mary Lou out of her mind. Turning into her driveway she sees her neighbor, Joan, across the street.

"Anne," Joan calls, "I've read it. I've read *To Kill A Mockingbird*. It's so wonderful. I can't wait to hear what you have to say about it."

Anne nods and waves. "I've always loved it. We will have a great discussion," she says, turning away to hurry inside. When the semester is over she will have more time. But now she has papers to read and classes to prepare for.

She takes off her jacket and slips her feet into sandals. She puts an old Cat Stevens CD on the stereo and pours herself a glass of chilled chardonnay. In the kitchen she seasons a chicken breast with lemon pepper, tops it with apple and onion, and puts it in the oven. She puts on the rice, then washes a handful of strawberries as a topping for yogurt. She's determined to lose five pounds. Along with straightening her teeth and the single parenting course, getting in shape is part of her plan. She believes outward change is often a prelude to inward change.

For dinner she will have a glass of sparkling water with a slice of lemon rather than a second glass of wine. Glancing at her watch she walks toward the phone just as it begins to ring. She stands by it counting the rings and on the fifth ring she hears Allen's voice as she had known she would.

"Are you there? Out jogging? I'm calling to say I'll be a little late Friday. Oh, and I've found a new wine. Inexpensive but good. A merlot. See you then. Bye."

Listening to Allen's message, she folds her arms. *I'm not so sure I want to try your merlot,* she thinks.

Allen is not yet aware that ending their relationship is her most drastic change. If she does nothing to prevent it he will come on Friday, "a little late" as usual; they'll have a glass of wine while he reads the *New York Times* and she prepares dinner, as usual; they'll sit at her table and talk cursorily (she can never remember what they talk about), and then, depending upon the wine, the music, the light in the room, depending on who knows what, they'll go to bed or they won't, as usual. But when he comes this Friday she is going to tell Allen that it's over.

As soon as she wakes up Friday morning, she begins to steel herself for the evening. She had thought of calling and saying, "It's over. It's finished." But this is a coward's way out. And she wants to be fair. She will be especially reasonable (Allen is always reasonable). She will simply explain that she wants, *needs,* something more. In the shower she soaps her arms, her breasts, all the while remembering the passion in Browning's poems, the yearning to be more, to reach higher. When Joan talks about her adopted Nikki's potty training, her face lights up as if her two-year-old has composed a sonata. A passionate marriage, a child to love. Even at forty-three, either or both is not out of the question.

This evening she dresses leisurely—a long, green linen dress and sandals. She has time. Allen is always late. His saying he will be "a little late" has wide variance—as little as fifteen minutes or as much as an hour—in it. Accordingly she usually prepares a meal that can be warmed up or served cold. Tonight it is celery soup. Creamy. With a dash of nutmeg. The bread, seasoned with garlic and olive paste, is in the oven ready to heat. And the asparagus for the salad, steamed for seven minutes, has been chilled but not dressed. It isn't until after she has almost finished preparing the meal that it occurs to her that celery soup and asparagus salad do not make a balanced menu. She can hear Allen's comment: *Vegetarian are we now?* The desert is a rich chocolate mousse cake she picked up from the City Café. Allen likes chocolate.

Sitting before her mirror she consoles herself. Brushing her hair, swooping it up into a careless swirl, she tells herself she has not been a fool. Allen had been honest with her, had said from the first he did not want children, did not want to be married. To anyone. Ever. His own parents, he told her, had wrecked whatever ideas he might have entertained about marriage. She leans forward to check her teeth. Definitely straighter. Four years ago a mostly tepid relationship, such as she has had with Allen, was fine with her. But not now.

When Allen comes he is twenty minutes late and, as usual, bustling with good cheer. When he leans to kiss her she turns away so that he only brushes her cheek with his mouth. She hands him a glass of wine. He picks up the paper, sits in a chair by the bay window, and reads. The light becomes gray, the air thick. She opens a window to breathe.

Studying Allen she stirs the celery soup. The light comes over Allen's shoulder and shines on the gray newspaper filled with the pain and horror of current and impending wars. The rubber band holding up her hair hurts. She pulls it off, releasing her hair, and runs her hand through it. She turns on the oven, lowers the burner under the soup, and begins to mix the dressing.

When Allen had arrived they had exchanged greetings, but now, just five minutes later, she cannot remember how his day had gone. After mixing the dressing she turns up the heat and stirs the soup again, willing him to look up, to smile at her, to come into the kitchen and touch her. *If he does something, anything, different, I might not tell him we're finished until next Friday,* she thinks. Now there's the odor of scorched milk. She feels the anger that slowly envelops her. The soup is ruined. Her face feels flushed. She touches her cheek. Surprisingly it feels cool. When she shifts the spoon to her left hand, her right hand trembles. She studies her trembling hand. She studies Allen.

He gets up, walks to the bar, pours himself another glass of wine. Newspaper in one hand, his wine in the other, he returns to his chair without a glance or a smile. *Can't he smell?* she wonders. *Can't he see?* She is invisible to him. This is it then. It's over. Grimly she opens a drawer, takes out a sack. She pours the ruined soup into a plastic dish, snaps the cover. She cuts the cake, encloses half of it in another container. Then the asparagus salad, still undressed, is snapped in. She puts the sack on the floor; one-by-one she drops the containers—*food bombs for Allen,* she tells herself—into the sack. Realizing the absurdity of her actions she lurches toward the sack on the floor and stumbles. "Damn," she says. Taking off a sandal to examine her scraped toe, she looks into the room where Allen sits. He leisurely turns a page of the newspaper. Angrily she kicks off the other sandal.

She walks into the living room. "Allen?" she says to his bald head. He does not look up. He will finish the paragraph before he looks up. She knows this.

When he does look up his black eyebrows lift with surprise.

He has seen her bare feet; seen her hair gone wild around her face. "What is it?" he asks in a voice filled with reasoned calm.

"Here," she says.

"What?"

"Here. Take it. It's your dinner. Take it home. Take it to the park. The soup's ruined. Throw it away. Throw it all away. I don't care. The wine's uncorked. I'm keeping the wine."

Wincing at this miserly last, she shifts the sack to her right hip and sweeps hair out of her eyes. This, what she's doing, is beyond absurdity. She knows it. She's gone mad. And Allen sees that she has. It's in his face, his Aristotelian calm as he looks at her, at this barefooted woman with her Medusa hair.

"Anne, what's the matter? What's happened?"

"It's finished between us. It's over."

Now he is on his feet. "You don't mean this. Anne, you don't mean this. Look at you. Standing there barefooted, looking pretty in your long green dress."

His voice is calm, soothing, as if talking to a cat, enticing it to come, soothing it, soothing her, ready to put down his paper, to hold her, pet her, help her with dinner, put her to bed.

"Anne, is there something burning?" he says, sounding faintly alarmed.

She shakes her head wondering what there was that so appealed here. His smile? The smoothness of his movements? Now his hands are on her waist. "You, you little . . .

Shorthand. Allen's shorthand: *Let's drink the wine; let's go to bed.* He's holding her close, nuzzling her hair. "You smell so good," he murmurs.

"No, Allen," she steps away. "Not this time."

She takes his hand, puts it over the sack.

"You're just upset now. Let's sit down. Let's talk about this.

Come over here," herding her toward the couch. His hands console, beseech, draw her close.

"No. No. No."

"Then just tell me. What is it?"

"It's everything. It's this. It's this evening. It's every Friday evening. This is not what I want."

"What do you want? Just tell me."

"I don't know. But this isn't it. I want you to leave. It's over."

"OK, then. It's over. Fine with me." His voice is tight with anger, all tenderness drained away. He starts toward the door, turns, and comes back. "I'll call you tomorrow. Anne, you'd better check the stove. You're not yourself now."

"Go." Hearing the front door close, "Oh, I am, Allen," she whispers. "I've come to myself. I am myself."

Hearing his car door slam she pours herself a glass of wine. She takes a deep breath and drinks the wine. Strolling—she's done it, she's ended it—into the living room, she begins to whistle an old song her brother used to sing. She doesn't know the name of the song, doesn't know the words, but they'll come. And it's over. Oh Lord, she hopes she can let it be. Oh, that's it! "Let It Be." That's the song her brother used to sing.

Anne's drive to the Lone Oak Community College from her house in Dallas is a long one, over thirty miles. This evening she lowers her car windows and turns up the sound system. It's Mozart. Perfect for planning. In her Single Parenting class she will be careful not to open old wounds. Wounds that have healed, scarred-over, are better left alone. But the fears the students have written about, these, when confronted, might shrink to a manageable size or possibly disappear altogether. And when their fears have been processed (she tries out the word on her tongue, likes the scientific sound of it), the real lessons of parenting can begin.

She considers the fears expressed by the students. Mary Lou's that her daughter will never come home. A runaway, probably fourteen or fifteen. She could be anywhere. But she'll probably come home. The percentages are with her. Ed is afraid his daughter will forget him. Ed with the swagger when he walks. The slightly petulant mouth. The anger at his ex-wife, who moved with their daughter to Colorado. An anger transferred to her as an authority figure? They can talk about Ed's fear, and she will suggest an arranged visit to Colorado, perhaps a visit to Texas by his daughter. The class will be supportive. Betty's fear of cancer is so strong she cannot say the word. Anne needs more information to determine how real the fear is. But cancer is insidious. It *might* return. Still, better to get the fear, the word *cancer* out of the closet into the full light of day. Rosie's fear is realistic. Her child has no father. She does not know how to comfortably explain the facts of his birth to him. Having a child through artificial insemination is uncommon, but Rosie is a good mother by any standard. Dylan's fear is that he will somehow be separated from his son. The root of this fear is probably an acrimonious divorce. Dylan has the look of an alcoholic. If that's true there is probably some basis for his fear. Tony believes he can never be a good father or a good husband. And Maggie's fear? Maggie is trying out for a part in the college play and she is afraid she won't get it. Anne suspects that beneath Maggie's lighthearted approach she has serious concerns. A single mother with three children? How could she not? But thinking about Maggie's play the thought comes that the members of the class are like characters in a play, and she is the director who, while exerting firm control, need not get involved in any one part.

And there's this small triumph: It's been three days and not one time has she been tempted to pick up the phone when she's heard Allen's voice on her recorder.

3

When Mary Lou reaches the campus and steps out of her pickup, she looks up at the sky, still full of light even with the sun gone. The leaves on the trees around the parking lot are still hanging on. The bois d'arc growing at the edge of the creek is beginning to turn; even the air has turned. Yesterday it had been too lazy to move, but today it feels like the nose of a dog. The weather is changing, and what Mary Lou likes the most about living in Texas (true, she's never lived anywhere else) is the way the seasons change. She's always loved the fall, but not this year. Not this fall.

Later, with the class in a circle looking grave and worried, Mary Lou listens to Betty tell of her struggle to overcome her fear that the cancer might come back. Then they think of ways to help Betty, and Anne puts their ideas on the board. Mary Lou wants to help but Ed says, "Go to church and talk it over with the Lord," before she gets up the nerve to say what she thinks. When Maggie suggests that Betty write the word *cancer* on a piece of paper, set it on fire, and watch it burn up, the class looks doubtful and Ed shakes his head. But Mary Lou likes the idea.

"Well, I can see some use to that," she says, while Anne writes it on the board. "You could try it. It might work. Gypsies do things like that. Not Gundren, but his family. Well, maybe Gundren, too."

All this just pops out of Mary Lou's mouth, causing Anne to look at her. *Oh, lord, here it comes!* she thinks. She sits very still, so still that the long-stemmed orange chrysanthemum earrings she wears come to rest against her cheeks.

"Betty, why don't you jot down these ideas and process them," Anne says, still looking at Mary Lou. "Now Mary Lou, can we talk about your fear?"

"No," she says, but then relenting, "Well, it's just that Echo ran away about a week after Gundren died. She's my little girl. She's not so little, really. She's almost fifteen. But when she's gone at night she seems little. I'm just afraid she won't ever come home." Her chin quivers. She puts her hand over it to hide the quivering, biting her lip to make it stop.

Betty, in the middle of her list, opens her eyes wide and shakes her head. Her head, going from side to side, says, "Oh, you poor thing! You poor, poor thing!"

Frowning, Ed crosses his arms and settles back in his chair. "You don't look old enough to have a fourteen-year-old kid," he says.

"Well, I am. Plenty old enough."

"Have you called up the police?" Maggie asks. "They might put your girl's picture on a milk carton. They do that now."

This, coming from Maggie, surprises Mary Lou. Maggie is the one she likes best. "Why?" she asks.

"Why, what?" Maggie says.

"Why would I want to go and call the police for?"

"So they'd find her. A lost girl. They'd help you look," Ed says, leaning forward again.

Well, here you go again, Mary Lou thinks. *Sounding like you know everything.* "Echo's not lost," she tells him. "I know right where Echo is. Why, do you think I'd be here in this classroom, would be anywhere but looking for her, if I didn't know right where she is every night of the world?"

"Well, where is she?" Ed says, like he doesn't believe her.

"In a tree house," Mary Lou says, not a bit embarrassed. "She can't live at home right now. Not with me. And that's all there is to it."

"In a tree house on your property?" Anne asks.

"No, in a tree house on the old Roseborough place. But Echo doesn't know I've found her."

For the first time Anne doesn't nod and go on to the next one. She looks at Mary Lou, and then she smiles and looks out the window. The members of the class gaze at Mary Lou.

Ed frowns, bites his lower lip. He leans forward but before he can say a word, Anne says slowly, "This class is just about over. Use the next five minutes to write your responses in your journals—your thoughts, questions, comments. Anything you wish."

And very slowly, out of the corner of her eye, Mary Lou sees that Ed is the last to pick up his pen; they put their heads down and begin to write.

4

When Echo ran away Mary Lou had been frantic with worry. But when she began to miss things—Gundren's canteen, a hammer, a pillow—from the house, she knew Echo was close by. But where? At night she walked from room to room, each time hoping that when she opened the door to Echo's room, she'd be there, asleep, her hair spread out on her pillow, her dark lashes curving against her cheeks, looking like an angel. And each time she called softly into the darkness of the backyard, she prayed that she'd hear her voice, "Here, Mama. I'm out here." Not working at all—well, how could she, not knowing where Echo was?—she had looked every day, driven every back road in Lone Oak, each time hoping that when she turned into their driveway Echo would be there. Home.

Then, driving past Old Man Roseborough's cow pasture that was bounded on three sides by the Roseborough woods, she'd seen a flock of birds, headed right into the heart of the woods, suddenly veer off in another direction. Could have been a wind shift, an owl, something on the ground. But then standing by the microwave waiting for the coffee to heat, it came over her all of a sudden. *Well, that was Echo's red sweater!* she thought. *That splash of red high up in the tree . . . why that was Echo up there in that old tree house!*

She ran the whole way down to the woods, climbed the fence, and found the old path. There she had to go slow, what with the path grown over with honeysuckle and grapevine. Poison ivy, too, probably.

Years ago kids used to play in there, and Gundren and Mary Lou, before they married, had walked there, and once climbed up into the old tree house for a picnic, but since Old Man Roseborough had started hanging dead water moccasins on the fence, even threatening to shoot a surveyor five or ten years ago, no one went in there. Ever. But hurrying down the path, pushing a small branch away from her face, stepping over a fallen tree trunk, Mary Lou knew that Echo would go there. Why, that's right where she would go.

When she got to the tree she saw a thick rope ladder going up, up, about twenty feet or so, maybe thirty, up to the tree house. And there it was! Echo's red sweater!

For a minute Mary Lou stood there filled with relief. Oh, the wonder of it! The joy! Her relief so great at seeing the sweater, she felt there was not one bone in her body.

But then what in the world should she do? Wait for Echo? Tell her to come home right this minute? "I can't, Mama. Right now, I just can't live at home." She could hear Echo say it, clear as anything. Or she could leave her a note: "I love you, Echo. Please come home."

She had settled on that. The next day she'd write the note and leave it in the tree house. But for now she moved back, back into the thickness of the goldenrod, the sweet gum and elms, and the old broken oaks. Underneath a sweet gum she brushed aside the leaves and twigs making a smooth place to sit, and the rich sweet smell of moldy leaves and black dirt came up. A comfort. She sat there watching the sky through the trees fill up with bright orange and pink colors and, for the first time since Gundren died, she put her head back against the trunk of the tree and let the tears come, feeling easier for it. Shy little things rustled through the woods and the birds called and leaves drifted down, and then she heard Echo's quick light footsteps coming down the path to the tree.

When she saw Echo, looking even skinnier than she remembered, it was only Gundren's voice saying, "Let her alone," that kept her from jumping up and running to her. And Echo never paused. Up the rope ladder she went, and, stepping into the tree house, she pulled the ladder up behind her.

So Echo was all right, just as safe there as in her own bed. Mary Lou's chest that had been squeezed tighter and tighter every day, all of a sudden felt light, and she breathed real easy. She could hear Echo moving around up there. A branch at the top of the oak shook, and then the one next to it, taking Echo's weight as she settled in for the night. To Mary Lou it seemed just like always, when she'd be clearing up in the kitchen at night and hear Echo in her room right next to it, opening her closet, sitting on her bed to take off her shoes, settling in for the night. The best part of the day. Peaceful.

Dusk came on and then it was dark, and she felt pretty happy, almost like humming. After five days of looking and calling and asking, to know where Echo was! She had sat right there until morning just wishing the night would go on forever. Not until dawn's first light had she slipped down the path, climbed over the fence, and run home.

Hearing Gundren's voice, "Honey, let her alone," as strong and sure as ever, she hadn't written the note the next day. Or the next. Now here it was. The whole story out. But hurrying to her pickup, Mary Lou isn't sorry she told it. It had been some relief.

5

Driving home after class Anne leaves the freeway to drive through the old section of Lone Oak. Here remnants of a small town remain—the courthouse-centered square, and on the east side, Wright's Drugs (ice-cream sodas, twenty-five cents), then Ben. F. Smith's Dry Goods, a post office, Dr.

Nemeth's Shoes Like New, Roger's Antique Store, and the Lone Oak Bank. This part of Lone Oak is the kind of town that almost everybody had known as children. But when the population of central Texas mushroomed, the giant wave of the city of Dallas rolled over towns like Lone Oak, leaving behind the fast-food chains, the liquor stores, the giant discount stores, the topless bars. But here the past remains. And it occurs to Anne that a vague atmosphere of this past envelops Mary Lou. Her wide-eyed amazement over the intimate revelations of the other students, her own old-fashioned reticence, her formality in class—like the haunting by an old tune one cannot quite remember—all evoke the past. Mary Lou does not seem to have grown beyond this part of Lone Oak. In spite of her youth she seems a quaint relic, quietly mourning her husband's recent death.

Anne slips a Copland CD into the stereo and turns up the volume. She intends to put Mary Lou out of her mind. And the tree house! It's all so unreal. But if she could paint, she would paint Mary Lou, perhaps with binoculars, watching over Echo in the tree house as one would watch over the nest of an endangered species. *Perhaps Echo is endangered,* Anne thinks wryly, *endangered by all the shocks and uncertainties of this world. Too many changes, too fast.*

Anne is beginning to feel comfortable with this new class she is teaching. Briskly, she runs over their fears and strengths. Mary Lou's traumas, the death of her husband and her runaway daughter. Betty's fear is that her cancer may return and although revealing this in class is good therapy, telling her doctor about it would also be helpful. And there's Rosie. At the age of forty-five, yet unwilling to settle for marriage to just any man, she has managed to have a son, now three years old. Because Tony lost his father as a child, he is fiercely determined to be a good husband and father. Ed is stereotypically tall, dark, and handsome. And he knows it. His self-image is revealed in his swagger, but underlying the bravado, the petulance and anger he feels is manifested in all he says, all he writes. Dylan's fear is separation from his son. And finally there's Maggie, a beautiful African-American with three children to support.

All these problems. Still, Anne believes she can help them. And they will help each other.

Enough, she tells herself. Enough mental and emotional energy spent on this class. Determinedly, she turns up the stereo and turns away from thoughts of her class.

But when night falls, although she follows her usual routine—a light supper, jogging, a warm shower—she finds herself unable to sleep. Imagine a place, she tells herself, slipping into an exercise that almost always works. There is water nearby. A mountain stream. And along the stream there are yellow flowers. A butterfly. She watches it stretch its wings, slowly, tentatively, its yellow wings centered with circles of bright blue. Then it lifts itself from the flower and, fluttering aimlessly in ever-widening circles, slowly disappears into the branches of a tree. But then the stream below begins to widen, becomes a torrent, engulfing the flower, the butterfly, engulfing Anne. And she is drowning. She cannot breathe. Suddenly she's wide awake, sitting up straight, her heart beating wildly.

She gets out of bed and walks to the kitchen, gets a glass of water, sets it on her bedside table, and plumps up her pillow. Still, it is sometime after two before she falls asleep.

When Anne enters the classroom the following Monday, the students have arranged themselves in a circle.

Ed is speaking as she walks in. "Doc, you're the counselor," he says, swinging his chair around toward her, "supposed to know things." His voice is harsh. "You just gonna let that girl stay up in that tree?"

"Let her? Ed, that girl is not my . . ."

"Echo. Her name's Echo," Mary Lou says softly.

Why, she's very pretty, Anne thinks, looking at Mary Lou's light brown hair that, in the sunlight coming through the window, shines with a rich golden color. Today she wears it in a braided roll held in place on the side of her head by a green cucumber clip. Her earrings are small yellow squash. Her eyes sparkle with flakes of gold. All at once, Anne remembers a marble her brother John gave her the night they celebrated her tenth birthday. For years she kept it in her purse, a talisman.

"Thank you, Mary Lou," Anne says, then, taking in Maggie's upraised hand, she nods, "Just a minute, Maggie," and, looking again at Ed, "Ed, Echo is Mary Lou's daughter and she must decide what's best for her."

"Well, I let my wife take our daughter out-of-state to live. And I'm sorry."

"Let's keep our focus on Mary Lou's daughter just now. What, Maggie?"

"Well, we could maybe help. Just listening. Sometimes it helps."

Betty leans forward. "Honey, I know just how you feel. My girl ran away right after I had my surgery. But she came home. Your girl will, too."

Anne leans toward Mary Lou. "Are you comfortable with this discussion? Mary Lou, how do you feel about all of this?"

"I don't mind it," Mary Lou says, looking down at her folded hands. "But I don't know what to do. I just don't know. When Echo ran away it was summertime, and it just seemed like she was camping out. Echo's safe at night, up there in the tree house, but I worry about her in the day. I wonder where she is right now. Where *is* she?"

"Well, tonight, why don't you holler up there and tell her to come home?"

Ed again. He's comfortable with confrontation, Anne thinks. But now Tony opens his mouth to speak. *Ah,* Anne tells herself, *it's about time Tony found his voice,* but before he can begin, Mary Lou answers.

"She won't come home!" she says. "And I can't make her because that last day, that very last day, right before her daddy drove away to get hisself killed, we had a fight. And Echo heard it. She heard every mean word I said."

Mary Lou's face is flushed. Lifting her chin, crossing her arms, blinking away tears, she shifts her position in her chair. Again the class, surprised and bewildered, stares at her. Raw emotion fills the room. Anne has not meant it to go this far. Perhaps it is the image of the torrent of water sweeping away everything in its path that has caused her to allow it to go so far. Quickly she rises.

"You are all single parents," she says firmly. "Today we've focused on Mary Lou's dilemma, but each of you has faced challenging situations. Think carefully about one such time in your life when you, as a single parent, have not known what to do and write about that experience. Write with as much detail as possible." Now her voice is gathering strength. "Often we don't know what we think about an event until we've written about it. So please do that now and if you'd like to share this experience, just put what you've written on my desk when you leave."

Chapter Two

1

THE days are getting shorter. By the time the class is settled the shadows of twilight fill the halls, but there's still light enough for Mary Lou to see the glow of Anne's white dress as she moves, mothlike, from her desk to a film projector, makes adjustments, comes to sit beside Mary Lou in the circle.

Then Ed, wearing a "gimme" cap and his fancy boots, arrives. "We gonna sit here in the dark?" he says, switching on the light. Now the room is too bright. By the time Rosie arrives Anne is talking about prejudice and ignorance and sexual harassment. As Anne talks, Ed shifts in his chair. "Well, I just don't understand what you mean when you say sexual . . . ," he begins. Anne shakes her head, "Not now." He leans back, crosses his legs, crosses his arms. "Ed, I know you have comments and questions, but let's watch this film first. We'll react to it later."

After they watch a film about people getting into elevators and people sitting around a table and people walking down the street, Anne suggests they write about their attitudes toward the opposite sex. "I am interested in how you think of yourself in relation to members of your own sex and in relation to members of the opposite sex," she says.

Mary Lou doesn't know what she means. All she knows for sure is that Anne is wearing one black shoe and one navy shoe with her soft white dress.

"Is there a question?" Anne asks. Everyone frowns but no one, not even Maggie, asks a question. "I realize that this sounds a little vague," Anne says, struggling on. "Let me give you an example. Regardless of your sex, would you prefer a female or a male lawyer?" She reaches up and pulls her hair back and up, lets it fall. The top of her dress strains across her breasts. Ed is momentarily silenced by those round perky breasts. "What do you notice first about a member of the opposite sex?" she asks.

At this Ed emits a loud guffaw. "Your amusement tells a lot about your thinking, Ed," Anne says dryly. She moves to the green blackboard and picks up a piece of chalk. She puts it down and dusts her hands together. "Thinking along these lines will lead to a better understanding of how you perceive your child's mother or father, and hopefully this will lead to a further understanding of how he or she perceives you."

"Before you leave," she says, "just take a minute to write down, informally, your thoughts, attitudes about the opposite sex. Specific examples would be helpful."

Mary Lou considers attitudes. She doesn't have one. Since Gundren died she is *careful* about the opposite sex. For her it's strictly business at the Dairy Queen. No jokes. "What's got into her?" the truckers growl, loud enough for her to hear.

She writes all this. Then after a minute she adds: *If you happen to notice that you are wearing a black shoe on one foot and a blue shoe on the other, don't think a thing about it. Sincerely, Mary Lou.*

Then she thinks about Gundren's funeral. She can't stay away from it. But some things she will never write. Or tell. Deciding not to write anything more about the opposite sex, she picks up her books and walks out of the classroom.

"Hey, you forgot your sweater!"

Turning around, she almost bumps into Tony. He is holding out her blue sweater. "You forgot this," he says.

"Thanks."

"You parked out here?" Tony asks, keeping up without even trying.

Well, this question she doesn't mind answering. "Yes."

"I didn't have anything to write," Tony says.

This interests Mary Lou. How could anybody not have anything, something, to write. The trouble with her is she has too much, but some she doesn't want told. "Don't put your business on the street." She hears Gundren saying it.

"It's nobody's business?" she asks. "Is that why you don't write?"

"That's not it exactly. I got into this class by mistake. I'd just get out, but it's too late to get into another one. Well, what the whole thing amounts to is, I'm not even a parent."

Mary Lou wants to look at him, but she hates it when the class looks at her like she is a bug on the wall.

"Well, a lot of people aren't parents," she says. "What of it?"

"I'm afraid I wouldn't be considered single either, since I've never been married," Tony says, chuckling. "Can you figure that out?"

This sounds so crazy it stops her right in her tracks. "Well, what did you take the course for? 'Course I don't care, but with all those drawbacks, I just wonder."

Tony, kicking at a crack in the sidewalk, seems to be wondering about this himself. Mary Lou wonders why he doesn't ever wear boots. Tony is the first man she has ever talked to who doesn't *ever* wear boots.

"It'll sound pretty foolish to a person like you, a serious parent, but I signed up because my sister read a book about single parenting and she doesn't have a child. And I just thought, who knows, I might be one someday. A parent and single. When I have a kid, I'm going to be a good dad. Mine died when I was eight. And I have a drawing class right before this. That makes it easy to hang around and learn something."

Some of it makes sense. "What did Anne say?" Mary Lou asks.

"She doesn't know about it yet. I guess I'll tell her when we have our conference."

It all sounds doubtful, but here they are, at Mary Lou's pickup.

"See you next week," Tony says, opening the door for her before he walks off.

Well, he's got manners, Mary Lou thinks, and she likes the way he talks. Her English is another thing she wants to work on.

Mary Lou gets in her truck and, giving it a minute to warm up, adjusts her rearview mirror so she can see herself. She cares about her looks. Even after all she's been through. Looks have always mattered to her side of the family. She, like her mother and her grandmother before her, knows a lady should look like a lady. Her grandmother's voice when she was mad could be shrill and shrewish, but at the sound of a doorbell it would become soft and pretty: "Just a minute"—almost cooing—"I'm coming," and by the time she'd walk down the hall and through the dining room (where she used to sleep at night on a little rollaway bed) to the door, her hair would be smoothed into place, her apron whipped off, and there she'd be, answering the door. A lady!

Echo has never looked like any of them, any of her people. At fourteen, no *fifteen,* Echo's fifteen now! and she's missed her birthday. She can't believe it. Echo's probably taller now, but she'd still be so skinny you could count her ribs, easy. Echo is dark, darker even than Maggie (the class wouldn't have known *what* Maggie was, but she told it). Anybody would know Echo was white though, by her eyes. She has the bluest eyes, like sapphire stones. People turn and look at her. Oh, Gundren was proud of that girl. Right now the thing that makes Mary Lou feel the best (and the worst) is thinking about Gundren and Echo.

Gundren's hair was black, coal black. His eyes were brown, but the pupils were so big that his eyes looked black. When he made love to her his eyes *were* black. When Mary Lou ran her fingers over his chin, or when he burrowed it in her neck, it always felt scratchy. He said that when he was forty he would grow a nice soft beard just for her. Not in a million years did Mary Lou think he would die before that.

The memory of that last night is a wound she can't stay away from. She's been over it in her mind a thousand times, remembering how, as she cleared the table, she had listened to Echo moving around in her bedroom right off the kitchen. Echo's bare feet pattering down the hall to the bathroom as Mary Lou filled the sink with warm sudsy water. Her footsteps returning and Mary Lou putting the stacked dishes in the sink. The door opening into the kitchen. The "Good night, Mama. I love you," and "Good night, darling. I love you, too," as she rinsed the plates and glasses. Then the sounds of Echo settling, the bed creaking, the springs scraping against the headboard a little, and Mary Lou drying the dishes, putting them up.

That last night she had known Gundren would be home. She had felt it in her bones. She had felt it the night before, too, but not as strong. Tonight Gundren would be home. She'd warm up the soup while he showered, and then he'd eat. After that they'd make love, and then, her head on his shoulder, they'd talk, mostly about Echo, wondering at how pretty Echo was. And smart. And at how stubborn she could be.

All that evening Mary Lou was getting the house ready for Gundren. And going from room to room, turning on lights, opening curtains (Gundren hated anything closed up), putting the soup back on the stove ready to heat as soon as she heard his truck pull in, Mary Lou felt herself getting ready, too. For Gundren.

Along the back fence there were a few roses left and some honeysuckle, and she got out a pitcher (the one with the mother hen and baby chicks painted on it), filled it with the roses and honeysuckle, and put it by their bed. Then she filled the tub with warm water and poured in a little baby oil. Stepping into the tub, for no clear reason, the words *attar of roses* popped into her head. She wondered what "attar of roses" was. Were the words in the Bible? She stepped back out of the tub and, going back into their bedroom, she broke off a full-blown rose and scattered the petals in her bathwater. When she had bathed ("in attar of roses," she'd tell Gundren) she put on her gown and robe and curled up in Gundren's chair by the window to wait.

So she was there half asleep, not hearing him when he came, until he opened the back door.

"You're home," she said. "Oh, Gundren, I'm glad you've come home."

"I'm glad, too, honey, but I've got to eat and run. I'm taking Plumb Easy to Mineral Wells."

"Gundren, you just got home. You're tired. Stay home tonight," she told him.

"I can't, Mary Lou. Plumb Easy's in season and I got a free breeding."

"You can take her Saturday," she said. "I can get off a little early and go with you. Echo and me."

Leaning against the kitchen table Gundren grinned and poured himself a cup of coffee that was not even warmed up. "I've got to be there early in the morning. Pat's taking the stallion out to New Mexico tomorrow," he said, slipping his hands underneath her robe, pulling her to him. "Besides, Plumb Easy's ready now. Mary Lou, don't you know nothing about nature?"

That flew all over her. Him talking about nature and her curled around his pillow every night, waiting for him, for the wild horsemint smell of him, the feel of his hard round shoulder underneath her head. Without thinking about it, she picked up the coffee he'd just poured and threw it in his face.

"Go on!" she screamed at him. "Go on off to Mineral Wells! All you ever think about is horses, anyway. That's all you care about! You and Plumb Easy just go! And don't bother to hurry back here neither!"

Gundren was not listening, not noticing even. Looking beyond her, smiling, he said softly, "Sweetie, go on back, go on back to bed." And it was only then that Mary Lou had seen Echo, wide-eyed and staring, at the kitchen door.

Without another word Gundren had pulled his boots on, loaded Plumb Easy in the trailer, and left.

The highway patrol came and told her. They said, "Sit down." Then they said, "Your husband's dead."

She was numb for a while. Knowing what dead meant slipped in, little by little, through unexpected cracks.

Her mama had come right away, and then her neighbors, with food and whispering. "How did it happen?" they asked each other softly, and gathering courage, they asked her mama: "Mrs. Carter, how could such a thing happen? A man like that, knowing all about horses. Stomped to death in a trailer." And then, "Poor thing. Can't even open the casket."

"Mary Lou, you want us to notify anybody? What about Gundren's family?" Tom Davis, their next door neighbor, asked.

"No, no, thank you, Tom."

"Mr. Davis, Gundren's family is all traveling in the South right now," her mama added, putting everything in its best light. "And we are trying to get in touch with them. But you could ask Brother Tinsley to come over here. Mary Lou will be wanting him for the services." Sighing, her mama settled onto the orange sofa in the kitchen.

"No, Mama. I don't want Brother Tinsley. Gundren was Catholic and I already called the church. The priest from All the Angels is coming out here this morning."

"Now Mary Lou. Think of Echo. You don't want that. All that mumbling. For Echo's sake you want a real service."

"Mama, Echo's gonna be Catholic, like her daddy was. She's already started on it."

"Don't tell me my own granddaughter's gonna be a Roman Catholic. We've never had that in our family."

"You're embarrassing me, Mama. Talking like that in front of Mr. Davis."

"I expect Mr. Davis understands."

"Mr. Davis is one, Mama," Mary Lou said, wishing she could fall through the floor.

"A Catholic? Well, excuse me, Mr. Davis," said Mrs. Carter. "Don't mean to step on any toes."

"It's all right, Mrs. Carter. Some things are worse than being a Catholic. My ex-wife was atheist."

"No!"

"Yes ma'am, sure was."

"I never."

"Me neither, not 'til I married one."

Then Mary Lou's mama leaned real close to Mr. Davis. "Gundren was a Gypsy. You know that?" she whispered.

"I'd heard it," said Tom Davis, taking off his John Deere cap, bowing his head. "But we never missed nothing from our house or yard. Not a thing. Could leave a bicycle, mower, anything out."

Mary Lou could tell this was more than her mama had bargained for.

"Sad! Sad! Sad!" her mama declared.

And hearing her mama say it Mary Lou wondered if she meant sad because Gundren was a Gypsy, or sad because he was dead.

Mary Lou hadn't meant to tell one soul about the funeral. Ever. But at the next Single Parenting class, she does.

Anne's voice is soft and clear. "Close your eyes and, in your mind, go to a place," she says. "This may be a place you've been to or it may be a place you've only imagined. Now, what is the first thing you notice in the place?" Her voice is almost a whisper, "What is the first thing you see?" The words are almost a poem, only they don't rhyme. "Listen," she says gently. "What is the first sound you hear?"

Mary Lou's heart skips a beat. She can hear the rustling sound again and, all of a sudden, the place is right there: the sun coming through the stained-glass windows, the smell of incense, the strange strong words of the priest.

After a while, Anne says, "Would one of you like to tell us about your place?"

Mary Lou swallows. She'd like to tell, but she hears Gundren's voice: "Don't put your business on the street."

"Hush," she tells him and leans forward to begin, but Maggie jumps in.

"I am watching a concrete-mixing truck," Maggie says, nervously. "It backs into place and dumps an entire load of concrete on my husband's green Mercedes."

Right away Mary Lou can see the whole thing. The green Mercedes, the milky-white concrete spilling over it. Raw and dangerous.

"Interesting," Anne says calmly. "Would you like to tell us more, Maggie?"

Maggie swallows. "The whole thing tickled the shit out of me. My husband, the son-of-a-bitch, was fucking his secretary."

Such words! Mary Lou can't believe she has heard these words. And from a girl! She waits for Anne to call her down. But Anne only says, "You must be feeling great pain. And anger. How sad for you." Then Anne leans forward, opening her hands, not just to Maggie, but to all of them. "But how wonderful to handle the pain in such an imaginative way. It's a creative, positive way to handle anger."

"Didn't feel so creative when I had to stay downtown all night. Took a lawyer that long to get me out."

Ed laughs, a loud guffaw. Tony smiles. Anne's mouth trembles into a big smile.

"You mean this really happened? You poured concrete on your husband's car?" Anne asks.

"I did," and now Maggie is laughing. "That was why I had to spend a night in the slammer. I borrowed a concrete truck."

"Aw, get out," Ed says. "You can't drive a concrete truck."

"Any fool can drive a concrete truck." Maggie says, daring him.

Now Maggie is really laughing. Then the whole class is laughing, and Anne is laughing as hard as anybody. All this laughter pries a laugh from Mary Lou. Surprised by the sound of it, she lifts her hand and touches her lips with her fingers.

After that Anne asks them to write about their place. It takes a minute but Mary Lou hears the whir and buzz again, the thumps of settling, and it is all there. She writes:

I know when they come. The church door opens and stays open. There's a rustling sound as they all come down the aisles. The Family. Ten, twenty, maybe thirty, fastening themselves onto the empty places. Settling in. Their dark skins and black, black hair. The way they move so quick even in church. I hold my breath knowing something strange and terrible is about to happen. Aunt Labelle is in a seat right across from me, her perfume, heavier than gardenias right before a thunderstorm, filling up the church.

After the church services, walking to the open grave, I try not to see them—the women with red and gold and purple shawls over their black dresses; their hands, for once, still. The men with their young bodies and their old faces. Like iron. Then the graveside service is over. I lean forward and break off one of the roses (maybe this is the attar of roses) from the casket spray for a keepsake. I get up and take Echo's hand to leave. As we walk away I hear the rustling again. After a few steps I turn for one last look. The red, all of it, is being stripped away. The Family is tearing the roses from the coffin. They are like locusts. They tear the roses off until every last one is gone, broken off. The stems are left jutting out, bare and spiky. That was the hardest part. The Gypsies had taken Gundren. Once a Gypsy always a Gypsy.

Mary Lou puts down her pencil and looks out the window. She sees the tree house and Echo in it, Echo swaying back and forth in a breeze that has just sprung up. And Gundren. So far out there she can't even imagine it. A Gypsy angel driving his truck round and round, trying like anything to find his lost way home.

2

Later that night, drawn by its lyrical quality, Anne reads the passage again. Mary Lou seems to know intuitively that truth, or a kind of truth, often reveals itself in the emblematic. Mary Lou's first journal entry had puzzled Anne, and she was concerned about the words she might find in this one. But there was no need. There is pain here but there is more. In the pure energy behind the young woman's search to find meaning and beauty after her loss, in the energy itself, there is healing and solace.

Anne looks down at her hands. Once long ago Donald had said that just to look at her hands made him sad because they were so beautiful.

Restlessly she rises from her desk and walks down the hall to her bedroom. Curious, she looks at her face in the mirror. She is still pretty even though she's forty-three. But there are a few strands of gray in her hair and small pouches under her eyes. *Gravity's on the job,* she thinks wryly, remembering how funny she had thought the comment was as a child whenever she or John dropped a dish and broke it. Then their father, to offset the dismay, even sorrow, her mother would express at such times, would chuckle and say, "Gravity's on the job." As a child she had felt mild sympathy for all those children whose fathers were not like hers.

Seeing the moon reflected in the mirror, she walks over to the window and looks at it, a full moon in a storm ring. She dislikes stormy weather. But tonight she almost hopes that high winds and a hard rain will come. A storm has a way of washing away the past.

But what about Echo? Echo in a storm being pelted by the wind, endangered by lightning. Maybe Ed is right. Perhaps she should be more direct. Echo can't stay in a tree house indefinitely. She'll have to come down. And what if the weather suddenly turns cold. Good Lord! What has she been thinking of? Echo needs to be at home. Someone needs to help Mary Lou get her daughter home.

After dinner (as a reward she had added a generous dollop of butter to the baked potato) she takes a brisker walk than usual, and then a warmer bath. In bed that night she lies awake thinking of Donald Lewis. She enjoys thinking about Donald now. It's not a betrayal now that Allen's gone, although still calling, leaving messages—*he's glad it's over, she was right to end it;* on another day, *he misses her, he loves her, although he doesn't know why he should;* and the last one: *why couldn't they just be friends*—she feels safe remembering Donald. She has no idea where he is, how he is, but now she can safely remember that she once loved him.

An English conference. The poetry section. Arriving late, she had slipped into the last row of seats. A paper on Browning's "My Last Duchess." But this tall slender man, in a beautifully cut tweed jacket, was not reading his paper. He was talking about a woman. Talking tenderly about the woman in the poem and about Neptune, this mighty god, taming a sea horse, surely one of the loveliest and most delicate of creatures. And all the while he spoke, in his slightly British accent, he was confounding her with his deep understanding of her, of Anne Hamilton, as he talked about the Italian woman of the poem.

That night, completely flummoxed by the intimacy she had felt hearing this stranger, she had gone to bed early but awoke in the middle of the night, imagining the woodsy smell of his jacket, hearing the intensity of his voice, recognizing the brilliance behind his intimate knowledge of the Browning woman. And of her, Anne. Fully awake, she had dressed, taken the elevator down, and walked into the bar. The bar was empty and then Donald came in, surprisingly alone and saying, "I knew you'd be here." And before the night was over they were together in her bed, tangled by passion in bedsheets and clothes, where they stayed the rest of the night and all the next day, ignoring the conference, even ignoring a book signing of his latest poems that afternoon.

Their affair had lasted five years and seven months, and while she never asked and he never said he was married, she had known it. Still, she loved him. His quick mind, his ardent body, the sound of his voice. They met three or four times a year, usually at English conferences (these always out of town), and always the struggle to get there—driving alone or with a friend or sitting up all night on a bus—until the year the conference had been held in Nashville. And Donald lived in Nashville. His wife Sarah, his children, his two dogs and a cat lived in Nashville. And one evening Anne, mistakenly, as she has come to believe, met his wife (actually nicer than Donald in most ways), a warm intelligent woman with intense brown eyes and a perpetually worried expression. Sarah had insisted that she come out to the house for dinner and, caught off guard, she had gone. After the children, trusting and vulnerable as only children are, had taken her to see the barn and the barnyard cat, their dogs, the garden, their neighbor's dogs, the grave of a deceased rabbit, she stopped seeing Donald. It was one thing to understand that Donald was married but another to have seen the innocence on his children's faces and the friendliness of his wife's smile. And after dinner, watching him pass around a box of Cadbury chocolates, without realizing the irony of it, she had determined not to see him again.

And then six months later: As if entering on cue, there was Allen. Unmarried. Not at all interested in poetry. Without children. Attractive, although balding and sensitive about it. A predictable lover. *And what's wrong with that?* she suddenly thinks. *What's wrong with me?* she demands, hearing the clock strike twelve and, dismayingly, one, before she falls asleep.

The following Monday Anne showers, washes her hair, and slips into panties and bra. For a minute she stands in front of her closet, longing for something different to wear, something new. She enjoys buying things for her house and plants for her yard, but for herself, she shops only when it is necessary. She flips past her skirts—the long green one, the short black, the black-and-white checked—and pulls out a soft blue skirt, a softer sweater. Also blue. Allen had liked the blue. *Forget Allen,* she tells herself, stepping back to look at herself in the mirror, pat her stomach, stand up straight.

Satisfied, she has a light lunch, looking through English essays as she eats. Hurrying! Hurrying! Deliberately she slows her pace. It isn't good to hurry. But tonight she has decided to speak more directly to Mary Lou about her daughter. And there is Tony. He got into the class because it fits into his schedule. But he has told the class that he is staying because of loneliness. She will talk to Tony about the advantages of being lonely at times. There are studies that show that periods of loneliness are often followed by periods of intense creativity.

After lunch she listens to Allen's latest message: *What about Friday? We'll order in. I'll bring a movie. One of those British films you like. If I don't get a message, I'll assume it's OK. Be over about seven.*

She'll deal with Allen later. It's only Monday. And her class is waiting.

Chapter Three

1

MARY LOU is in the loft of Mr. Roseborough's barn by six, waiting for Echo. It had taken a week, but after moving around from one spot to another looking for the best place to watch for Echo, she found the right place. The only thing was if Mr. Roseborough had looked out when she was climbing up the ladder to his hayloft, he would have seen her plain as day.

The whole place is full of signs: No Trespassing. Keep Out. Private Property. No Parking. Nothing On This Place Is Worth Your Life. She hopes he won't shoot. She doesn't think he means it. Even with all the mean signs around there is a red geranium in one of his windows, and some aluminum pie pans for feeding the birds are hanging in the sycamore trees in his front yard. Mr. Roseborough must be old and sad, just worn-out, like his place. She almost hopes he is sick, too sick to get out of bed. Then he couldn't see her climbing up into the hayloft. She doesn't hope that. Not really. Anyway she knows he isn't sick. Someone feeds the cows and chickens, although the cows look awful. When she sees them moving slowly up to the barn to drink and eat, with their ribs sticking out, first on one side and then on the other, they remind her of Echo. She can see her ribs, too, plain as day. Settling back she puts her binoculars to her eyes. Anne had thought up the binoculars the last time the single parenting class had talked about Echo. It isn't quite time for Echo, but she looks toward the tree house anyway. She doesn't know what to do about Echo. Everybody in the class believes she should make Echo come home. Her mother thinks so, too.

"Don't say a word about this to Tom Davis," her mother had said when she told her Echo had moved to a tree house. "Don't tell any of your neighbors about all this. They'll think we're crazy."

"Mama, I don't care what the neighbors think. And especially Tom Davis. We've just got to let Echo alone for a while." And she doesn't care. Not in the least. All in the world she really cares about is knowing Echo is safe when the sun goes down.

She will have to do something sooner or later, but Gundren had always been so sure. And suppose he was right, saying, "Let her alone!" Gundren was right a lot of the time. And besides that the weather has held. October is usually one of the best months in Texas, and this evening there is not a cloud in the sky. That has made it easier to just let things go.

Carefully she focuses the binoculars on the woods where the tree house is. A soft late-season haze hangs over the cluster of scrub oaks. Most of them look terrible, their limbs hanging, broken and gray. Like they haven't tried hard enough. Trash wood. But there! Right in the middle of the scrub oaks, that old live oak is growing, bold and green, making its way toward the sky. In the oak, almost hidden by its own leaves and by the bare limbs of the scrub oaks, is the tree house where Echo has set up housekeeping.

Each day Echo adds to the house—plastic bottles for water, then, a blanket and two quilts, and one day, candles. Yesterday she had brought rope from the barn and tied it across the part of the railing that, like the scrub oaks that cradle the tree house, was hanging broken and swaying in the wind.

Echo has her own money, and when she ran away she took all the money from all three piggy banks. Gundren had started the banks, filling up the first one before Echo was four. The last one, a pink unicorn with purple ears and mane, must have had well over a hundred dollars in it because on Echo's twelfth birthday Gundren had taken to putting dollar bills in it. Nothing small.

Echo has stopped going to school. Mary Lou hates that. But she knows what Gundren would say. "School can wait. It'll be there. Echo knows what she's doing. She'll go back to school when she's ready."

When the principal called about Echo's absences, she told a lie, feeling bad about it, even though in telling it, she had made it white. "Echo's been so upset about her daddy," she had begun (and that was true), "that she just had to have a change" (and that was true). "So she's with her daddy's family for a week or two," she'd said finally, sighing. That last was the hardest but Mary Lou feels it is almost true. Echo, in a way, has always been with Gundren's family.

That is what worries Mary Lou the most. She is sure that if Echo knew where the Family was she might go to them, and behind that idea is another one: If they heard she was living in a tree house, they might come and get her. And Mary Lou cannot bear the thought of losing her. Echo is all that keeps her going now.

A sudden noise, like glass breaking, from inside Old Man Roseborough's place causes Mary Lou to turn sharply and focus her binoculars on the house. Blurring the worn-out path that leads to the back door and the kitchen steps, she stops at the kitchen windows. They reflect the reds and pinks of the sunset sparkling out at her like two big Christmas ornaments. She cannot see past the sparkle into the house. When the sunset fades, she might. Or if Old Man Roseborough turns on a light. Right now the house is quiet, so still and quiet, she believes she may have only imagined the glass breaking.

Still, she moves a little farther back into the hayloft. She looks again toward the tree house. Echo is not there yet. What if she never comes! Suddenly she sees the highway patrol at the door, hears them saying, "Sit down, Mrs. Burgandy. We've come to tell you that. . . ." No! She whips away the thought. Echo is all right.

When Echo comes it is late and she isn't wearing her red sweater. Mary Lou is accustomed to seeing the red, first thing. Through the bare branches and green foliage, the red is always noticeable, and without it Mary Lou almost misses her. But then she sees the patches of white (Echo's shirt) and blue (Echo's jeans) and black (Echo's long hair) moving up into the tree, like a patchwork quilt.

Relieved, Mary Lou leans back against a bale of hay. She watches a barn swallow fly down and perch itself on a board that juts out from the loft, looking this way and that, turning its head fast, almost all the way around. It reminds her of Echo. Well, now Echo is home, and she can relax.

Mary Lou hasn't told the class about her lookout. In class it would all sound wrong. She knows how disgusted Ed would look if she told it. But up here in the loft with the cows just below and the smell of hay and dust settling (even the smell of barn manure is not so bad) and the soft lowing of the cows and the barn swallows flying in and out, it seems right. The loft makes her feel better.

Pretty soon Echo will be in her own room again, just off the kitchen, and Mary Lou will be getting ready for . . . what?

Not for Gundren. Never again for Gundren. The wave of sorrow she feels when she finally knows this just about washes her away.

2

In class the next day Mary Lou feels like she's walking in her sleep. Nothing seems real. Maybe it's because she is so tired out. On Sunday she had gone back to the hayloft after work. She had meant to go home but the hayloft, being closer to Echo and all, was beginning to seem homey. And then Mr. Roseborough's light had come on, first in his bedroom and then the kitchen, and stayed on a long time. With her binoculars she had been able to see the blue teapots on the wallpaper in the kitchen and the pumpkin-shaped salt and pepper shakers on the kitchen table. Then she saw the old yellow chair. And looking at the chair she saw ahead of her a lifetime of breakfasts and dinners and suppers, a lifetime of sitting at her place at the kitchen table and looking, day after day at the other two chairs, always empty, and she hadn't been able to get rid of that idea all night long.

When she had put her binoculars on Mr. Roseborough she thought, at first, she had made a mistake. Maybe all this time it was *Mrs.* Roseborough who lived there.

Maybe Mr. Roseborough had died. But she knew it was hard to tell about old, old people, and she thought that, even with the long gray hair and real rosy cheeks like a woman's, that it was Mr. Roseborough. The old man opened a cabinet and set out three bottles, got a glass from the cabinet, held it under a faucet, shook some pills into his hand, and took them with the water. After that, he shuffled over to the window and stood there a long, long time, looking out. She could have sworn he looked right at her. Then he looked toward Echo's tree house like, *I know you're out there! Trespassing!* It had made cold shivers go down her spine. And all this had kept her in the loft most of the night.

And now here is Betty in class, saying, "Mary Lou, October's nearly over. And there's a cold spell coming down from Canada." And Dylan saying, "Listen to your heart, Mary Lou." Dylan, limping into the classroom with a cane, looks terrible, the black circles under his eyes darker. And Ed, sounding as brisk as the cold spell on its way, says, "Mary Lou, remember what we talked about last week? Anne said not to take a risk is sometimes the biggest risk of all."

Ed, tall and dark like Gundren, and wearing boots and a hat like Gundren's, and sounding sure, like Gundren—what he said made her think. The idea that not doing anything at all about Echo was chancy is something to think about. She has felt safe letting it go a while, but with Gundren gone for good, she reminds herself, she has to do what she thinks is best for Echo.

"Mary Lou?" Dr. Hamilton, *Anne,* is looking at her. "Mary Lou?"

"Yes?"

"I asked if you would like to stop by my office before class next week. I'll be free then, and we can talk." And when she hesitates, Anne says gently, "Betty's right. Colder weather is predicted."

"All right. I will."

Mary Lou is tired, but stopping by Anne's office does seem like the thing to do. And even if she is tired, when Tony had told the rest of the class that he wasn't a single parent, and added, "I've already talked this over with Mary Lou," it made her feel like somebody. Last week Ed had leaned over and said, "Let me know what happens. Hell, I've got a kid that age. Haven't seen her in three years. She lives in Utah with her mother."

Well, Mary Lou, you're not the only pebble on the beach, she tells herself sternly. With that she puts Echo out of her mind for the time it takes Betty to tell them about a book Anne asked her to read about a woman who had cancer. The woman got so interested in a pair of pigeons outside her window, she wrote a book about them and forgot the cancer. And Mary Lou noticed that in talking about the book Betty says "cancer" four times without flinching.

3

Anne walks out of the covered walkway into the mild sunshine of late October. At six o'clock in the evening the day seems as fresh as early morning. The students at the tables around the courtyard are animatedly talking and laughing. The sound of a plane, high enough so that its engines are no more than a faintly audible drone, blends with the water from the fountain, water that laps easily from one smooth step down to the next. The predicted cold spell doesn't seem possible.

She sees Christopher Ryan walking toward her. Christopher. The campuses are full of rumors about Christopher. Having been invalided out of the navy (or was it the army?), Christopher had arrived with some import late in the semester. He limps slightly because, it is said, of a bone-shattering wound that slightly shortened his right leg. Others discount this, saying that a problem with his lungs caused by the Gulf War was responsible. However, they go on to say, anyone who can run three miles in forty-five minutes has not much wrong with his leg. And his long gray hair, tied back with a leather thong, his slouchy clothes, his relaxed bearing, totally nonmilitary, cause the cynics to doubt that he was ever in a branch of the military.

At any rate it is a fact that Christopher is tall and slender to the point of thinness. His brown eyes are brilliant and intense. Now, walking toward Anne, he is smiling. And Anne sees that he has a very nice smile.

Whenever he sees Anne, Christopher smiles, always remembering that first time. It was early in the second semester. The entire faculty in attendance and he, the newly hired physics professor, sitting in the audience waiting to be introduced by the college president. The flash of a silver needle in the row just ahead of his had caught his eye and he leaned forward. And there she was, Anne, bending over her work, a needle in one hand and a slender thread in the other, so that a narrow ribbon of lace appeared from her quickly moving fingers and enfolded into her lap. With the sun shining on the flashing needle and on a jeweled clasp in her hair, she reminded him of a cameo, an old-fashioned miniature. This image, amid the businesslike pencils and papers and textbooks on the other desks, suggested serenity. And caused him to smile. As she bent over her work her black hair fell forward obscuring her expression; still, the generous mouth, the swell of cheek, the slender hands, even the blue shawl around her shoulders suggested a certain serenity. And wasn't this why he had come to teach in this small college? To find a measure of mental as well as physical recovery?

When the meeting ended he had hurried to catch up with her. "Christopher Ryan," he said.

"I know who you are. I'm Anne Hamilton. Welcome," her blue eyes openly appraising, mouth curving in a smile. An extraordinarily pretty smile.

"I'd like to know what you are making. What is it called?"

"I'm tatting," she said. "My grandmother taught me." And then a quick smile, mischievous, "I find it relaxing. I dislike meetings, so I tat through them."

Now in the faintly decorous courtyard light, he smiles again when he sees her. "Whoa!" he says. "Anne, wait a minute! A man was just here looking for you."

"Do you mean Allen?"

"Well, yes. His name was Allen. I told him you'd be here tomorrow. But he said you had a class tonight and he'd wait."

"Thanks."

"I should tell you that he seemed pretty steamed up."

"Allen?"

"If you would like me to hang around, I will."

She laughs. "In case Allen's violent? That is so funny. Allen's the most gentle man I know."

"Oh, sorry," he says. Leaning forward slightly, he smiles again. "OK then. See you."

Within the community colleges gossip travels from one campus to another faster than e-mail, but Christopher is so new, he is probably not yet privy to gossip. He wouldn't know about Allen. She wonders how Allen would have described their separation. *She just lost it. Threw me out.* No, too much pride for that. It would be more like: *We decided to cool it for a while.*

Hurrying to her office she notices that her stomach feels more than a little upset. If Allen has come looking for her, he must be angry. But threatening? No.

Deliberately she slows her pace. When she arrives at her office Mary Lou is there, just outside her office door. She stands primly, books in one arm, the other at her side.

Anne unlocks the door, swings it open. "I'm glad you've come."

"Are you?" Mary Lou says. "Well." Her voice drifts away, uncertain as smoke.

Inside her office Anne sees the yellow tulips in a crystal vase on her desk. A saucer containing two lemons sits beside the tulips. A blue bowl containing a single white hyacinth that Dylan brought sits on a small table by the window.

"Yes, I am glad you're here," Anne says firmly, slipping her purse into a drawer, looking at the tulips. "How about a cup of tea."

"No," Mary Lou says softly. "It smells nice in here. Is it the flowers? The lemons? Do you keep lemons in your office?"

"For tea. I like fresh lemons. It's probably the hyacinth you smell. Dylan brought it. He drew it in an art class. My mother used to say, 'If you have two loaves of bread, sell one and buy white hyacinths for your soul.' "

"That sounds nice," Mary Lou says solemnly.

Anne flips the card on the crystal vase. Sees Allen's signature. He must have persuaded someone to unlock her office and put the tulips on her desk.

"Well, I came about Echo. Right now, Echo should be in school. I know that."

Anne turns away from the flowers and Allen's handwriting and sees that Mary Lou is standing, one arm behind her back reaching to clasp the other arm that hangs down by her side. Involuntarily touched by this—the posture that of a young schoolgirl—Anne gestures to a chair. "Please," she says. "Sit down." Then she moves to her desk chair. "I agree. Echo should be in school."

"Well, she's stubborn. I can't make her go to school, can I?"

"I don't know. Let's think this through. The two of us." She puts a pencil behind her ear and crosses her legs. Wriggling a foot, she says, "By the way, Mary Lou, thanks for the note about my shoes."

Mary Lou smiles. Her teeth are straight and white. She's wearing jeans, a yellow shirt, sunflower earrings, old-fashioned loafers. "I'll bet you laughed at yourself when you looked down and saw that," she says.

"No. Not exactly," Anne says, shaking her head. "I felt rather foolish." A small wrinkle appears across her forehead. She takes the pencil from behind her ear and puts it on the desk. "Now, what do you think you should do about Echo?"

"I wish I knew," Mary Lou says, her voice filled with longing. "Can't you tell me?"

"I need more information," Anne says. "Tell me what this week's been like for you."

"It's been the worst week of my life. You see, I saw this chair," Mary Lou gasps, bursting into tears.

Opening a drawer, Anne pulls a tissue from a box. "Here," she says crisply.

"In my whole life," Mary Lou sobs, taking a tissue from Anne's hand, and then another, "I've never seen anything so lost and sad as that old kitchen chair," she says, and, burying her face in her hands, she sobs.

Deep shuddering sobs. All restraint gone. Anne waits while Mary Lou's hiccups become gasps mixed with long shuddering sighs.

"Can you tell me about the chair?" she says gently.

"Gundren told me he had to leave and I didn't want him to go and I threw a cup of coffee in his face and Echo saw it and he left and the highway patrol came and said, 'Sit down,' and he told me Gundren . . ."

Now her cries are high notes of pain, the sounds of a dog hit by a car. Finally she continues, gasping out the words: "Echo was quiet after the funeral and wrote a note: 'Mama, I love you. I can't stay here. Don't worry.' "

Mary Lou puts the box of tissues on the floor by her chair, takes one out, and blows her nose. "Excuse me," she says. "I don't know what came over me. I haven't cried. I don't cry, usually."

"I think you needed to cry," Anne says.

Nodding her head Mary Lou wipes her nose. She takes a deep breath, and then she tells about the tree house and about finding her way into Mr. Roseborough's loft. She tells about waiting for Echo to come to the tree house each night and about looking into Mr. Roseborough's kitchen, about how helpless and sad seeing the one chair at Mr. Roseborough's table had made her feel. As she talks the words spill from her mouth along with the damp balls of tissue that fall, unnoticed, from her lap. "And I hate to think about looking at nothing but two empty chairs for the rest of my life," she finishes, with a deep shuddering sigh.

This whole thing is incredible to Anne. A girl in a tree house. Her mother in a hayloft. Watching over her with binoculars. Binoculars *she* suggested.

"Let me think about all you've told me," she says, and when Mary Lou makes a motion as if to go, "No, don't go. I just want to process everything you've said."

But Anne doesn't know where to begin. Mary Lou is hunched over in her chair, her arms crossed over her stomach as if that is the source of her pain. She looks fragile, as if the act of expelling all that fear and grief has left her physically smaller. Anne feels somewhat responsible. She takes a deep breath. She will first explain the idea of projection. Then the logistics of getting Echo back home will be relatively simple.

She leans forward. "Mary Lou, in thinking about those two empty chairs, you're doing something we call projecting. You think now that tomorrow and next month and next year you'll be the same person, but you won't be. We, all of us, change a little, every day."

Mary Lou shakes her head, denying Anne's credo. "Do you change? Every day?"

"I hope so. I'm working at it."

"The braces on your teeth?"

"Exactly," Anne says, laughing. Then after a minute, "Let's get back to Echo." She folds her hands on her desk, leans forward. "Can you imagine that tomorrow, next month, next year two empty chairs might make you feel good?" she continues. "Just suppose that someone whom you don't even know right now might be leaving your house. If you're tired, tired of that person, seeing them leave, seeing two empty chairs, might make you feel good. Does that make sense to you?"

Even before she finishes Mary Lou is nodding. "Yeah. I can see how that might happen." Frowning she says, "Already, I'm not the same. In some ways, I'm more of a scaredy-cat. Well, when my telephone got turned off (Gundren paid the bills) that scared me. But sometimes I'm so brave I don't know myself. I never thought twice about going up into Mr. Roseborough's loft. Can you believe that?"

Oh, dear, Anne thinks, her *telephone,* but then, reminding herself to stay on track, she says, "Certainly I can believe that. Now the next thing we, *you,* have to do is get Echo back home so you can get down from the hayloft."

Pleased with her joke and, in spite of the new problem of an unpaid telephone bill, pleased that Mary Lou has grasped the idea of projection so quickly, Anne sits back in her chair and smiles. She will recommend an experienced psychologist, that is, after she gets Echo home. And this should be relatively easy.

She makes a pyramid with her hands. Her thin bracelets slide toward her elbow. Her blue eyes open wide. "Mary Lou," she says, "if Echo left home because she thinks, however wrong her thinking is, you had something to do with her father's death, she might be more open, more willing to listen, to someone else. Why don't you ask someone she trusts, her grandmother or your friend at the Dairy Queen, to talk to her?"

"I'm not sure," Mary Lou says, frowning. "Oh, I know it's probably the right thing to do, but Gundren . . ."

"Gundren's dead," Anne says firmly. "And asking a friend to talk to Echo might help. I believe it would." Saying this, Anne feels freer, even a little reckless.

But Mary Lou is not the sort who carelessly turns the fate of her daughter over to someone else. The part in her hair is too straight, the angle of her chin too determined for that.

"Mary Lou, it's supposed to be in the fifties tonight," she presses.

"All right. But you've got to be the one. You'll know how to talk to her, what to say."

And as Anne shakes her head, begins to say, "Oh, no, I couldn't. . . ." Mary Lou reaches for her hand, clutches it between the two of hers. "But you said yourself it might freeze tonight. Oh, don't you see? You have to talk to Echo. You're the only one smart enough to think how she feels, to know what's right to say. Why, just look how you helped Betty. You've got to help Echo!"

Confused by the sudden turn of thought, Anne withdraws her hand from Mary Lou's and walks to the window. The creek is running almost dry. A heron pecks at its edges, then steps forward, lifting high one foot and then the other one just as high, carefully stepping into the slow-running creek and, finally, sinking into it for a fluttering bath. Perhaps she should talk to Echo. She herself said that someone other than Mary Lou would be better. Someone not connected with her family, better still.

"All right, Mary Lou," Anne says. "I'll come out there. I'll talk to Echo."

Looking at Mary Lou she sees a brief tentative smile, followed quickly by a huge grin that crinkles up her eyes and fills out her thin cheeks. Then Mary Lou shivers as if a shower of joy has washed over her, and at that moment Anne remembers how it feels to be unreservedly, deeply happy.

"Oh, thank you! How can I ever thank you?" Mary Lou says, grinning broadly. "Now, you come on out to my house about five-thirty, and I'll show you where the tree house is."

Well, now. The where of the meeting with Echo has not occurred to Anne. The responsibility she has felt toward Mary Lou and her daughter has suddenly deepened. She needs to disentangle herself.

"The tree house?" Anne says. "Oh, some other place would be more suitable."

"I don't know where. She likes movies. She may have hitchhiked to Dallas. I doubt that we could find her there. I don't know where she is or where she'll be, but she always comes back to the tree house."

"Oh, Mary Lou, that's so dangerous. A girl hitchhiking."

"Well, don't I know that! But I can't lock her up, can I? Well, the hardest thing is that Gundren, well, he loved her. And I know what Gundren would say. He'd say, 'Let her alone!' "

Well, here we are, Anne thinks, *back to square one.* "Perhaps he would have," she says, "but you love her, too, and you must do what you think is best."

"I know that and I know Echo needs to come home. If anyone can talk some sense into her, you can. Well, there's Mr. Mac's grocery. She'll probably go in there between four and five, but there will be some other people in there buying a Coke or a Lotto ticket."

The tree house is beginning to sound like the best place, indeed, the only place for Anne's talk with Echo.

"I'll be there at your house around five," she tells Mary Lou. "And you can show me where the tree house is."

But after Mary Lou leaves Anne walks again to the window. The water bird has gone. The creek is empty. *My Single Parenting class is taking too much of my time and emotional energy,* she thinks. She needs to focus on her own life. Her new life.

4

By five o'clock Anne is on her way. For her excursion into the Roseborough woods she is wearing her jogging suit and running shoes. Carefully following the directions Mary Lou has given her, she turns off the familiar expressway just east of town. All at once she feels inexplicably anxious. Everything she sees—the trees, the meadows, the long-horned cattle—all seem partially obscured by hazy unfamiliarity. Grimly determined to keep her promise she tightens her grip on the steering wheel. She stays on the hardtop road for a mile, and then, following Mary Lou's directions, she takes the first turn to the left.

"I can't believe I'm doing this," she tells herself when, a half-mile later, she turns onto Gilly Road. Here the land is slightly rolling, Gilly Road cutting straight across what looks like a meadow. Now the houses on each side are becoming more sparse, until, on the right, they disappear altogether leaving only a barbwire fence to run skimpily alongside a narrow pasture. Then on the left, here it is: 4815 Gilly. Mary Lou's house.

Easing the car up the dirt driveway Anne decides that the house, recently painted, had probably been built in the fifties. Set on an acre or more of land without shutters on the windows or trim over the door, and with the screen door ajar and sagging, the house itself looks bare and unpromising. And there is the stinginess of the unmown grass in the small yard, the meager hedges under the windows, and in back the barn that has never known a coat of paint. But overshadowing and softening the starkness of the house there are magnificent old pecan trees, their untrimmed branches weighted down by sprawling grapevines spreading generously over the rough ground they shade, and in the patches of sunlight there is the luxurious growth of waist-high grasses and weeds.

Anne looks again at the address: 4815 Gilly. Yes, this is the right house. Before she can open the car door Mary Lou is out of the house coming quickly down her steps to her car.

She wears a yellow cotton sweater and, instead of her usual jeans, a skirt. The clinging skirt, a black background with yellow daisies scattered across it, makes her seem taller. Her earrings are even more curious than usual: a little brown-and-yellow dustpan in one ear and, yes, a tiny broom in the other. Dressed for housecleaning? Where does she find them? Anne wonders, each pair stranger than the one before and all worn so matter-of-factly.

Anne sees immediately that while the task ahead has caused her to feel grimly determined, it has had an opposite effect on Mary Lou. Flushed with excitement, her usually pinched face seems fuller. And as Mary Lou eagerly hurries along the worn path to her front door, first leading the way, then falling behind, now at her side like an eager puppy, Anne has the notion that if she were not careful she might trip over her.

"Oh, I'm so glad you're here," Mary Lou says breathlessly. "I got to thinking you might not come. And it's already colder. See? You can feel it. I've been so excited all day just thinking that tonight Echo would be in her own bed. Would you like to see her room? Do we have time? Well, what time is it, anyway?"

Careful, Anne thinks, almost says. All this happiness is premature, but despite herself, she smiles. "It's exactly five-thirty," she says, looking at her watch.

"Then we do have time," says Mary Lou, turning back up the steps. "Come on in. We've got about ten minutes. I've been working on Echo's room all day, and I got her a surprise. Come see it. Just see what I've bought for her!"

Mary Lou reaches for the screen door, which screeches open and then falls slowly down to the porch. "Dern it," she says cheerfully, kicking it aside.

Entering the living room, Anne's first impression is of a room in mourning.

"I keep these on for the cats," Mary Lou says, pulling off a bedsheet from the sofa, and then, moving over to a chair, another one. "They're for Sugar and for Sugar's babies," she says airily.

Although the furnishings are sparse, when the sofa and chairs are undraped the room is transformed into a riotous carnival of color. A floor lamp, its red base shaped like a pencil, with a fringed red lampshade resting on the point of the pencil; a dressmaker's dummy dressed in a bright purple, ruffled gauze skirt and a pink blouse, also ruffled, stands against the wall behind a sofa covered with pillows—a purple one embroidered with the word *Paris* and the Eiffel Tower in gold, and a blue one embellished with gold stars.

Mary Lou stops at a table, picks up a photograph, and hands it to Anne. "Here we are," she says proudly.

In the picture Mary Lou leans against a tree, her arms crossed, smiling broadly. A young girl, Echo, her expression solemn, hangs upside down from the lowest limb of the tree, her arms crossed like her mother's. Behind them and off to the side, Gundren stands, slightly out of focus.

Frowning, Mary Lou looks over Anne's shoulder at the picture, studying it. "Gundren looks like he's already on his way. Out of our lives. Echo's and mine," she says wistfully. "Oh, I wish we had a good one of him," she adds. Shrugging her shoulders, "Well," she says, her voice now surprisingly cheerful, "come on. I'll show you Echo's surprise." Two steps and they are down the hall, and Mary Lou is grandly throwing open the door to Echo's room. "See! It's a bedspread," she says. "Isn't it pretty! I know Echo will like it. 'It's tasteful,' the salesgirl said. It was real expensive but I think it is worth every penny. Doesn't it make the room look like, 'Well, hello, Echo! Come on in!' "

The spread is nice, Anne thinks. Blue-and-white-checked cotton. She says, "The salesperson was right, Mary Lou. I think Echo will like it."

Standing just inside the door, Anne looks at Echo's room. A teddy bear and doll lying side by side on the bed look as untouched, as pristine as the spread. A bird's nest with three small blue eggs in it is on her dresser, and a pink vase with pinker roses sculpted around its base holds a collection of feathers. A *Harry Potter* book is on the floor by her bed. Missing is the usual paraphernalia Anne thinks most teenage girls would have—the ribbons draped over the mirror, the fingernail polish and lipsticks and emery boards, the posters on the walls, the smells of perfume and polish remover.

Anne, wondering how far into the woods she must go, looks at her watch. "It's five-forty-five," she says, "do you suppose . . . ?"

"Oh, yes. We'd better go. I'll take you down there, and then I'll go up in the loft and wait," Mary Lou says. "No, I won't. I'll sit right here on the front porch steps. That way I can see you coming out of the woods. I can see you both coming out of the woods and up to the house."

Satisfied, happy, Mary Lou hurries down the steps and, almost skipping, follows the path across a vacant lot that leads to the pasture. Reaching the barbwire fence she stops. "Here," she says, putting one foot on the bottom wire to hold it down and pulling up the top two with her hands.

Anne steps through and turns to help Mary Lou. "When was your phone disconnected?" she asks.

"Oh, I don't know. I don't need it. I was spending too much time on it anyway, talking to bill collectors and whatnot," Mary Lou says, dismissing it all with a wave of her hand.

"Whatnot?" Anne asks, her mind still busy with bill collectors.

"Oh, bill collectors and Mama and such. Mama'd talk all day if I'd just stay on the phone."

Now they are in the woods. "It's right over there," Mary Lou whispers, pointing. "Watch out along here. There's a thorn tree," and pointing to a tangle of vines growing across the path, "I think that's poison ivy. There!" she says, stopping so quickly that Anne almost bumps into her. "It's up there right in the middle of that old live oak. Do you see it?"

Anne, following the line of her sight, looks up through

the bare branches of the scrub oaks and higher still through the thick leaves of the live oak, until, there it is! A rectangular shape, heavy, and with the leaves thick beneath it, dark green, almost black.

"Ah, yes," Anne says. "I see it. I'd never imagined it would be so high."

"It's high all right," Mary Lou says. "Now you can get real close. And if you listen hard you can hear Echo when she comes. But if you don't hear her you can see her when she climbs the tree. OK?" And moving quickly along the path, she turns once, waves, and is gone.

For a few minutes Anne stands as if immobilized. The woods that had seemed so quiet when she and Mary Lou had walked in are now filled with the thud and buzz of insects, the chirps and liquid trilling of birdsong, the dry rattle of tree frogs. Her breathing slows. She smells damp bark and water and the healthy compost of leaves and, over all, the scent of things growing and green.

Turning off the little-used path she now follows one so lightly trod that only crushed tufts of grass, leached yellow by the scrub oaks, show any wear. Then a path, even less worn, turns away from the tree and for a few steps, ten or more, Anne follows that and, yes, here it is, the flattened grass at the base of a sweet gum tree, probably the very place where Mary Lou has waited.

She bends over to brush the leaves and twigs away, and then at her feet, a small eruption, a blur of dark green and yellow, flying up, flying straight up, disappearing into the branches of the live oak. For an instant Anne watches the place where the bird has disappeared, and then she settles at the base of the tree to wait. The sun reaches in to touch the topmost leaves, slanted yellow, of a bush just in front of her. Then a swarm of small yellow butterflies appears from a cluster of small brush, moving as one, swinging this way and that, dipping and swaying in front of her, and then hanging in midair, so close she could have touched them had she reached out to them. She does not, but even so, she feels a kinship.

A shadow falls over her. She looks up. *Why, Echo looks exactly like a Gypsy,* is her first thought. The dark bronze of her face, the thick black hair, like coal, even here in the shadows, glistening, and the eyes sapphires blazing out from the mass of tangled hair. A face as lean as her body, high cheekbones, hip bones jutting out. Beautiful. Strikingly beautiful. *So this is Echo,* Anne thinks, *fathered by a Gypsy.*

The girl is poised for flight; bracing herself, only the tips of her fingers rest against the trunk of the tree. Another minute and she'd be gone.

"You're Echo," Anne says. "My name's Anne. Anne Hamilton."

Echo does not move. She looks directly at Anne's face. Her expression is one of extreme seriousness. Anne, with an effort, gathers her thoughts to tell why she has come, to persuade Echo to come home, but before she can speak, Echo, turning swiftly, runs to the base of the giant oak. Up and up she climbs seeming to fly up the ladder before disappearing into the tree house.

Jumping to her feet Anne is abruptly halted by the loss of feeling in her right foot. She shifts from one foot to the other until she feels the needles of returning circulation, and then she walks to the base of the tree. "Echo!" she calls.

Silence. After a minute she walks around the tree's magnificent trunk wondering at its age. Thinking of hers, she feels ridiculous. Here she is. In the woods. She seems to have treed Echo. Now what?

She calls again, looking up. A branch shakes. Leaves tremble. A face appears. "Echo, please come down. I want to talk to you. Come down."

"You come up here." A young voice issuing a friendly invitation.

"I don't like heights. Please come down."

Over the side of the tree house two legs appear, swing for a minute, before crossing primly at the ankles. Again silence returns to the forest.

"Echo, do you have a telephone? I could call you."

At this the merriest of laughs rings out, high across the treetops. This is not the Echo she has imagined.

"Are you coming down?"

"No."

A *no* full of laughter.

Now Echo steps from the tree house and into the tree. She sits comfortably on a huge limb, one blue-jeaned knee flung impudently over the other.

The sun's rays have left the forest floor where Anne stands and are now bright against the red sweater hanging from the limb on which Echo sits. *Echo's happy up there,* she could tell Mary Lou. *And she is really, really safe.* She could walk out of the woods and tell Mary Lou that.

No. Damn it! She has begun this process; she's come all the way out here and she's going to finish it. "Echo, I'm coming up," she calls and, holding firmly to the rope, she sets one foot on the ladder and then the other a rung higher and then she's climbing and climbing up, up into the bright sunshine toward the girl who seems more sprite than girl and it's like a Ferris wheel and she's rising up, up into the green leaves and tumbled clouds and now she's here, at the platform, and crawling over it and is on her knees and bending over, holding her chest and catching her breath. Triumphantly she turns to look over the edge down, down, far down to the spinning ground below. Her knees go weak, the ground swims below; her head swims. And she's falling, falling toward the center of the platform, reaching for its center, stretching, scratching to hold on, tightly closing her eyes against the whirling clouds and the whirling tree and the whirling girl who stands over her.

"Oh my Lord," she groans. "Good heavens."

"Are you OK?"

"No, I'm not OK, Echo, I'm dizzy. I may die." She sighs heavily.

"I'm sorry."

Sorry. The word was not one she would have associated with Echo. Lying carefully still she hears a bird's call and the faint rustle of leaves surrounding her. After a while the whirling stops. She turns over, careful to inch closer to the middle of the platform as she does so. Slowly she sits up.

"Here." Echo's hand is at the nape of her neck, a water bottle is at her lips. She swallows, then watches Echo cap the bottle and put it into a basket that hangs from a limb. The sense that she is dizzily disconnected remains. She draws her knees close and hugs them.

"Echo, you'll have to call the fire department to get me down."

Again the merry laugh. "You're fine."

Her eyes are dreamy. Her teeth are white against dark skin. Her long black hair seems unreal.

"Well, I'm up here now. And we need to talk."

Echo leans against the trunk of the tree, her feet carelessly anchored. Clearly she's willing to listen.

"Your mother needs you. She loves you."

"I know that."

"Echo, the night your father left, that last night when she was so mad, you remember?"

"She threw coffee in his face."

"She did that even though she loved him. She wanted him to stay at home."

"I know that. But Daddy had to leave."

"Then, then why did you run away?"

"I don't know. Daddy isn't there. He's gone and . . ."

Echo frowns, shakes her head.

Anne knows her question is difficult. Waiting for Echo's answer she looks up into the high overhead canopy that, even from the vantage point of the tree house, towers above them. The wind gathers. The clouds tumble together, banking above the tree.

"I don't know *why*." Restlessly Echo walks to the furthermost edge of the tree house. "Up here, this is where I am. I'm Echo."

The conversation seems to be veering off onto an existentialist plane. Struggling to help Echo better express herself, Anne says, "Do you mean this is where you have your being?"

Now Echo's expression is one of embarrassed amusement. She covers her mouth and giggles. Anne laughs. The tension fades.

"It's nice up here," Anne says. And it was. Now that she is beginning to relax she finds the view unlike any she has ever known. It is wonderful.

As if acknowledging her comment, Echo begins to move

lightly, easily, around the tree house. She rehangs her sweater, lowers the basket to set a fresh water bottle into it, stoops to pick up a caterpillar and carefully place it in the tree. Together they watch its slow crawl upward. A fat raindrop splats onto the wood.

Anne looks up and sees no sign of rain. But she has lost track of time. She looks toward the red blaze of setting sun. *It's gorgeous up here,* she thinks. But now she's suddenly impatient to be down, to be done. "I'm going now," she says. Dropping to her knees she crawls toward the edge. She looks down. "Oh, my God!" she says. "I can't do this."

"You'll be all right. I'll help you."

Echo steps into the tree, moves to a lower limb, and then steps back to the rope ladder. Now she's below Anne. "You come down backwards," she says soothingly. "Turn around. I've got your foot. Put it here. Now the other one. Down. And another. Down. Put your hands on the ladder. Good! Now you're almost there. Now down a few more rungs. Now just three more. And now, you're down."

Anne's heart pounds, trying to escape her chest. Feeling the ground beneath her feet, she breathes deeply. In and out. In and out. Forest yoga. Ten times. Ten more. Echo waits, her hand on the tree.

"OK? Are you all right now?"

"Yes," Anne said, managing a smile.

"Look" Echo says. "That was so cool the way you climbed the tree."

"I want you to come home."

Echo takes her hand from the tree and hooks a thumb over the edge of her blue jeans pocket. She looks at Anne, her expression one of friendly interest.

Anne, for the moment speechless, searches to find the words to bring Echo home to the blue-and-white welcome of her room. She wants to say, "When your mother thrusts her chin into the air defying an entire class that thinks you should be forced to come home, it somehow pierces the heart." Or "Your mother, however mistakenly or awkwardly, loves you more than you can possibly imagine." She wants to shake her, to ask, "Doesn't love count for anything with you? Don't you know what love means?" Instead she says, "You lost your father. And your mother lost her husband, and oh, Echo . . ."

But Echo, shaking her head, is already retreating.

"Echo, your mother's waiting. Please listen to me for just a minute. Let me listen to you!" she cries.

Now Echo turns away, begins to run. "Tell Mama I'm OK," she calls, running down the path that leads away from the tree house. "Tell her that you climbed the tree," she calls, disappearing into the woods.

"No, wait," Anne says. "Echo, please don't run away. Oh, don't run away," she calls. But there is only the empty path, the silent forest.

Chapter Four

1

THE days passed slowly. Mary Lou did not return to class. Anne had not thought that she would. The following Monday she told the class about her encounter with Echo, although she did not mention the terror of her climb to the tree house. "I saw Echo," she said, telling nothing of the girl's wild beauty, of her animal grace. "And I talked to her," she said, hiding the despair she had known when she could not find the words to help Echo, words that would have made her listen. "She's safe. She seemed happy but she refused to come home. She ran away again," she had finished, not allowing herself to see again the desolation of the empty path, to feel its emptiness.

This evening she opens her book to begin a discussion of the assigned reading. But Ed—it would be Ed—will not have it. "Wait a minute!" he says, looking more puzzled than angry. "You gonna leave it at that? What about Mary Lou? That must 'a just broke her heart." Then, glaring at Tony, "Well, I'd like to call her. You got her number?"

"She doesn't have a phone," Anne says, and forestalling his

next question, "and it's against our policy to give out addresses or phone numbers."

Frowning, slumped in his seat, Ed crosses his arms over his chest and allows Anne to begin the discussion.

Turning into her driveway the next afternoon, Anne sees that Joan, her neighbor, is clipping a small hedge. Her eighteen-month-old, Nikki, is swatting the hedge with a stick. In her straw hat and denim skirt, Joan is reassuring. Anne calls out a greeting to her.

Joan stands, takes off her hat, and waves it. "Hello!" she calls. "Come on over if you've got time. We'll have a glass of iced tea."

"Give me ten minutes."

Slipping into her sweats, tying her shoes, she tells herself, *After that Alice-in-Wonderland adventure in the woods with a runaway girl, a glass of iced tea with a neighbor will be like stepping into the real world.* This is what she needs. And the minute she steps into Joan's yellow kitchen with its smell of freshly baked cookies, she understands that Echo's world is more fantasy than real.

"Have you thought any more about it?" Joan asks, watching Anne sweep the baby up into her arms.

"May I give him a cookie?" she asks, ignoring the question. Anne knows what the *it* is. She and Joan have talked about adoption for three years, and now that Joan has adopted Nikki, she's a proselytizing convert to motherhood.

Holding Nikki in her lap, Anne watches him eat. He chews, swallows, drops whatever he's eating with drunken abandon. Considering Joan's question, Anne gives herself over to the mess of his runny nose, the wet cookie-crumb mouth he wipes on her tee shirt, the cheerful *uh-oh*'s when crumbs fall to the floor.

"Well, have you? Have you thought about it?"

"I think about it. Of course, I think about it. There's an agency you can go through. Single, I could go to China and adopt a baby girl. They prefer boys in China. If I could find another Nikki, I'd do it in a minute," she says, squeezing an *oomph* out of him.

But she's not quite ready to begin the process of adoption. The Single Parenting class has made her aware of the difficulty of parenting a child alone.

After a few weeks the class stops asking about Mary Lou, but without her presence, it seems as if the energy and the sense of possibility is gone from the class. Anne tries to recover some of the momentum of the discussions. Knowing that money is a problem for most single parents, she asks Jake Harrison from the business division to come in and help her students become better money managers. She feels a small gratification when the session helps Ed realize that it costs his ex-wife, who has custody of their daughter, four times as much to take care of their child as the amount of his child support payments. But when Ed asks Anne to help him determine the fair amount he should pay for child support, "Talk to Jake Harrison about that," she says, carefully drawing back from involvement with her students.

When she jogs she often meditates about the changes she has made. Allen no longer calls. She misses him the way one misses the familiarity of a doctor's office where one goes for a checkup. But she does miss Donald. She misses the excitement of their time, always brief, together. She misses the anticipation of those times. *My teeth are straighter,* she thinks ruefully. She has lost, maybe, half a pound. And she still has her soap opera.

Almost every Tuesday she has a sandwich in front of her television, perversely enjoying the complexity of relationships she observes each week. Who's married to whom. Has the husband or his son fathered the stepmother's child? And there is an occasional murder. And loss of money. And divorce. Still, the characters manage to rise above anything and everything, always brightly (often hysterically) talking, always beautifully dressed. She loves seeing the characters grow older, grow fatter. And even though she knows she's being manipulated she occasionally sheds a tear or two over the reuniting of mother and daughter or husband and wife.

The symphony series has begun now and midway through the series, Zubin Mehta appears as guest conductor. On that November night Anne arrives early and is soon lost in the exquisite sounds of instruments coming together in their resolution of themes, in their resounding codas. Caught up in the energy, the exuberance of Mozart, she is surprised to find tears rolling down her cheeks when the final movement comes. She has always enjoyed the symphony, finding the kind of satisfaction in music that she does not find in her teaching. For example, the unobtainable passion of Mary Lou for her dead husband, her strange daughter—she does not intend to give herself to that frustration again.

During the day, oh, she maintains her routine during the day. By keeping to a careful schedule of classes, papers, meals, jogging, she controls her thinking, guarding herself against any thought of Echo or Mary Lou. But on cold nights she sometimes stirs and, half-awake, frets that Echo might not be warm. Once, too restless to sleep, she had risen and walked through the house. Peering out the windows, she had imagined Echo walking along some dark Lone Oak street, easy prey to lust. To violence. And as the night passed, Mary Lou's face, in her mind's eye, became more pinched, more colorless, her hair dull and faded, even her earrings bleached by sorrow.

One bleakly cloudy night, following a bleak gray day, she walked through her house, turning on lights to see her Dufy, her Meissen china, her neatly shelved books. She had changed her life. But to what purpose? Looking at her *things* she knew that, in spite of her makeover, all she had left is a dust-covered accumulation of a lonely life.

On the last Friday before the Thanksgiving holidays, Tony stops by her office. "Are you real busy?" he says. He puts a hand in his hip pocket, takes it out again, and crosses his arms.

"What is it, Tony? I was just leaving."

His blue eyes are without guile. "Dr. Hamilton, if you're tired, well, I know it's late and I could stop by another time."

"I am a little tired. But today is fine. This is a good time."

"I hate to bother you, but is there any way you could just tell Mary Lou I'm thinking about her? Tell her I'd like to see her, and oh, here," he adds, taking a postcard from his hip pocket, "here's a card for her. If you don't see her, how about mailing it to her?"

"I'll do what I can," Anne says, taking the card, as he backs out of the office and softly closes the door. Sinking back into her chair, she does not think she will do anything at all.

But she puts the card in her purse. Then a few days later she takes it out to throw it away but, instead, she puts it in her coat pocket. One morning, waiting for the car to warm up, she reaches into her pocket for her driving gloves and feels the sharp edges of the card. She pulls it out and straightens it, pressing it flat against the steering wheel. Tony has written:

A Poem for Mary Lou

Your eyes are the color of a stormy sea,
Your hair is the color of wine;
If you'd only go out with me,
I'd show you a mighty fine time.

Anne smiles. She had said she would do what she could. She'll address it and drop it in the mailbox. No! She will take the card to Mary Lou. She will deliver it, and, in doing so, free herself from this nagging sense of responsibility. She will tell Mary Lou again that she regrets not having been able to help. Then she can focus on her own life. Allen has stopped calling. Lorene, her colleague, had told her he was dating again. Some woman from the North Lake campus.

Walking to the parking lot that afternoon, Anne shivers, draws her coat closely around her and turns up her collar. She is surprised that a cold front has blown in since morning, but then, when Echo disappeared she had stopped listening to weather reports.

Maybe Echo's home by now, she thinks, turning off the hardtop onto the road that led to the Gilly Road. On a day like this, surely, she would be at home. Anyone with any sense would be, and Echo, obviously, has some sense. She cannot remember when she has seen a young girl with a more intelligent face. And so alive! Then, too, the bond between mother and daughter is strong. Obviously that is why, when Echo ran away, she had only run as far as a tree house close to home.

Echo is probably home now, perhaps even in school. Anne is beginning to feel foolish.

As she pulls into the driveway she sees that the house looks shabbier than she had remembered. But even the weather is shabby today, the sky overcast, the wind strong and right out of the north. Most of the leaves have fallen from the trees, and, walking across the yard, the grass feels dry and brittle under her feet. As she climbs the steps a dry leaf falls in front of her and is blown, skittering off the edge.

The house feels empty. Mildly disappointed, Anne realizes that she has been sure that Mary Lou would be there waiting on the steps, just as she had been waiting when Anne had come up from the woods, alone. She knocks on the clumsily repaired screen door, so loosely latched that it bumps against the door frame each time she knocks. She waits a minute and knocks again, this time calling, "Mary Lou. Oh, Mary Lou. It's Anne."

No one answers. Then she remembers. Of course. Mary Lou would be at work. At the Dairy Queen. Vaguely she remembers seeing it in Lone Oak. Just off I-30. She will go there and if Mary Lou isn't there working, she will mail Tony's card to her.

Driving to the Dairy Queen she sees again the pinched expression on Mary Lou's face when she had come back from the pasture alone. Anne had expected sorrow, anger, but Mary Lou had offered sympathy.

"Echo wouldn't come," Mary Lou had said, making it a statement.

"No. She wouldn't listen. She just ran away. But maybe she'll go back to the tree house."

"No. She won't. I know Echo. She won't ever go back

there. She'll get as far away from the Roseborough place as she can." Then lifting her head, squaring her shoulders, "Well, you tried," she had said softly. "Nobody could do more than that. Don't you worry. I'll find her. Wherever she is, I'll find her."

Now driving into a parking space at the Dairy Queen, Anne believes that Echo is probably on her way home from school this very minute. Opening the door of the Dairy Queen she steps into the warmth and the smell of hamburgers frying, the sounds of dishes clattering. Off to the right somewhere there is the sound of breaking glass.

"Oh, damn! Chester! Come clean up out here. Hurry, 'fore someone gets hurt!"

The woman is tall, unusually tall, and thin. Her hair, as red as carrots, flames out past narrow shoulders. She wears overalls, at least the top looks like overalls, but no, the bottom is a skirt, short, a flowered print, revealing stemlike legs. Turning she sees Anne.

"Help you?" she asks.

"Just some coffee. Is Mary Lou here today?"

"Mary Lou? Oh, yeah. Squirt," she calls, her Adam's apple bobbing up and down. Then lowering her voice, "We call her Squirt," and raising it again, "Mary Lou, someone here to see you."

Suddenly Anne regrets having come. What good will it do to see again Mary Lou's pinched face, the faraway look in her eyes?

Now. Here she is.

Her hair tied with a red ribbon into a frizzed clump on top of her head, brown and gold honeybees swinging from her ears, her nose pink as if she's just come in from the cold.

Seeing Anne she comes over, smiling ruefully.

"Gosh, I've been meaning to call, tell you I'm still planning on coming back to class, as soon as I find Echo again," she says, shaking her head in mild embarrassment, setting the bees to furious swinging. Then clicking her tongue, "Well, I'm pretty sure we'll find Echo this week, and oh, Maudie," she says, interrupting herself, "Maudie, this is Anne. My teacher. She's the one who tried to get Echo to come home. Came all the way out here to do it."

It is Maudie's protruding teeth that makes her smile so generous, Anne decides, holding out her hand.

"Boy, have we heard a lot about you," Maudie says. "Well Squirt here sure thinks a lot of her teacher! I'd like for you to meet my husband. Chester! Come on out here. Bring the broom and meet Squirt's teacher."

Chester, as tall as Maudie, comes from the kitchen, broom in hand. He could easily be Maudie's brother except that his hair is a light brown. And natural. But his smile is every bit as generous. *Same teeth,* Anne thinks.

Shaking hands with Chester, going over to a table, sitting down with Mary Lou, "Take a break, Lou," Maudie says magnanimously; Anne suddenly feels an intense benevolence toward Mary Lou and Maudie, toward Chester, who is now sweeping up the glass, even toward the Dairy Queen. *This is Mary Lou's home,* she thinks. Maudie and Chester are her family.

"Chester's bringing you a hamburger. And French fries."

Anne lifts her hand to protest, to say she'd had a late lunch.

"Don't worry," Mary Lou says expansively. "It's on the house." She takes a sip of her Dr Pepper. "Coffee just gives me the willies," she says. "I've been thinking about you, and I haven't forgotten the class, either," she says, lowering her head.

Now the honeybees are resting against her cheeks. "Tell them just as soon as I find Echo, I'm coming back, unless," frowning, tightening her lips, "I'm too far behind to catch up."

"If Echo comes back this week, or even the next, you come right back. This isn't a credit course. And the dean has agreed to offer the class for another semester. It's to be called Single Parenting II. Almost all the students currently enrolled in it have signed up again," Anne says, taking up her role as a teacher, feeling at ease with it. "But getting Echo home. That's the important thing right now."

"Well, I've looked all over Lone Oak. I went up to the Roseborough place, past all those No Trespassing signs, to ask if Mr. Roseborough had seen her, but he thought I was from the electric company and wouldn't say a word. Yesterday I decided I'd let it go long enough."

"You went to the police?"

"Better than that!" Mary Lou says, leaning back, putting both arms on the table, setting the bees into a dizzy swing.

Anne shakes her head. "What?"

"I sent for Gundren's family," Mary Lou says triumphantly. "They'll find her. They can find anything."

Oh, I wish the class were here now, Anne thinks, seeing them all, Ed, Tony, Maggie, Rosie, surprised again by Mary Lou, seeing them listening to her. Looking at her. Enjoying her, too.

"Gundren told me they found his great-great-grandpa's grave way out in the country on a farm in Tennessee. Just nosed it out," Mary Lou says.

Anne shakes her head, unable to comment. She takes a bite of hamburger and dips a French fry into catsup.

"And dogs," Mary Lou continues, "they are real good at

finding dogs. Once Joey, that's Gundren's uncle, left his dog in New Jersey, just forgot all about him for two hundred miles. He drove all the way to Virginia before he realized he wasn't asleep in the backseat. When he missed him, he doubled back, 'course, but the dog was gone. Then, four weeks later, he found that dog! Guess where?"

"Well, I don't know. In New Jersey?" The hamburger is good. Surprisingly good.

"No, sir. Washington, D.C. was where he found that dog. One month to the day, he found him on the Dupont Circle. That was when he changed his name to King. Before that, he'd always called him Pup. Just Pup."

"When he found his dog, he changed the dog's name?" Anne asks. She dips another French fry into catsup, wondering why the conversation seems difficult to follow.

"Yes. Sure did," Mary Lou says. She leans forward; her tone becomes confidential. "Well, when Joey found King (that's his new name), he was driving a taxi for a cousin. His landlady said, "No dogs!" so he rented a room for King in a low-rent part of town. He had to give a name with a deposit, and he thought, well, not every dog has his own rented room, so he wrote down Mr. King. That's how he got the name."

"The dog has his own room!" Anne is incredulous. "But how does he, how does Joey manage?" Anne asks, unable to frame a single question that would address all those that, one after another, stream through her mind.

"Well, King living three miles away was trouble, but Joey would make it over two, three times a day to take King for a walk. And sometimes King would ride in the taxi all day. Joey's customers liked it."

"And now, does King still have his own room?" Anne asks.

"Oh, as far as I know, he does. But wherever Joey is, there's old King, too, setting, sitting (I'm still working on my English) right beside him. You can be sure of that."

"So you think they can find Echo. What about asking the police to help?"

Mary Lou drew herself in. "I couldn't do that! That might give Echo a record. No. The Family can find Echo." Reassuringly she smiles at Anne. "Don't worry. Echo's not really lost. Most likely she's someplace nearby this very minute."

Mary Lou pulls a bee earring from her right ear. "I never have liked their ways. Never will," she says, studying the bee, "but they get paid to find horses. Some have the power more than others. Gundren's aunt is the best one at finding horses. I know they will find Echo."

Anne nods. She has read of psychics who find things. She supposes what Mary Lou is suggesting is possible. She slips into her coat. The drive out to Lone Oak had been foolish, all this expending of energy and emotion on a student. But in Anne's own defense, Mary Lou's problems are unusual. And now she is released from all responsibility. Mary Lou is fine. Filled with hope. Confidence. Anne can return to an orderly life, go home to a pleasant evening. She puts her hand in her coat pocket, feels the postcard.

"I almost forgot the reason, one of the reasons, I came," she says. "Tony asked me to see that you got this card."

Reading it, Mary Lou purses her lips. "That's real nice. It's the first time anyone ever wrote me a poem," she says shyly. "Tell him I said hi." Lifting her left shoulder, setting the bee in her left ear into a gentle swing, she smiles.

Driving home, Anne turns on the radio. Beethoven. The piano is her favorite instrument. She considers Joey and his dog with a rented room. She wonders how the family will go about finding Echo. Wonders how Gundren's aunt finds horses. All at once her heart lightens. She feels buoyant, as if she has had a good swim.

Chapter Five

1

ANNE draws her routine around her shoulders. Teaching, reading, attending various meetings, she distances herself from Mary Lou's unsettled world, feeling relieved that she will not be visiting it again.

Still, certain words, words like *dappled*, or *myth*, or *forest*, or sounds, like the strum of a guitar, a crow calling, an oak branch blown against the eave of her study, evoke an astonishingly clear image of Echo standing in the shadows of the live oak tree, her slender neck seeming scarcely able to support the dark cloud of hair that frames her narrow face.

Driven inside by December's cold, Anne putters around her house. At an estate sale she picks up a nice old tilt-top table for her study. She finds, however, that when she puts it at the end of the love seat in front of the windows, the study looks crowded. She takes out a footstool and a small chair. Then she has to rearrange all the furniture, finally moving her desk away from the wall, where the Dufy hangs at eye level, to the windows that look out over her garden in the side yard. She likes the change. She can imagine the earliest blooms of the jonquils and narcissi, followed by the antique roses. Today it looks bleak, but as early as March everything will begin to green up.

Just before the holidays begin Christopher, surprisingly, sticks his head into her office. Wearing jeans and running shoes, he leans against the door frame, pulls a handkerchief from his pocket, and wipes his forehead. "Three miles," he says. "Now, how about lunch? You can't say no. It's too close to Christmas. I'll meet you in the cafeteria at one," and without waiting for an answer, he is gone.

She looks at the papers waiting to be read and marked. A stack of papers at least a foot high. *Later,* she tells them. She opens her file drawer, takes out the lunch sack filled with carrots, almonds, and tofu and drops it into the wastebasket. *Tomorrow's soon enough to diet,* she tells herself. And she's curious about Christopher. Rumors about him have begun to fade, but still he remains mysterious. Obviously bright, good-looking in a craggy way, he is always alone. She imagines the woman with whom he lives—a woman who appreciates the sensual world and all its refinements. She believes that Christopher is a very sexy man. It's his attitude, indefinable, but very much a part of the way he moves or watches a woman or leans into a conversation with her. But what she needs is a friend.

Over beef tacos—they're so greasy, so good—Christopher tells her about his plans (she notes the singular) for Christmas. "I'm looking forward to it. Can you imagine a more beautiful place in the whole world! The snow falling, the music, the city of Vienna. I've always wanted to be there at Christmas."

He probably lives alone, she thinks. *His description of Vienna is lovely.*

She imagines flying off to Vienna. She would be dressed in her most casual clothes, but with tickets in her purse to the operas and the balls. "I'm flying to Vienna," she would say, checking in. The woman behind the ticket counter would lift an eyebrow and smile. "Ah, Vienna," she would sigh. But merely imagining sets Anne's heart into a faster beat and she places her hand over it. "I think that sounds absolutely wonderful," she says. "Someday, maybe. But I've never flown. I can't. I'm totally neurotic about flying."

Without launching into the series of questions that usually follows this revelation, Christopher simply nods. Tempted by his reaction, *so cool,* she thinks, she almost tells him about Mary Lou and Echo. About climbing up to the tree house. It would amuse him, draw on his experience as someone who lives alone, almost certainly alone, but some reticence makes her hesitant to serve it up like an appetizer on his luncheon plate. Anyway the whole thing with Echo is beginning to seem unreal.

After lunch she hurries back to her office determined to finish her papers and get her grades in early. But her ideas about Christopher have not changed, she decides, picking up a freshman paper. He is very, very sexy. And nice. Out of the corner of her eyes she sees a flicker of yellow outside her window, a yellow balloon drifting lazily over the parking lot, until finally it escapes over the treetops. She watches until the yellow disappears into the shimmering haze of the sky. Impulsively she puts the stack of papers into her briefcase and drives home.

That afternoon Tony Orchard appears on her doorstep.

She had been reading the journals from her single parenting class. Maggie, with a part in the college production of *Crimes of the Heart*, writes that she has fallen in love with her director and that she is suing her husband for nonsupport: "Better him in jail than me with children that need coats and new shoes," she writes. Dylan writes of the deep comfort he feels when his mother reads *Goodnight Moon* to his little son. Betty, having been pronounced free of cancer at her six-month checkup, describes how, driving home from her doctor's office, weeping with relief, she got two tickets: one for not stopping at a stop sign and the other for driving over the speed limit. "Do you want to get yourself killed?" the police officer had asked her when he wrote out the tickets, thereby setting off uncontrollable laughter from Betty. Ed's daughter is coming from Utah for a holiday visit. He writes about the places he will take her, the things he will buy her. He wants the visit to be perfect. His expectations—a perfect daughter, a perfect vacation—are high. Rosie is trying to get her son into one of the best private schools in Dallas. Knowing that Rosie's funds are limited, Anne hopes the school can help with the tuition. And she hopes, she *believes*, that Rosie's artificially induced pregnancy will not affect the school's decision.

When she finishes reading the journals she leans back in her chair. In this light the Dufy is losing its color, the reds and blues and yellows becoming darker in the darkening room. But in her garden the pink remnant of a late-blooming rose blends with the colors of the setting sun. Although she is surprised that it is so late she feels satisfied with the work she has accomplished. Rubbing her shoulders, stretching, she decides to pour herself a cup of tea and walk out into the garden.

Just as she gets up from her desk the doorbell rings. "It's probably Joan," she tells herself. But when she opens the door, she sees that it's a student. Tony Orchard.

"Dr. Hamilton, I would have called first, but I couldn't get your telephone number." He retreats, frowning, a little ways from the door. His blue eyes widen in a mixture of hope and uncertainty.

"It's unlisted," she says, mildly resentful. "How did you find my address?"

"Rick, the man who delivers your wood, gave it to me. He told me where you lived."

"The man who delivers my wood?" She is incredulous.

"He's in my drawing class, and we got to talking. I told him about your class. He wants to take it. He's getting a divorce."

"Tony, I'm rather busy."

Holding out a paper sack in both hands, "Mary Lou sent this to you."

The wind lifts his blond hair above round blue eyes, one with a slight cast. His face is tanned, his cheeks made ruddy by the winter's wind. Wisps of blond hair hang below his jacket collar. He's wearing jeans, a leather jacket.

"Here!" He hands the sack to her. "I stopped by the Dairy Queen in Lone Oak, just dropped in. Mary Lou's working, but she sent me over with that." Nodding toward the sack she now holds, he adds, "It's a Belt Buster and fries."

She looks down at the sack, still a little warm, and catches a whiff of onions. She hasn't realized she is hungry. "Thank you."

"She sent enough for two and I also have an invitation to deliver."

"You're here," she says. "Come in."

Leading the way into the kitchen she decides, with some amusement, how like Mary Lou this is, sending the hamburger and a guest along with it.

"Mary Lou's sent for Gundren's family," Tony says, watching as she takes plates and glasses from cabinets and divides the contents of the sack. "They'll all be here soon. Maybe by Saturday. Out at Mary Lou's place. They are looking for Echo."

"A good many people have been looking for Echo," she says crisply, putting the plates on the table.

"Mary Lou really wants you to be there when they come," he says, easing gracefully into the chair toward which she gestures.

"I'm sorry. My weekends are usually full," she says vaguely.

He nods. "That's too bad." He picks up his hamburger and frowns at it. Then he replaces it, untouched, on his plate. His mouth straightens. "Dr. Hamilton, I'd sure like to help Mary Lou find Echo, but I don't know where to start."

"I saw Echo only one time," she says. "I know her only through her mother's eyes. When I saw her she seemed fairly happy. And safe. She was certainly safe," she adds wryly.

"When Mary Lou talks about Echo it's a little like reading *Catcher in the Rye*," Tony says. And now he seems years younger. "That's a book about a boy named Holden who runs away."

"I know the book" she says. "I hope Echo has better luck than Holden."

"So do I."

The hamburger is very good. "Tony, would you like some coffee? Decaffeinated?"

A frown appears. "I guess I'll try decaffeinated," he says, seeming younger still.

While she grinds the coffee beans Tony takes the plates from the table and puts them in the dishwasher. Again she wonders at the almost preternatural familiarity she feels in his company.

When they are again at the table Tony drinks from his cup,

replaces it, and looks somberly out the window. "I've been out there a lot, at the Dairy Queen where she works, and when she's not busy we talk."

"About Gundren."

"Yeah. God, she was crazy about him," he says. "She told me the first time she saw him was at a rodeo. I've fallen off every horse I've ever been on, but he was a good rider." He picks up his coffee cup, puts it down. "She was married sixteen years. That's a long time."

"I believe Mary Lou's doing just fine now."

"I guess. But she'll never care anything about another man. I'm sure about that." For a minute, despair, or something close to it, sweeps over his face. He shrugs. "Everybody has to love somebody, and she loves Echo. That's why we've got to find her." His face brightens. "She told me one time Echo left, disappeared looking for her cat. Two days later she came home safe and sound. With the cat. She says Echo has a knack for taking care of helpless animals. 'God's creatures,' she calls them."

Touched by Tony's eagerness to help Mary Lou, Anne says, "Echo and Mary Lou are close emotionally, and my guess is that Echo will stay geographically as well as emotionally close to her mother."

"You mean somewhere in Dallas?"

"Closer. She's probably still in Lone Oak," she says. Encouraged by the trace of a smile, "Well, surely you don't think Echo's made her way to Dupont Circle in Washington?" she says teasingly.

Tony grins. "So she told you that story," he says. His mouth curls. A dimple appears in his cheek. "Well, it could be true. Mary Lou told me that Joey did rent a room for a dog, but"—and now his eyes are shining—"I've never thought the dog he found was the dog he lost!"

Anne bursts into laughter. Still laughing, she glances at her watch, stands, and pushes her chair away from the table.

"I know you're busy," he says. "But thanks for talking to me."

"Of course."

"Gosh, it is late. I've kept you too long."

"It's all right. Next time, if there's something . . ."

"I'll stop by your office."

"Thank you."

"If you change your mind come on out to Mary Lou's when the Gypsies come. She will let you know when. Mary Lou says Gundren's family can be a lot of fun. Gundren's aunt says she has 'seen' the place where Echo is. She says it's filled with air and light. Open, but musty and old. Sounds like a barn to me."

"You think his aunt knows?" Tony is so young, so serious, she has to smile.

"I don't know. Maybe. Maybe some few are born with the veil."

Dismissing the idea with a wave of her hand Anne leads the way out of the dining room, through the kitchen, and into the apricot warmth of her entrance hall.

"Gypsies. Perhaps you can write about them." She opens the front door, ready for him to leave.

"Mary Lou's just a friend. I realize that. But she's different. Her voice, I don't know, everything she says, she's honest. Sometimes a night comes around, you know, like in that song about a warm wind blowing the stars around, and I think about her." Hands in his hip pockets, he says, "I guess everybody has to love somebody." Taking the keys from his pocket he jingles them in the palm of his hand. "So long," he says. He walks to his truck, turns, and waves. "If you change your mind, come on out," he calls.

Hearing Tony's hopeful footsteps, she wonders about the Gypsy gathering. By the time she walks down the hall to her bedroom she has decided that if she were a sociologist, even an anthropologist, then certainly she would go out to Mary Lou's. What a rich and original study an evening spent in the company of Gypsies would be. But as an English teacher it would be ridiculous to go.

I'll never be able to sleep tonight, she tells herself in the shower and is asleep almost as soon as she feels the pillow beneath her head.

In the night she dreams. And in the dream Tony Orchard is swimming out to sea, and she, Anne, is surprisingly happy in the dream. Laughing, he urges her to follow him out into the bright blue water. Then he lifts his hand and waves and the droplets of water falling from his raised arm sparkle in the sunlight. But now it is her brother, John, John waving and laughing . . . then . . . he is gone! John is gone. Gone forever in the vastness of the empty sea.

Awakened by the sound of her own cry she sits up in bed, feels the pounding of her heart. When she is fully awake she realizes the dream, the nightmare, has been made more terrible by the feelings of happiness immediately preceding it. *Even in dreams,* she thinks sadly, *one seldom knows supreme happiness.*

She rises and goes into her study, turning on lights as she passes. The Dufy sailboats bob reassuringly on the water. She reaches up to the highest shelf and takes a worn leather album down. Curled up on the sofa in her living room she slowly turns the pages, carefully studying the snapshots of her parents. Here they are reclining in beach chairs. And another picture around a Christmas tree. Lighting candles on a cake. And here's her brother John. Tanned by the sun. Blue eyes made bluer by the tan and by his sun-bleached hair. Here he is again. Waving. Like Tony had waved. Of course. That was why she had felt the closeness to a student.

Funny. It has been years, over twenty, since she has looked at the album. Now she touches the photographs. Studies the faces. In the stillness she hears the sound of their voices. Now here is the picture, the last picture she took before her family—laughingly excited and teasing her about her seashells—left her that last time, left her alone. Forever.

Her family had taken a cabin on Padre Island for a month. The golden days of July had passed; each one different, yet each one the same. Waking to the sound of the waves breaking, the seagulls crying, her brother calling, "Anne, get up. Hurry! The sun's up. Let's go!" And they were usually on the beach before breakfast, walking along the seashore, sometimes talking, sometimes not, looking for seashells. And always the salty smell of the sea and the sound of the waves and the steady wind. Endless. Everlasting.

Until that last day. Her father had charted passage on a glass-bottomed boat, a new experience for vacations at Padre. But she had chosen to spend her last day searching for shells, hoping to find something special, maybe a chambered nautilus. Taking their pictures, hugging them for the last time, she watched her mother and father and brother step happily into a boat to be taken out to sea, where from Anne's vantage point the flat-bottomed boat they were to board was hardly visible, a child's toy bobbing on the vastness of the Gulf.

All that day as she read and sunbathed and searched for a seashell, and for years after as she searched for survival, she grieved over not having gone with them. She might have seen the wave. She was a strong swimmer. She might have been able to help.

She was in therapy for years, and she emerged basically sound. This is what the therapist had told her; this is what she has believed. Until now. Now she feels unsure about the decisions she has made, especially when she yearns with such longing to see Donald Lewis once more.

2

Restive beneath awakened memories of her lost family, Anne struggled throughout the weekend to regain a measure of tranquillity. She lectures herself: *It's not been a year since Mary Lou's loss and she manages better than I do. Not knowing one thing about the stages of grief and without self-pity, she just puts one foot in front of the other and goes on with her life.*

Despite the bitterness of winter's wind she makes her usual round of Saturday errands—the cleaner's, the shoe repair shop, the fresh fish market. After spending her customary hour in church on Sunday, she hurried home to the beauty and order of her house, and to the hermetic world of Meissen china, Oriental rugs, and her beloved Dufy.

But the comfort she usually feels there is still missing. Even the talismanic sight of the sailboats in the Dufy watercolor fails to offer its usual solace.

Walking through her silent house she finds herself monitoring the unpleasant sounds with which the outside world seems to be filled—the insistent whine of a dog, the harsh rattle of a power saw, the boom of a car's sound system. Changing into gray woolen slacks and a silk blouse she sits at her dressing table brushing her hair. *Everybody has to love somebody.* She hears Tony's voice and the sound of his footsteps on her driveway. But when her thoughts drift rebelliously toward Donald and the sound of his voice reading Browning, she turns to a task that, although unpleasant, never fails to satisfy some inner (masochistic?) need. Turning the refrigerator knob to defrost she opens its door and begins to throw out leftover food with prodigious abandon. Carrots beginning to dry. Lettuce with a single wilted leaf. Milk a week from spoilage. After half an hour of frenzied work she is able to view with some pleasure the gleaming, almost bare refrigerator.

And all the food that she had shopped for the day before seems unappetizing. Suddenly, without even the pretense of a list, she rushes to the grocery store. First potatoes. Then she recklessly tosses in a pound of butter and sour cream. *To hell with health food,* she tells herself. But after adding whole milk and a marbled steak she finds herself aimlessly roaming the aisles behind her grocery cart, feeling estranged from the other shoppers and uninterested in the vegetable or fruit sections of the store. When she notices, in her basket, carrots dryer than those she had thrown away and lettuce as wilted, she finds a clerk and motions toward her half-filled basket. "Sorry," she says and hurries out to her car.

A flyer is wedged under her windshield wiper. Irritably she

snatches it out, tearing it in her haste. Looking at it as she crumples it into a tight ball, the words *Who do you love?* leap from the torn pamphlet. Startled, she gets in her car and smooths the torn paper out across her steering wheel. She reads:

WHO DO YOU LOVE?
"I want to help you," says Sister Alicia.
I AM A SPIRITUAL READER.
AMERICA'S MOST GIFTED AND BELOVED PSYCHIC
NOW REACHES OUT TO MILLIONS IN NEED.

And at the bottom of the flyer:

She will lead you to a richer, more satisfying life.

Satisfying. Anne says the word aloud, rubbing her finger across her lips. She looks at the address: 1711 Lemon Avenue. A few blocks away. She can drive by the house, see what the house of a psychic is like.

The house is frame, the yard bare of grass. An old basketball has come to rest in the middle of the sidewalk. A huge piece of metal stands in the left side of the yard, twisting and turning in an elaborate asymmetrical gyre.

Finding herself on the slightly sloping front porch, she rings the doorbell and hears chimes, a few notes from what? Is it "Morning Has Broken"? The door opens wide. A woman stands in the doorway. Her gray hair a cloud below her shoulders; her pink slip falling unevenly below her dark dress; her stockings gathering in gentle folds around her ankles.

"Come in, child. You need my help. I had this feeling you

would come today," she says, gesturing toward the front yard, the street, Anne's car, the whole of the universe! Anne thinks wildly.

"I'm Sister Alicia," the woman says warmly.

Only the aura of warmth and Anne's own unwillingness to offend prevent her hasty retreat.

"Come in, child. Sit here. By the fire. I'll be right back. Chancey wants out. Come on, Chancey. Come on, baby." And a small brown dog obediently jumps from the sofa and trots from the room.

Anne sees that the chair she has been invited to sit in is stacked with newspapers. Looking for a place to deposit them Anne notices that the logs in the fireplace are fake, as is the fireplace itself. And the room is filled with clutter. An old box of Valentine candy, empty, lies on a coffee table by a stack of magazines. On top of the magazines sits a large box of matches and an ashtray with the city's skyline etched into its brown glass. Cushions from the sofa lie carelessly about the floor and the lampshade of an old brass floor lamp sits crookedly on its base. In the window a red sequined Christmas ornament hangs from a shade's pull.

"This is ridiculous," Anne tells herself, but before she can gather herself to leave, the woman is back and shifting the newspapers from the chair to the floor. Then she takes Anne's hand, eases her into the now empty chair, and, in a single motion, pulls another chair so close that Anne finds herself sitting knee-to-knee with the woman.

Anne looks at her face—the smooth brow; the deep vertical lines around the mouth; long gray hair; brown eyes with flecks of gold; and in her ears, large golden hoops.

"Now, baby," she says, taking both of Anne's hands and placing them on her knees, "you are not malicious. I see that right away. You've done many, many good things."

Her voice chimes. *Blackbird has spoken,* Anne thinks.

A tear runs down Anne's cheek. And then another. Amazed at the tears, chagrined by them, she opens her purse and briskly takes a handkerchief from it. "I don't . . . I know I'm not malicious," she says. "I never thought I was."

The woman nods, takes her right hand, pats it, takes her left hand in both of hers, and smiles. "Well, you're not," she says reassuringly. "Honey," she says. "I don't charge for my services. My talent is a gift. But I have to pay the church for the candles. The reading is ten dollars. That's just expenses. The candles, and I do think you need the yellow candle ceremony, the candles are fifteen."

"I think just the reading," Anne says, as another tear rolls down her cheek.

She opens her purse and watches the ten dollar bill she has placed on the table disappear into Sister Alicia's bosom.

"Now, child," Sister Alicia says, taking up her hand again, "Honey, there's so much to see here. But what you need will unfold."

"What do I need?"

"Nothing much. All you really need is trust. Baby, then you can let your life unfold. It will. Trust. That's all, honey. Trust."

Baby. Honey. Child. Anne tries to remember if her parents had called her such names, said them as tenderly. Another tear falls into her lap. "Trust what?"

"Life. Let life unfold. Open your heart to life. Doors close. Windows open. Honey, what's your name?"

"Anne."

"Little Orphan Annie. You're all alone. That's what you are now; it's why you're crying. Well, you never mind all that. Things are changing."

How did she know I'm alone? Anne dabs at her nose that now seems to be running.

Spreading Anne's fingers wide, Sister Alicia continues, "Now some folks read palms. I read between the fingers. That's my gift. Reading between the fingers. Now there's bright karma at your door, Annie Rooney. It's there. Good karma. Honey," she says with a firm nod, "we're gonna need the yellow candle ceremony. Never mind the fifteen dollars," she says, retrieving a half-burned yellow candle from the folds of her skirt. "We'll use this one. For ten."

Feeling somehow blessed, foolishly blessed, less orphaned even, Anne opens her purse, finds a five dollar bill and five ones. She places the money on the table, sees it whisked away.

Now just a minute," Sister Alicia says, and returning Anne's hand gently to her own lap, she leaves the room.

Anne hears the opening of the refrigerator door. Its closing. Then Sister Alicia is back, the small brown dog trotting at her heels. Thinking the reading is finished Anne starts to rise but Sister Alicia places a hand gently on her shoulder, resumes her place, and, knee-to-knee again, as if there has been no interruption, says, "You have carried many, many burdens."

Anne supposes that, in a way, she has. But isn't that a part of the human condition? Doesn't everybody carry heavy burdens?

"Yes," says Sister Alicia firmly, as if Anne has spoken the thought, "but a burden can be light as a feather or heavy as a rock."

"Oh," Anne says, unsure of whether she has, in fact, spoken aloud.

"Your burdens will be light, no more than a butterfly on your shoulder. Your future is bright. It's coming. Doors close. Windows open." And chuckling, she opens her hand wide to reveal a plump red tomato in her palm. "Now you put this tomato in a brown paper bag and sleep with it under your bed tonight. And tomorrow go to your bank, get a hundred dollar bill, and keep it under your left breast, close to your heart for a week. Then . . ."

Then come back and give it to me. Anne finishes the sentence in her mind.

Again, as if in answer, "No. You don't need to come back," Sister Alicia says. "Trust. That's all you need. Let your life unfold."

Let your life unfold. The words become a refrain as Anne drives home. Smiling at her own foolishness she feels almost her old self. The thought that she has been driven by some extremity of the soul to a kind of craziness—an existentialist crisis—comes to mind, but it has all been harmless, and now she feels herself to be in charge of her emotions, her impulses again. Turning into her own driveway she experiences an inordinate relief. When she has changed into jeans and a faded-blue cotton shirt, she works in her study, savoring the feeling of relaxation and contentment that had swept over her as she drove home and that remains with her still. And as she works the words Sister Alicia had spoken, *Let your life unfold. Trust. That's all you need,* become entangled with the Beatles songs she plays that evening. She sits a long time listening to the music and hearing Sister Alicia's chimey voice. After a shower that night she drinks two glasses of wine and has her supper in the study, enjoying the birds who come again and again to drink at her fountain. And smiling at the foolishness of it, she puts the tomato in a sack and sleeps with it under her bed, sleeps soundly all night long.

When morning comes she breathes a sigh of thanksgiving, relieved to be free of the woman she had become the day before, for clearly that woman had descended for a brief time into a kind of frivolous madness. But now here she is! Herself again, in her own bed, her own house, in charge of her own life. She takes the brown paper sack from under her bed, pads barefoot down the hall to the kitchen, and puts the ripe tomato into the almost empty vegetable tray of the cool clean refrigerator.

Driving to work that morning she analyzes her weekend behavior. And more importantly its causes. First Mary Lou's life is disorderly to the point of messiness, and she has allowed it to intrude into her own. And then there is the problem with Echo. Seeing the girl again, as she had seen her in the woods, seeing her running away from the help she had been willing to provide, Anne realizes she had experienced the futility of misplaced charity. And most recently there had been the encounter with Tony Orchard and the reawakened memories of her family. But the visit to Sister Alicia had been strangely helpful.

After she stops at the bank she feels so lighthearted that she purses her lips into a cheerful whistle of an old Cat Stevens, or whatever his name is now, song.

Hurrying to class she sees Christopher. "How about lunch?" she asks.

"What! Oh, sure," he says.

"See you at twelve, then." Smiling at his raised eyebrows, she feels giddily conscious of the hundred dollar bill in her brassiere.

3

Except for Mary Lou the class is in full attendance and discussing various ways to meet single persons: Internet chat rooms, grief recovery programs, single parenting classes (the response to this is laughter), shopping at a *social* grocery store. "I meet guys," chuckles Maggie, "fingering the cucumbers." Ed grins. Betty's grimace is halfway between a smile and a frown. Tony blushes.

At that moment, Dylan, breathing heavily, limped into the classroom holding a cane in one hand and guiding a small boy with the other. "I want to talk to you all," he said, "but first I want you to meet my son, Lennon. Lennon, these are my friends."

What is Lennon thinking? Anne wonders. This small boy with the red hair and freckles. Unsmiling, Lennon stands close to his father. Staring solemnly at the floor he reaches for his father's hand, and finding it, allows his own to disappear into his father's much larger one. Lennon frowns, gazing down at Anne's shoes. She leans over to be sure they match. He is serious, too serious for a small boy.

"Lennon. That's a pretty name," says Maggie.

"He's named after John."

"Are you named after Bob Dylan?" Tony asks.

"No. That name belonged to my grandfather."

"How old are you, cowboy?" Ed's voice, the artificial voice sometimes used by adults when talking to a child, is high, squeaky.

"I'm not a cowboy," Lennon says, his astonishment causing the gap left by a missing tooth to be visible. "I have to grow up first. See, I'm growing." Up on his tiptoes, his shoulders lifted almost as high as his ears, "See," he says.

The class smiles in unison.

"Lennon, could you tell my friends how old you are?"

"I'm six*th*," he says, the word whistling through the toothless gap.

More smiles. Bigger smiles. Maybe she should turn the class over to Lennon.

Dylan turns toward Anne. "Lennon and I talked about this. He's going to sit right outside our window and read his book. He can see me and I can see him."

Holding the boy's hand, Dylan turns to the door, but before he reaches it, Tony is there opening it for the two of them. After a minute the two appear outside the window. Dylan opens a book, places it in his son's lap, and gives the small shoulder a pat. Then he hurriedly limps back into the classroom. His breathing is raspy. Standing, he angles himself so that he can see everyone in the room. He looks at his son, framed by the window, and smiles. Looking directly into Anne's face he says, "The first time you asked us to write what we were afraid of I wrote that I was afraid of being separated from my son."

"I remember," she says.

"This week I realized that my fear is coming true. We are going to be separated."

They wait. How separated? A divorce? An illness? An illness.

That's it. Dylan is very, very ill. It is suddenly a common knowledge the class holds, has held for some time without realizing it.

"I have AIDS," he says. He uncaps a bottle of water and drinks from it. He glances toward his little son, now so motionless he seems a portrait framed by the window. He swallows, clears his throat, and then continues. "Tomorrow I'm going into the hospital to be treated for pneumonia. I'll recover. The doctors think I have some good years ahead."

Dylan. Always the gentle one exuding kindness. As they absorb what he is saying, Betty sniffs, blows her nose. Tears run down Maggie's face. Anne feels the shocked grief of the class.

Dylan looks toward the window, turns quickly away from the glimpse of his son bending over the bright illustrations of the book he holds. As he continues to speak he is no longer able to look into their faces.

Anne feels the ebb and flow of ache and question.

"There are practical things," Anne says. "When you go to the hospital who will take care of Lennon?"

"My mother," Dylan says. "She loves him. She's strong. I'm thankful they have each other."

"Tell us," Rosie says. "What can we do?"

"I guess I just wanted you to know. When I come back, it will be easier for me. I won't have to be guarded. I can be honest. I'm going into Baylor Hospital. You could call me. I'd like that."

"Oh, we will," Betty says.

"We'll come see you," Maggie says. "I have a friend, a nurse, I'll tell her you're there."

"I've got a small flask," Ed says. "I'll put some really good stuff in it and smuggle it in."

Dylan laughs. "Bring me flowers."

"Are you kidding? I'm not gonna bring you flowers. Carrying flowers in public. Man, are you crazy?"

"All right," Dylan says, smiling. "Bring the flask. Now I'm taking Lennon home, but I'll be back. But wait just a minute. Lennon brought you all a surprise."

And when the two of them reappear, Dylan carrying a tray of cookies and Lennon handing each a paper napkin, the somber air fades from the room.

When Dylan has eased himself into a seat beside Lennon, Anne picks up her cookie and takes a bite. "It's delicious," she says.

Most of the cookies remain untouched. "Dylan, are these safe cookies?"

"Mom made the cookies and look, Lennon's already eaten one."

The class smiles. They get it. The cookies are safe. They are safe. For now they are all safe. They can raise their children. Worrying, relaxing, tasting, they ease into the knowledge that one of their classmates, young and a single parent, might not live long enough.

Chapter Six

1

WAKING up from his nap Mr. Roseborough rolls over and looks out the window. The sun is just about down. Before long the cows will be coming up to feed. They will eat slow and then they will drink long slow drinks of water. Afterward they'll stand around, shifting their weight and lowing. Mr. Roseborough thinks their eyes are right pretty, like coffee in sunshine.

Some days they have to wait a long time for him to get up strength enough to feed them. Thinking that now, he rolls back over, lets his legs drop over the side of the bed, and sits up. He has to sit quite a spell before the room stops spinning. Then he makes his way through the kitchen and, holding on to the screen door, steps off the back step and walks out into the yard toward the barn. Here it is hard going, getting up to the loft where he keeps the feed. He dreads it. He takes hold of the ladder and, "Well, here goes!" he says to himself. He puts one foot on the bottom rung that is a good ways off the ground, and gives a push, trying to get the other one up beside it. "Dad burn it!" he cries, when his foot doesn't make it. He pushes again, but before his foot comes up, he is flat on the ground, and here comes this girl, thin as a stick, flying over to where he is lying on the ground beside the ladder.

"Who in thunder are you?" he asks. Then he remembers. "This here property's posted. You're trespassin'."

Seeing that the girl just stands there, looking down at him, "Who are you?" he asks again.

"I'm Echo," she says, sitting back on her heels. "I was just passing by."

"Hurumpt," he says, to let her know he doesn't believe that last. "Well now, girl," he says, shoving himself to a sitting position, wiping his eyes that are watering some from the fall, "since you're here, you might as well give me a hand."

She holds her hand out to help him up. "No, no," he says, brushing it away. "I can git myself up. I just want you to stop the cows from their dadburned bawling. Climb up there and throw down some dadburned hay."

Before he gets the last word out she is up the ladder pulling open a bale of hay and throwing some down, while he calls up to her, "Not too much! That's about right. There. Now that pan on the nail just over that sack. Fill it about half full. No! Don't throw it down. Come down here to feed the chickens."

Then the girl, he can't think of her name (she has a funny one), is feeding the chickens. "Here chick, chick, chick. Here chick," she chants, making her way among them, carefully tossing handfuls of grain, first on one side and then the other, making sure that all are fed.

Watching her, all at once, it seems like it might be Stella, the way she was years ago. How many? He's lost track. But later that night he knows it was that, seeing Stella so plain, that made him say yes when the girl, Echo, asked if she could sleep on his front porch. And dern if she hadn't, all wrapped up in Stella's quilts that he had pulled out of the old trunk in the closet.

The very next day she throws all the hay down from the loft, the chicken feed, too, and drags it into the garage so he can feed the cows and chickens his own self.

Since then she's been his right-hand man. But he can still do things for himself. "Now, girl, you don't have to be over here so much," he tells her. "You better go on home. Your mama's likely worried." And she leaves without a word, but when she leaves, the fear comes flying back to roost, like some old crow, on his back. Then dragging himself out of bed he catches himself talking to an empty house again. "Folks get old, they take 'em off. Put 'em in a home somewhere," he mutters, and trying to buckle his belt, find the eyelet. "I'd rather be dead than off in one of them homes somewheres."

Today is one of his good days, and the girl is back for the night. Sending her out to get their supper, he says, "I'll just set on the front porch while you're gone, Echo. Now get what you need. And you get yourself something, too. You hear?"

He always says that, but he's noticed she has her own money. He is glad she does because he has been planning a long time for the day when he can't get to the bank. Or anywhere. He doesn't know how much money he has around the house. In cigar boxes, folded in newspapers under his mattress, in the ice-cream freezer. Now watching her take three one-dollar bills from the ice-cream freezer, he hopes he has enough. That money is all that stands between him and the welfare. And what will happen to his livestock and his chickens if they take a notion to haul him off?

While he is waiting for the girl he reads his letters. He has every single letter he has ever got his whole life long. But it has been a while since he has got a letter. He doesn't remember when he has got a letter last.

Now she is back, handing him a bologna sandwich, an orange drink, and thirty-one cents in change, and telling him she'll be staying a while, if it is all right.

He hates for her to know just how all right it is. "What about your schooling?" he asks. "You know I believe in schooling for youngsters."

But when Echo just smiles and shakes her hair out of her eyes, he drops it. That night sitting on the front porch, listening to the night sounds, like they do a lot, he feels like trouble has left his shoulders, flown off like an old black crow.

"Listen," she says.

She has good ears, better than his have ever been.

"What? I don't hear nothing."

"A dragonfly, tick, tick, tick, like a church organ, warming up."

"I can't hear it," he says.

"And a bee finding its lost way home."

He smiles. Can't help it. "Next thing you'll be saying you hear the grass growing."

But Echo goes right on with what she is hearing. She is serious. "There's moths' wings. Like candles just lit and fluttering in church." Then she says a thing that goes through his body like lightning. "The sounds of God," she says.

2

Mr. Roseborough and Echo are eating bologna sandwiches and chips on the front porch, he in his rocker, a quilt thrown over his shoulders against the chill, and Echo sitting on the steps. In the three weeks she has been in and out of Mr. Roseborough's house, they have eaten outside every night. It being the end of November, or thereabouts, it's a bit chilly, but Echo likes it. Now Mr. Roseborough puts his untouched plate down on the porch beside his chair, lights his pipe, and looks out into the darkness.

Echo pops the last bite of her sandwich into her mouth. "Aren't you hungry?"

It takes a minute for him to shift his eyes from the darkness to Echo, who is standing before him in the light that comes from the living room lamp.

"Trouble takes a man's appetite. And I'm in trouble. I'm gonna have to get out of Lone Oak, maybe even out of the state."

"What kind of trouble?"

"Two of those welfare folks was out here this week," he says slowly. "I think it was yesterday. Could have been the day before. But it don't matter when it was. They're getting ready to take me off, and I ain't going."

"Take you off! Who would feed the cows and the chickens if you left? Do they know about the kittens?"

"Echo, those folks don't care nothing about kittens, nor nothing like that. They're just worried about my pension checks. Say I haven't been cashing them. Why, the dern idiots. Even say they's no food in the house."

"They got that right," Echo says.

"We get food everyday," he said, "and I could cash my checks. But that's a fool thing to do. Cashing checks when a man don't need the money."

"Can't you explain that to them?"

"Then there's the electricity," he says. "Some dern fool from Texas Electric drove all the way out here the other day just to tell me they were getting ready to turn it off."

"Why?"

"I haven't paid the bill. That's why. But I told that man, 'Turn it off! I don't need it. Got plenty of wood for heating the house, plenty of lamps for light.' "

He sighs, a long exasperated sigh.

Echo walks down the steps and out into the yard. "It's sad, real sad, that they can do that."

For a minute he thinks she might be leaving, but she comes back up on the porch and picks up the paper the sandwiches had been wrapped in.

He takes a swallow of his drink. "Well, there's no getting around it. They're gonna try it."

The next morning Echo has just returned with their doughnuts and coffee when the green Chevy comes, bumping slowly along the dirt road. Then a big yellow-haired lady is coming up on the porch taking one step at a time and saying she is Mrs. Robinson, the county health nurse.

"Come in. Come in," Mr. Roseborough grumbles. "No use standing outside. Come on in and state your business." Standing as tall as he can Mr. Roseborough leads the way into the living room.

"Mr. Roseborough, how have you been feeling?" the woman asks, setting her handbag down and bending over to rummage in her flowered satchel.

"Fit as a fiddle. Never felt better in my life."

"Who's this here?" she asks, looking hard at Echo, then looking out the door again at Echo's pallet still on the porch.

"This here's my right-hand man."

"Where do you live, young lady?"

"Up the road a little ways."

Mrs. Robinson frowns and Mr. Roseborough can tell she is not going to like a one of their answers.

"Mr. Roseborough," she says, taking a pad of paper from her satchel, closing it. "Mr. Roseborough, do you know what day this is?" She opens her purse, feels around in the bottom of it. "Mr. Roseborough, do you have a pen or a pencil I could use?"

"Echo, run get a pencil out of the pencil jar," he tells her.

Echo returns and hands the woman a pencil.

"Now," she says, "do you know what day it is?"

"What kind of fool question is that?" he asks angrily.

"What day of the week is it?" she asks again.

He believes it might be Friday, but he isn't sure. "What difference does it make what day it is? Next question!"

"How old are you, Mr. Roseborough?"

It is a trick. If he says his real age they'll take him off for sure. He frowns and then Echo pitches in. "My grandfather's seventy-two," she says.

"Your grandfather? I hadn't understood that this was your grandfather."

Pleased with the idea Mr. Roseborough nods his head vigorously.

"Mama sent me over to help out," Echo says. "I'm going to be cooking some soup today."

"Our information shows Mr. Roseborough has no relatives in Texas."

"Well, your information is all wrong. My relative is standing right in front of your nose," Mr. Roseborough says.

"And may I have your name?" she asks, her pencil hovering in the air like a snake about to strike.

"Sally," Echo says, picking one she's always liked. "Sally Roseborough."

"Address?"

Here Echo isn't quick enough. "Four-eight-one-five Gilly Road," she says, and as soon as she says it, Mr. Roseborough knows they'll be after her, too. Echo will be back in school where she ought to be and he'll be in a nursing home.

Just as soon as the car is out of sight Mr. Roseborough and Echo begin to count. There is $387.23 in the ice-cream freezer. They count $821.16 in his left boot in the clothes closet and $642 in the coffee can. No change. They count the money in the laundry hamper and the top dresser drawer and in his billfold and under his mattress. When they finish they have counted $3,746.87.

"Well, I'm mighty tired from all this," Mr. Roseborough says. "I'm gonna lay down and rest awhile. And when I get up I'll tell you what I got on my mind."

What he has on his mind, he tells her when he wakes up, is going to live with his nephew in Arkansas. "I've thought this through," he says. "Now those bureaucratic folks move real slow, and I probably have a month, maybe longer. Howsomever I don't intend to sit here and wait. I'm going to Arkansas to live with my nephew, Elvis Lee. Haven't seen him since Cora (Cora was my sister) died, but being family he'll take me in. And I don't intend to live on him, just with him. Now Echo, go in there and get me those letters. I need that address, where Elvis Lee lives. I'm going to write him a letter, and then I guess I'll write Joe Bob. I'm fixing to sell my livestock. Echo, when you reckon your mama will be home? Well, since you been taking care of yourself and me, too, you can see to yourself until she gets home."

It has taken some doing, but a few days later Mr. Roseborough's business is all squared away. Joe Bob White had come one day and paid cash for the cows. "I'll pick 'em up just as soon as Son gets back with my trailer," Joe Bob had said.

"Anytime," Mr. Roseborough told him. "They'll be up here at the barn or in the pasture. And, Joe Bob," he calls as Joe Bob was driving away, "if I'm gone, just take 'em on."

Joe Bob laughs. "Oh, I guess you'll be right here."

"Nope," says Mr. Roseborough under his breath. "I won't."

Four days later Mr. Roseborough and Echo take the bus to Dallas to buy his ticket. He enjoys the ride, the cows and people and houses coming faster and faster, then the cows dropping out, then the people, until it was just cars and tall buildings. Then downtown Dallas and the bus station. They step off the bus and go to the window that says Tickets.

"One way to Pocahontas, Arkansas," he says.

"That name again?" says the man at the ticket window.

He spells it. Even after that it takes quite a while. Then the man says, "Mister, it's gonna be, let's see, seventy-six dollars. Even."

He counts out the money.

On the way home he looks at the ticket. Greenville, Hot Springs, Jacksonville, Searcy, Bald Knob, Tuckerman, Hoxie, Walnut Ridge, Pocahontas. Knowing that each stop will put him farther and farther away from the welfare, he chuckles with pure pleasure.

The next few days Mr. Roseborough says he hasn't felt so good in a long time. His bones don't ache as much, and once he gets his legs going he can step along. Sometimes he catches himself whistling, and every time he thinks about how surprised the welfare woman will be when she finds out he's gone, he laughs out loud.

The night before he leaves they pack the money in an old suitcase. "Pick an old one, Echo," Mr. Roseborough directs. "I got to watch out for thieves and robbers."

"That's easy," she says. "Old is all you've got. What about your nephew?" she asks. "You haven't heard from Elvis Lee."

"I'll find Elvis when I get there. And he'll be glad to see me."

That last night he is journey proud and can't sleep. Sometime in the night he gets up and wanders through the house. Bumping into the table by the sofa in the living room, he hears Stella's picture fall. Doggone it! He'd almost forgot to pack it. Taking the picture he goes into the kitchen, strikes a match, and lights the lamp. He holds the picture close to the lamp and looks at it. Stella sits on the grass and looks young. When Echo had seen it she had thought it was his daughter in the picture. He had thought they'd grow old together, and it worries him some that when he dies and gets to wherever Stella is, he might be too old for her.

After a while he goes back to bed, but he can't sleep. And the next morning he can't seem to get his legs going.

"I'll carry the suitcase for you," Echo says, holding his hand as he comes down the steps. "It's a ways to the highway."

But before they have walked any distance at all, they both know he'll never be able to make it to the road.

3

After the ambulance had come with its sirens full-blast, and then (a good hour later) had eased slowly down the parking ramp and driven away with the body, the driver of the bus, sitting in the small office behind the luggage room, made his report to the police. "I was running a little behind schedule, and there was this low-lying fog carrying enough mist so I had to run the windshield wipers now and then, when I saw the three of them, this dark, thin girl leading a white heifer and the old man on its back. They came slowly out of the mist, just stepped out of the woods. The passengers and I, we all saw them at the same time, and there was a murmuring went through the bus, seeing this girl with her hair all the way down to her waist and the old man on the cow with his long legs almost touching the ground. With the fog and all, it didn't look real, the way they just appeared, stepping out of the morning mist." The driver's speech slowed. "I never saw anything like it before," he says carefully, "the girl and the old man on the cow and the fog, too. Before it happened, it was just me and the passengers almost into Dallas, yawning and looking forward to a hot cup of coffee. Then we saw them. The girl, with beads of mist in her hair and the old man on the cow and the fog swirling around them. Why, it was . . ." He pauses again, a look of wonder on his face. Then he found a word he seldom used: "It was beautiful," he says. Impatient to finish his report and get back to his unfinished breakfast, the officer doesn't comment. "You stopped?" he asks.

Nodding, caught up in the wonder of it, the driver refuses to be hurried. "In no more than a minute the girl pushes the old man up the bus steps and then she goes back, opens a gate, and turns the heifer back into the woods. Well sir, things settled down and when we got to Dallas I thought he was asleep and that I was gonna have to get back on the bus and wake him up. It wasn't until all the other passengers were off that I heard this little cry from the girl and went back. Anybody could see he was gone. I ran to call nine-one-one and when I got back, the girl, why, the girl had disappeared."

The officer, hearing the softness in the driver's voice, stops writing and looks at him. He shakes his head. "Must have been something," he says, before beginning again on the report.

4

Echo sits on a bench in downtown Dallas. Thinking about the way they had taken Mr. Roseborough off made the wind on her face seem hard and mean. Shivering, she buttons her bright red sweater all the way up and pulls her blue jean jacket tight across her chest.

Earlier she had watched the ambulance come slowly through the crowd, watched them take the little bed out and put its wheels down, watched them roll Mr. Roseborough out and put him and his sad old suitcase inside. It was all wrong. They ought to have kept their sirens going, telling the whole world, here's a departing soul! Precious beyond all things. Maybe a choir singing "Amazing Grace." A trumpet playing loud. But the ambulance had left slow and quiet, like it was embarrassed at all the fuss.

Feeling the sudden cold on her cheeks Echo wipes the tears

away with the sleeve of her coat. She had thought she would be the one leaving him when they got to Arkansas, not the other way around. On the bus she hadn't thought a thing about it when she'd heard him coughing. But when she turned to say, "Here we are in Dallas, and I'm going with you, all the way to Pocahontas," she knew he was gone.

She looks up at the blue sky. Not a cloud in it and Mr. Roseborough on his way to heaven. That is a comfort.

She can't sit on the bench forever. Her fingers and feet are numb and her ears hurt.

Looking across the paved cobblestone way, she sees people going in and out of a building, the Dallas public library. She walks across the street and goes through the automatic doors. A lady with brown hair looks over her glasses at her and frowns.

"Yes?"

"My grandfather," Echo begins. But her throat suddenly feels so tight she can't finish so she points toward the elevators.

The frown disappears. "Oh," the woman says.

Knowing the woman is watching, Echo hurries to the elevator and punches the button for the third floor. Feeling herself being lifted through the air, she leans close against the wall. Then the doors open and she steps out into a place so quiet she can hear the birds' song in the trees outside the building. Making her way through shelves and shelves of books, she finds a table under a window big enough to see the whole sky. The books smell like her daddy's saddle.

She looks around the room almost expecting to see her daddy at one of the tables. Instead she sees this boy. Even sitting down he looks tall. Skinny. A gold earring in his left ear. No. Two earrings. Ears flat against his head. Sharpness about the cheekbones. Old enough to be in high school. Maybe older. When he sees her looking at him he straightens up and gives her a quick nod before she can turn her head away and look out the window. Hoping he isn't still looking she puts her backpack on the table and rests her chin on it. The sun comes through the windows. The hands of a clock click. The fluttering of turning book pages mingles with the birdsong. Echo closes her eyes and sleeps.

A hand on her shoulder is shaking her awake. It is the boy, his face so close she could touch it. He smiles; the sharpness vanishes.

"You can sit in here and look at a book, but you can't sleep," he whispers.

"What?"

"Look at a book. Don't sleep. They'll run you off," he says. "They'll think you're homeless." He straightens, stands back, frowning. "Are you?"

She shakes her head.

"I'm not either. I've got my truck. Soon as I get a couple of tires I'll hit the road again."

On the road again. The song pops into her mind.

Silently she rises from the table and, without a backward glance, takes the elevator down and walks out the doors into the cold bright light of the December afternoon.

"Hey!"

She looks back. Here he is. Taking long strides to catch her.

"Do you know where you're going?"

"No."

"Look. Something could happen to you. How old are you? Sixteen? Seventeen?"

She looks at him.

He smiles, encouraging an answer. "What about your folks? Can't you go home?"

Don't put your business on the street. It was what her daddy used to say.

Without answering, she walks on.

"Look, I know a place. There's a lady there at this shelter. You can stay all night."

Like he knows everything. Sounding just like the welfare lady. Echo knows about shelters. She went to a shelter with her daddy once to get Lady out. Lady was her daddy's hunting dog, dead two days after her daddy's funeral and buried in the middle of the night. Next to him. By the Gypsies. Echo won't be staying at any shelter. Not any kind. Not ever.

Throwing her backpack over her shoulder, she begins to walk faster.

"Let me take that," he says, and before she knows it, he has her backpack in his hand and is striding ahead. Like her daddy, carrying things for her. Just as she catches up with him, he stops so fast she bumps into him. He peers into a place with darkened windows. A red neon sign over the door reads "Red's."

"It's open," he says. "Come on. We'll eat here."

Looking at her backpack in his hand, she considers.

"Come on," he says again and they are inside before she can say Jack Robinson. Putting her hands in her jacket pockets she follows him into the warmth of cakes baking and onions frying and meat on the grill.

Chapter Seven

1

MARY LOU is on her way back to school, feeling like the school may have disappeared, or may not be like it was. It's almost Christmas and she's sure Echo will be home by Christmas. And it is almost the end of the semester, and she wants to be in class one more time, maybe just to tell everybody goodbye. Anne will be glad to see her, but will the class remember her? Will she know what they're talking about?

She is wearing an old-fashioned quilted skirt. It's not really quilted, but it looks like a quilt because it has flowers and stripes and checks and no two pieces the same. She has on a white peasant blouse, her hair twisted in a bun on top of her head. And earrings. They are the Eiffel Tower and look right with the skirt. Old-fashioned.

When she's almost there, at Lone Oak Community College, somewhere in her sore heart she feels this tiny surge of hope, rising up like yeast bread. And then she sees this long trailing of birds across the sunset, migratory birds they are, and the hope gets bigger. She thinks about Echo coming home pretty soon. She is almost sure this will happen. The Family is coming. She's sent for them. Gundren said they could find anything.

When she walks into class carrying her jacket, Ed whistles, and "Get down, Mama," says Maggie. "You are so cool," Rosie says. And on the faces of everybody, the nicest smiles of welcome.

The class is excited about Christmas. They have all pitched in and bought a bicycle with training wheels for Dylan's little boy. She hadn't known Dylan was sick. Well, she had known it, *really.* From that first day he looked sick. But not that he was in the hospital, not that he has AIDS. The class is happy because Dylan is now at home and working some. She unzips her backpack and gets out her billfold to help.

"Later," Rosie says. "There's Valentine's Day coming up. And Easter."

When Anne comes in she nods like she doesn't know Mary Lou very well (*Well, a teacher can't be partial,* Mary Lou tells herself) and says, "It's good to have you back, Mary Lou."

Anne's hair is in a ponytail, no ribbon, of course, but she has on shiny lipstick, pearls in her ears, a suit, and shoes of the same color. Black. The ponytail is nice. She looks like one of those ladies on television who talk about the stock market. She says, "Today, we will discuss Chapter Four: Managing Your Finances."

Ed says, "Doctor, I thought we were going to talk about loneliness."

And Betty says, "Me, too."

"It doesn't seem that . . . I suppose I assumed we had moved beyond that stage of single parenting."

"I haven't," says Maggie. "I know I'm better off than Dylan and my kids are better off than Dylan's little boy, but I still get lonesome."

And they're all nodding their heads at once and Anne says, "Very well. We'll discuss loneliness. Anybody?"

"Anne, do you want us in a circle?" This from Rosie of the warm voice and dimples. Mary Lou is glad to see her.

"I don't think that will be necessary. Now, what about loneliness?" Anne is not one bit interested in the subject. Mary Lou can tell that.

Betty jumps right in. She says, "At first I wasn't lonely. It was months before I believed Robb wasn't coming back. Then I realized I had to move on."

Maggie shakes her head and grins at Betty. "I used to drive by Peter's house at night. One night there would be a BMW in the driveway next to his car and the next week there'd be a Volvo. I'd wonder about the woman in there with him, and I'd try to guess what she looked like. I knew I didn't look as good as those women with their fancy cars. But if he doesn't catch up on his child support, I'm gonna put the son-of-a-bitch in jail."

Even with her mad words, Maggie's voice is sad now and full of remembering. Mary Lou hadn't thought she cared about her husband after she poured the concrete on his car, but she does. Even threatening him with jail, she sounds like she loves him.

"Nobody cares about my wife walking out and taking my kid to Colorado," Ed says. "That's how I used to feel, anyway, but now, I guess I . . ." He stops in the middle of his sentence.

The class looks at Anne. "I care," Anne says. "And we can decide what changes we can make in our lives and then begin to make those changes. And Ed, I believe you'd be surprised by how many people care."

"I think Mary Lou and I are lonely in a different way. Our husbands are dead," says Betty, matter-of-factly.

"Maybe the rest of us, we're just mad." Ed's black leather jacket creaks as he slumps back in his seat. His mouth turns down like a little boy's.

"But the feeling one has, that nobody cares, nobody listens, nobody knows the pain of loneliness, that feeling has been experienced by all of us," Anne says, thinking that she really should send the entire class to the counseling center. What then would the dean say, she wonders? She had not wanted to talk about loneliness.

She moves to her desk, sits down, picks up a pencil, and holds it end-to-end between her index fingers. "Would it be helpful to choose a person close to you, perhaps a close relative or friend, and talk to that person or, if they're not nearby, write that person a letter?" And looking at Mary Lou, she adds, "It could be a daughter or someone you work with. Even a classmate."

"I could write my ex-mother-in-law and tell her she did a lousy job raising her son," says Maggie, grinning widely, joining in their laughter.

"Oh, Maggie, thank you for your sense of humor," Anne says. "Laughter gets our endorphins going." Warming to her idea, she continues, "Directing your thoughts to a specific person may clarify your feelings, may help you understand them, even get beyond them." Anne had been reminded of this in a psychology journal fairly recently. She notices that the class, opening their notebooks and getting out pens and pencils, is interested in the idea.

"If you'd like to share your thoughts, put your writing on my desk when you finish. And after the class break we'll discuss Managing Your Finances."

Mary Lou opens her spiral notebook and uncaps her fountain pen. She notices Tony Orchard frowning and writing fast. His shoulders are very narrow. She doubts he'd be strong enough to throw a saddle on a horse.

That's what Gundren was doing the first time she saw him. At the Mesquite Rodeo. She and her best girlfriend had gone because Helen, her girlfriend, had entered the barrel racing contest, and Mary Lou had gone because she liked horses. She had never been on one, but when she was a little girl she had brushed their neighbor's horse, and it was Gundren throwing the saddle over his horse, making it seem so perfect and easy, that made her say, "Helen, let's stay for the bull riding." Gundren's horse had come out of the gate fast and Gundren, waving his hat in the air with one hand, was sitting easy, like it was a rocking chair he was in. And when he won a silver belt buckle for first place, he had ridden over and handed it to her. After that she couldn't take her eyes off him. When the rodeo was over he walked them to the parking lot. Opening the door for Mary Lou he took off his hat and said he hoped she'd be there the next weekend. After that nothing could have kept her away.

Well, here goes, she thinks, and bending to her task, she writes:

Dear Gundren,

The class was real glad to see me when I came back today, all dressed up and wearing the Eiffel Tower earrings you gave me. And they were happy about the present for Lennon.

But listen. You did not need to take Plumb Easy to Mineral Wells and you did not need to get yourself killed, either. What were you doing in the trailer with Plumb Easy anyway? Even I know better than to get myself in a trailer with a horse weighing fourteen hundred pounds or more. Why, Gundren? Will I ever know why?

Last night when I got out of the tub, I stood in front of the mirror and looked at myself without a stitch on. Which I have never done before. I just stood there looking, and thinking what a shame! Gundren's not here to enjoy it, and Gundren, you always said I had the prettiest body in the world. Now what?

I don't know what. But I've about given up on you, Gundren.

Sincerely,
Mary Lou

P.S. I've still got Echo. She will be home by Christmas.

2

Driving out to Lone Oak Anne feels a frisson of excitement. She is going out to Mary Lou's because she can't resist going. She wants to see Mary Lou and Tony and Maggie, of course. But she really wants to see the Gypsies. She's curious about them. She's read about them in novels, especially English and Irish novels, where they're called Tinkers or Travelers. But until she met Mary Lou she hadn't known they were right here in Mesquite, Texas.

The invitation, delivered along with her wood, had been brought by a tall thin young man, obviously into body piercing. He had several earrings in his left ear and one in his nose. Looking at the nose earring had made her sniff. When she handed him a check, he said, "Mrs. Burgandy says to come anytime next Saturday. The Gypsies will be there."

"Oh, do you know them?" she asked, noting the man's formality concerning Mary Lou.

"No ma'am, I don't think I do. But we've got quite a few in Mesquite. They come and go."

Still wondering about the delivery man and the Gypsies in Mesquite, here she is, suddenly in front of Mary Lou's house. There are pickups and one or two SUVs and an old Lincoln parked along the street. Wearing jeans and a rather new, white cotton shirt, Anne feels appropriately dressed. Her hair is held back with a silver comb on each side. She gets out and, straightening her shoulders, walks up the steps. She knocks once. Waits. Knocks again.

The door opens wide, and a woman stands there, hands on her hips.

"I'm Mrs. Carter," she says. "And I know who you are. You're the teacher. Why, you're real pretty. Mary Lou will be glad you came. She just got home. She's in the kitchen with some of them, Gundren's people, and I'll say this: Mary Lou's in-laws are not one thing like we are. Can you imagine coming in on somebody like this? All those folks right before Christmas. Not to mention their dogs and such. All I hope is that Gundren's Aunt Labelle can tell us where Echo is. Then they can be on their way and we can forget we ever saw them. Now Mary Lou's family, our family, well, we're just ordinary folks," she adds proudly.

Even without the lengthy introduction the woman who has opened the door for Anne is clearly Mary Lou's mother. Chin raised, her eyes slits of energy—only the ears bare of earrings keep the resemblance from being complete.

"Well, where in the world are my manners!" Mrs. Carter exclaims now. "Come on in and sit down. If you'll excuse me for a minute I'll see about the pinto beans. We're having barbecue, at least Mary Lou said that's what she thought we were having. Well, I'll let her know you're here."

Comfortably seated in a wing-backed chair, Anne feels inordinately pleased that she has come. The very word *Gypsy* conjures up myth.

The entire week has gone smoothly—the students responsive and involved, the committee meetings shorter, a lunch with Christopher encouraging. He is certainly more contented than almost anyone she knows, single or not. More importantly she has realized that it isn't good to live such a scheduled life. *Let your life unfold,* Sister Alicia told her. She's working on this. She no longer wears a watch and she has stopped making lists.

Now Mary Lou, wiping her hands on a dish towel tied around her waist, hurries into the room. She wears a soft red dress splashed with yellow daisies. A small golden bug hangs from each ear. Seeing her pretty smile, her faintly freckled face, her hair catching red from the sun, "Mary Lou, you look wonderful," Anne says.

Untying the dish towel from around her waist, Mary Lou holds out her hand. "Thank you. Oh, I'm so glad you're here.

Gundren's Aunt Labelle is in the woods, under the tree house. Can you imagine? Eighty-six years old and she climbed through those fences better than I can. She is sure she can tell me where Echo is. That means everything in the world to me. By the way, Ed's here. He's been helping me fix up things around the house. He's out in back right now repairing the pasture gate."

Saying all this about Ed, Mary Lou feels a flush rising over her face. Ed wants to do it with her, but he hasn't said he loves her. She doesn't want to marry him, but since she wrote that letter to Gundren she's been so hungry for love. Oh, Jesus. Hurrying back to the conversation, she says, "Gundren's people are here; his sisters are in the kitchen. Would you like to come in the kitchen and meet them?"

When Anne nods Mary Lou happily leads the way, looking back over her shoulder. Anne has rarely seen a face so filled with hope. What if, somehow, this Gypsy aunt can tell Mary Lou where Echo is? Perhaps the skepticism she feels about parapsychology is nothing more than cynicism. Remembering her recent visit to Sister Alicia she quickens her pace and follows Mary Lou into the kitchen.

The room is moist with heat, a sauna steaming with the smell of tomatoes and bacon and rice, and filled with the murmur of three dark-skinned women. *The Gypsies.*

"This is my teacher, Dr. Hamilton. Anne Hamilton," Mary Lou announces.

The women, who have fallen silent upon their entrance, turn and, as if their movements have been choreographed, lift their heavy black hair back over their shoulders and, crossing their arms, gaze at Anne. Although they are all wearing black, their accessories—black sandals, golden earrings, brightly colored shawls—give Anne the notion that she would like to be a part of their more dramatic world.

One, the tallest of the three, lights a cigarette. "Hi," she says. Another, whose nose is long and thin, smiles quickly, looks down as if examining a long red fingernail before turning again to the onions she peels. The third one merely nods, and turning away, begins to stir the contents of a steaming pot.

"Hello," Anne offers.

"Let's go out back and tell Ed you're here," Mary Lou says, dismissing the women with a shrug of her shoulders. "He's been hoping you'd come. He gave me these earrings for Christmas." Stopping, she turns her head so her earrings could be admired. "They light up, come right on at night, like little lightning bugs."

"Mary Lou, they're wonderful," Anne says. "They seem just right for you."

"I know," Mary Lou says. "When it's dark, or if I run, they blink on and off and on and off."

Mary Lou crosses her arms, tilts her head. "I invited the whole class. I think Tony's coming. And Maggie. There's lots of time. We won't be eating until after dark." But then as she opens the back door, "Oh, my God!" she cries, and is out the door, down the steps, and running across the backyard.

What in heaven's name? Anne thinks, stumbling over the woman with the spoon in her haste to follow Mary Lou out the door and into the backyard. There she sees a small goat stagger to its feet and then, slinging blood with every movement, it begins to run. A man jumps to his feet and, holding a knife, takes up the chase. He, in turn, is chased by Mary Lou who, running like a gazelle, quickly overtakes him.

"Don't kill it! No! No! Don't kill that goat! Stop! Stop!"

Mary Lou screams and with both hands grabs the arm that holds the knife.

Watching the scene, unable to grasp its full import, Anne leans weakly against the wall of the house. The entire scene—the bleeding animal, Mary Lou's screams, the men (motionless shapes in the encroaching darkness) scattered about the grounds—all seems primal except for Mary Lou's earrings that, like minuscule Christmas tree lights, began, disconcertingly, to blink on and off.

In the midst of these impressions Anne feels some pride in the objectivity with which she watches the scene. It is good that she has come out to Mary Lou's. She has lived too long with poets and academics. She needs to experience the whole world, and some of that world is violent. And thinking this she puts her hands across her stomach, leans over, and throws up on the lilac bush by Mary Lou's back door.

"I'm sorry," she tells it, dabbing at the perspiration on her upper lip. Straightening she sees that Mary Lou and Ed have placed the small goat on a blanket and, holding it between the two of them, are intent on carrying it into the house.

"We're taking it to the vet's," Mary Lou says as they ease their burden up the steps. "You're just a baby," she croons to the goat. And then to Anne, "It's lost a lot of blood."

"Hello, Dr. Hamilton," Ed says then, his frown reminding Anne that, for most of the past two weeks, he has seemed angry and frustrated.

"Well, now look, Hon," he says as they cross the living room. "They were planning on barbecue. Now what about their supper?"

"Ed, I can't believe you said that! Darn it! We can go get hamburgers at the Dairy Queen."

"Now, Mary Lou," her mother says, "there's no call for language such as that. You weren't raised to talk that way."

"Ed, we'll go in your truck."

"Aw, Hon, I put on new seat covers last Saturday."

But as if she hasn't heard, "It will be a smoother ride," Mary Lou says firmly.

I feel unwell, Anne tells herself. *No, I feel unreal,* she thinks, following Mary Lou and Ed and the bleeding goat they carry out onto the front porch. There she sees that, from all around the parameters of the front yard, Gundren's family is watching the funereal cortege move slowly out to Ed's truck, watching in a puzzled silence that remains until the sound of Ed's diesel has faded into the distance.

3

Five deep breaths. Emptying her lungs. Than five more. In an effort to regain a centered state Anne concentrates on breathing deeply and rhythmically. When she had come inside to retrieve her purse and slip away, the living room had been empty, blessedly empty, and so she had sat down to regain her composure. Now a truck backs out of the driveway followed by another, their lights slashing through the windows, highlighting the vivid colors of the room. From the kitchen comes the ring of cutlery and glassware, the sounds of vegetables being washed, peeled, and chopped. And the smells! Smells of spices and herbs and chocolate drift from the kitchen.

Anne puts the blue pillow behind her head and relaxes against the chair's back. Closing her eyes she feels the return of tranquillity, except for a nerve that causes her eyelid to quiver spasmodically.

Sometime later—has she been asleep?—she senses a presence. Opening her eyes she sees Tony Orchard standing in the doorway. "Hello, Tony."

Smiling, he hands her a glass filled with wine. In her relaxed state Anne sees that now, apparent in his smile, his shirt unbuttoned enough to display chest hair, and in the gold chain around his neck, Tony seems to have taken on the coloration of Gundren's family. And when she takes the wine from his hand a faint odor of musk causes her to sit up in her chair and straighten her skirt. She drinks from the glass.

"Tony, you look different," she says.

"Well, I thought I'd dress for the occasion. It was just a guess. I don't know what Gypsies wear." He blushes, grins.

"All you need is boots," she says.

Grinning, he looks down at his shoes and nods. "I'm thinking about that, too," he says. Then, admiringly, "I heard that Mary Lou rescued their *cabrito*."

"She did. I couldn't believe it. It was extraordinary. I'm sorry I have to leave. But I really need to go. Please tell Mary Lou. . . ."

"She'll be back in a minute. She'll be disappointed if you leave before she gets back."

And as she reaches for her purse, here they are, Mary Lou and Ed, easing the unconscious goat through the house ("Forty-seven stitches!" Mary Lou whispers) and placing it gently in the bathtub.

When this is done, Mary Lou looks at Anne. "Are you all right?" she asks.

"I'm fine. I was startled. That's all."

"Who wouldn't be? I had no idea they were gonna barbecue that baby goat. I thought it was a pet. Well, it is now! And Dr. Hamilton, I've been thinking about what to do if Aunt Labelle doesn't know where Echo is. It's my alternative plan. Remember how we talked about alternative plans in class?" She turns to Tony and takes a newly poured glass of wine from him.

Anne takes another sip from her glass and, surprised by how good it tastes, takes another.

Mary Lou continues. "If Gundren's aunt doesn't know where Echo is when she comes out of the woods, I'm going to the police, and I want you to go with me. They'll listen to you."

Drained of all energy Anne focuses again on her breathing.

"Well, that can all wait for now," Mary Lou says reassuringly. "I'm gonna take the rocking chair out back. Tony, will you take it out there for us, and Dr. Hamilton, *Anne,* you can bundle up. Here's a shawl," she says. "Well, you look nice with a blue shawl! Now you sit close to the fire and enjoy the evening. Their music is the best part. Oh, I do miss Gundren. This is the first time I've been with his family since he . . . well . . ."

And somehow it seems the easiest thing in the world to follow Mary Lou out into the starlit night, sit in the chair Tony has placed there, sip the wine and watch the flames casting shadows under the wash of moonlight, and gaze at the star-filled sky.

Starry, starry night, she thinks. *A night for Van Gogh. Van Gogh at Lone Oak.*

One of the men picks up a guitar and, leaning lazily against a tree, begins a dark piece filled with the discord of minor keys;

another answers, sweetly melancholic, but the first, refusing to be comforted, repeats the theme of discord until a third interrupts with silver arpeggios insisting upon a harmony that reveals the melody until all three come together in joyful reconciliation. Then a woman begins to dance. And another. Dancing alone at times, then together, their soft skirts lift and fall around slender ankles adorned with golden chains. To Anne it seems that the music, the very music, has called up the dancing women.

"The music is beautiful," she says to Tony, standing behind her chair.

He moves to take her hand.

"Oh, no. I haven't danced in years."

"I'll show you," he says. Pulling her gently to her feet, he puts one arm around her waist, takes her right hand in his, and they are moving easily, lambently, to the strum of the guitars. And as they move around and through the other dancers, Anne feels a tenderness for these women who seem aware of the intense energy with which the men, just outside the circle of light, watch.

Returning to her chair Anne sees that two of the Gypsy women have pulled Mary Lou, protesting, into their circle.

Tony laughs. "That's good for Mary Lou. She needs to enjoy herself," he says, settling on the grass beside Anne.

As if Mary Lou's presence among the dancers has energized the musicians, "Ah . . . ha!" one calls, and the tempo increases. Mary Lou, in her red dress and flashing earrings, begins to dance, almost formally, among the whirl of black skirts and bright shawls.

"I'll bet this is the first time she's been able to relax and enjoy herself," Tony says.

As if to outdistance the dancers the tempo quickens still more and Mary Lou, her arms overhead, her hands clapping, begins to lose herself in the music, whirling faster and faster to the ever-increasing beat, becoming a red dervish, spinning in the center until one by one the other women drop breathlessly from the dance.

Then Ed, frowning, steps into the circle and puts his hands around Mary Lou's waist to stop her dizzying whirl. Steadying her he walks with her back into the house.

"Who in the hell does he think he is?" Tony says to no one in particular. He shrugs his shoulders and says, "Well, you stay right where you are, Dr. Hamilton. I'll get you something to eat."

Sighing, she looks up at the sky. Away from the lights of the city the night is deeply beautiful.

Now Tony comes gingerly down the steps balancing a drink and a plate of food. "I'm sorry. I've got to go. Mrs. Carter asked me to take her home. Anyway, I've got twenty windows to install tomorrow." Leaning over he touches her shoulder. "I'm glad you came, Dr. Hamilton."

But before he takes a step, he stops, frozen in place. Following his line of sight Anne sees the old woman stepping from the darkness into the firelight that flickers over the green parrot on her shoulder and the glittering green and blue beads entwined in long loops around her waist. And "Where is Echo? Where is she?" Mary Lou is crying. "Do you know?"

Good heavens! Anne thinks. *It's Sister Alicia!* Sister Alicia smiling and putting her hands on Mary Lou's shoulders.

"Echo's traveling, Baby," Sister Alicia says. "She's here. She's there. She's all right."

Mary Lou's answering wail, deep, a low keening that goes on and on, strikes at the heart.

"My little *gadje,* don't despair," Sister Alicia says tenderly. "You will hear from Echo soon. I named her. And I know."

"Oh, my sweet Lord," Mrs. Carter whispers to Anne. "I just can't get over Mary Lou's in-laws."

"But I know that woman," Anne says. "She told my fortune once. She called herself Sister Alicia."

"That's her professional name," Mrs. Carter says. "She's Gundren's aunt. Aunt Labelle."

As she listens to the woman, Mary Lou, nodding her head, seems to be drinking in every word.

"It just about breaks my heart about Echo," Mrs. Carter says. "But this is too much craziness for me. Tony, I'm ready to leave when you are. I don't hold with fortune-tellers."

"I'll walk out with you and Mrs. Carter," Anne tells Tony. Turning to leave she hears the Cat Stevens–chimey voice of Sister Alicia calling, "Annie, Baby, Child." The woman is walking toward her, arms outstretched. Reaching Anne she takes her hands in hers. "You see, honey, all you needed was trust. I see it in your face. Your life's unfolding. Now you just let it be."

"I've changed my own life," Anne says.

"Baby, that's good. Now just let it alone. Just trust."

Driving home that night Anne takes a wrong exit and has to double back, so caught up is she in the events of the evening. The bleeding goat. The firelight shining on the knife in the man's hand. The quiet wonder of Gundren's family as they watched their *cabrito* being taken away. The shock she felt when she saw Sister Alicia stepping into the light of the fire. *Maybe I was conned,* she tells herself. *But maybe it was worth it.*

4

After everybody leaves, Mary Lou moves the goat from the bathtub onto a pallet in the kitchen. Then she cleans the bathtub, fills it with water, sprinkles in some bubble bath (she makes it herself from Ivory liquid and rose geranium leaves), and gets in, all the time wondering *where is he? What's he doing right now?* The truth of it is she doesn't know why she told Ed he could stay all night. But when she had written that letter to Gundren, she had taken Gundren's boots out of her closet (where she had put them after the highway patrol brought them home, all bloody and sad) and put them back into Gundren's closet. Waiting in the vet's office for Stitch, the name she has settled on for the goat, to be sewed up, he had asked. "Ed, I've got too much on my mind," she'd answered. One thing she has on her mind is how much Stitch, with his perky mouth and yellow eyes, makes her think of her grandfather. To the day he died her grandfather looked like nothing but good had ever come his way. And Stitch, so sore he could hardly turn his head, had looked just like her grandfather when they had carried him out of the doctor's office.

Then in the middle of the dancing Aunt Labelle had appeared, and Ed had asked again: "Mary Lou, you know how much I like you. What about it?"

"Hush, now, Ed," she had answered. "I've got to put my mind on Echo."

When Aunt Labelle had first stepped out of the shadows, she had looked so pleased with herself that everybody was sure she knew where Echo was. Mary Lou most of all. But when she said, "Mary Lou, I can't tell you where Echo is,"

Mary Lou thought she'd die. Christmas nearly here and Echo who knows where. A Christmas without Gundren. She could get through it. But without Echo, too. Some things are just too hard.

Ed had brought her another glass of wine and an aspirin, and when she could stop crying, Aunt Labelle had hugged her and said, "Why, little *gadje,* there's nothing in the world to cry about. You'll be getting a message from Echo next week."

Then everybody, especially Gundren's family, had all been so sure Aunt Labelle knew what she was talking about that Mary Lou began to believe it herself. Pretty soon she'd processed it, feeling better and better until, with her heart light as a feather, "You can stay," she told Ed. The funny thing is, lately, it has seemed like both of them were out there somewhere. Waiting. Gundren and Ed. And in some ways Ed reminded her of Gundren.

Marrying at seventeen she'd hardly been touched by anybody else. Now sliding down into the tub so that the water ran over her shoulders, she thinks about loving Gundren. About when he had come home late one night and she had run out to his truck in her nightgown and hopped in and before they knew it, there they were, helpless with love, and Gundren laughing, stroking her face, her hair, kissing her, had drawn her closer and closer, and then they were together and she had known, oh, this is what it's all about. This. This is what we're here for. Gundren and me.

But after she wrote the letter to Gundren she had taken his boots out of her closet and put them in his. Gundren's shit-kickin' boots. He was buried in his nicest boots.

Loving Ed the way she had loved Gundren doesn't seem possible. But with him around so much, fixing her porch light, putting new rings in her truck, and wearing starched jeans and boots, lately, like a whisper, a feeling would come over her, and she'd find herself wondering how it would feel to bury her face in his neck, feel his bare shoulder beneath her hand. Sometimes she wishes she was too old for all that.

When the party had been about over Mary Lou saw her mama watching Ed, looking him up and down like he was a shoplifter. Then her mama said, "Young man, I expect you're about ready to leave, aren't you?"

"Mama!" Mary Lou exclaimed, mortified to death.

But Ed just smiled. "Yes ma'am," he answered, meek as a rabbit.

It was then that Mary Lou had whispered, "Stay," to him, and Mama, her nose out of joint, had asked Tony to take her home.

Shaking her head at the thought, she rinses the soap suds off. She has to get out of the tub sometime. She can't bathe all night. And what is he doing? Listening, she doesn't hear a thing. By now Gundren would have taken a shower while she finished the kitchen and would be lying in bed with the bottoms of his blue pajamas on, smoking and scratching his chest. "Oh, Gundren," she sighs.

She stands up, dries herself off, and looking in the mirror, which she has done a lot of lately, sucks in her stomach. Her stomach is nice and flat but her breasts look like, oh, like parched cantaloupes or something. *Poor things,* she thinks. Then lifting her chin and straightening her shoulders, she whispers, "Here I come. Ready or not!"

Slipping into her granny gown and robe, she fastens the robe and opens the bathroom door. "Ed?" she calls.

"Here, Hon," he answers. "I'm in here."

Echo's room. The lights are out, but from the kitchen light she sees that the bed has been turned down and Ed is in it.

"Come here, Baby."

She walks over and as soon as she touches the side of the bed his hands fly to her body and they are all over her, her face, her shoulders, her breasts. And his kisses. They are everywhere, too. She is caught in a storm of hands and kisses.

"Ed," she gasps "Ed, stop. Wait a minute. Stop!"

"Oh, Hon," he groans. "Oh, Baby."

"Ed, not here. This is Echo's room. Ed! Not here!"

"Aw, Baby, it's been too long. All right," he gasps, collapsing back onto the bed. "Where?"

And then he is following her down the hall and she is hurrying ahead, and then they are in her bedroom. Hers and Gundren's. And he is pulling her onto the bed, onto hers and Gundren's bed, pulling off her gown and his hands are touching her and there is the strange brackish smell of him, and "Ed, please!" she cries. "No, Ed. I've processed it! I've changed my mind!"

"Baby, what's the matter? What's the matter? God almighty, this is hard on a man."

"Ed, I'm sorry. But I can't. I just can't."

"Well, what are you? Frigid or something?"

"No. Yes. I don't know," she says. "It's not you. I think about Gundren. I can't help it."

Muttering under his breath so that she hears only "process, hell!" and "Gundren," and "damn," he gets out of the bed. "Well, what do you want me to do?" he says.

"Leave," she says. "I just want you to leave."

She turns away as he pulls on his jeans, his shirt, and with his boots in his hand, stumbles out the door. "Ed, I'm sorry," she says. And again, "I'm sorry," she whispers.

She sits very still until she can no longer hear the sound of his truck. Then she puts her gown back on and smooths up the bed. She goes through the house locking the doors, checking on Stitch, turning off the kitchen light. Then feeling some better she goes out to sit on the back steps to sit where she has so often sat, waiting for Echo. Waiting for Gundren. Hearing Stitch stumble to his feet and make his way to the back screen door, she opens it.

"You feel like coming out here with me?" she asks. "Well, come on. It's nice. Almost like a spring night."

Stitch takes a wobbly step and then another until he settles close enough to put his head in her lap. Rubbing his head she wonders where Echo is this minute. Never mind. She is somewhere, and Mary Lou will be hearing from her soon. Gundren's aunt said it, and she feels it in her bones. And Gundren? Where is he? Well, he is out there somewhere, too. A Gypsy angel driving his truck around and around, trying like everything to find his lost way home.

Chapter Eight

1

IT came late. It came after a Christmas that Mary Lou wouldn't let herself notice. Closing herself off from the garlands and trees and Christmas carols and bells and shoppers, she kept her head down and worked sixty hours a week at the Dairy Queen. She cleaned out closets and rotated the tires on the pickup. She paid off her bills and got her telephone reconnected. And somehow she got through a Christmas without Echo. Then it came. Mary Lou had known it would come. Aunt Labelle had said she'd hear. And she'd felt it in her heart. She reads the card again:

Dear Mama,

I miss you. I have a friend named Jamie. He is just like Daddy about the road. He likes being on it. Take good care of Sugar.

Echo

On the front of the card two lambs frolic in a meadow strewn with wildflowers. It is postmarked Geraldine, Montana,

January 2. She gets a road map from the pickup, finds Montana. Then Geraldine. Montana is a long way off but still it is a place, and she can put her finger on it. *He is just like Daddy.* She reads that again. *Like Gundren. Something like Gundren,* she amends. There was just one Gundren. She thinks about the name. Jamie is a good name for a man. Sitting on the back steps with Stitch, she looks up at the sky. A row of clouds puffs across it like a train. She has heard from Echo! Her mind touches the thought, veers away from so much happiness. The leaves of the pecan trees, stirred by a brisk wind, shake themselves free of their drabness. An old crow sings a scratchy song from the highest branch of a tree. She knows where Echo is! The thought touches her heart again and again until finally it rests there. She sits quietly, reading the card over and over until even her bones believe it.

Overcome, she jumps up from the steps. She has to tell somebody. She will tell Anne! But Anne will not be in her office. The college is closed for the holidays and Anne is probably on a trip somewhere. Anne is better than anybody at listening to a person's heart. She would know how lost somebody can feel one minute and then how a postcard—a little thing like that!—can make everything seem all right. She will drive by Anne's house and see if she's there. She won't go in if she's there. She will just stop long enough to tell her. Hurrying to collect her car keys and purse, she almost forgets her earrings. She opens her earring box, sees the frisky silver rabbits, and puts them on.

Forty-five minutes later here she is at Anne's house, and here is Anne walking out the door. Wearing a blue skirt swinging from side to side and her blouse unfastened a little at the top and tendrils of her hair falling out of a bun, Anne looks like a Lone Oak college student. There are plenty a lot older.

When they have settled themselves in Anne's kitchen ("You must come in," she had said), and Anne has read the card, "Think of it!" Mary Lou says. "Echo in Montana traveling and seeing the world. No telling where she'll be next. I'm glad she's getting all this out of her system. Then she'll be ready to settle down."

Anne smiles. "Mary Lou, I'm so glad you've heard from her. And chances are, since she's written once, she'll write again."

She's almost maniacally happy, Anne thinks. *But the wide smile does nothing to mask the dark circles under her eyes. And she's thinner.*

"Mary Lou, you look tired. Are you sleeping well?"

"Not lately. But I will now that I've heard from Echo."

"Of course. And you will hear again soon."

"I know I will. And asking about Sugar. You can tell she misses her cat."

"That is her way of saying she misses you, too. But she is so young," Anne says, frowning. "I wish we knew more about Jamie."

"She says he's just like Gundren."

"But she is a minor and he has taken her across state lines."

"But not for the purpose of . . . of that! Echo's a good girl. And she's almost grown."

"Mary Lou, how old is Echo?"

"She was fifteen last September."

"She's not yet an adult."

With her mouth in a straight line and her hand on her hip

Anne looks like she's been spray-starched. And sounds like it, too.

She'll have to explain it better. Explain about Echo. "I was seventeen when I married Gundren," Mary Lou said. "I thought I was grown, but I grew up after I married. Maybe Echo will marry Jamie. Maybe they'll grow up together."

Anne smiles. She thrusts the pencil behind her ear and now she looks like her old teachery self. "Now that you've heard from Echo, why don't you enroll in the spring semester classes? We're registering next week."

"As soon as she comes home, I'm coming back. I can go as fast or as slow as I want to in word processing. It's flexible entry. And Tony said our single parenting class will continue, same class, same parents. And I'm gonna take Automotive. There are lots of courses I want to take. But not until Echo comes home. I can't put my mind on it now."

Dis-appoin-ting! Mary Lou tells herself then, leaning back in her chair. Telling Anne about the best day she's ever had in her whole life and here she is frowning and talking like it is the worst thing in the whole world.

Trying again, she clasps her hands over her knees, leans forward. "Echo's not like anybody else. Not me. Not Gundren. She's not like anybody I've ever known. Echo's like . . . this!" she says, holding out her hands, opening them, palms upward, toward the sky.

With startling clarity, Echo is before Anne—the merry laugh, her exotic beauty, her swift flight, running, running, disappearing into the Roseborough woods. Anne's face softens into a smile. "Mary Lou, you're right. Echo is exactly like that."

Satisfied, Mary Lou looks around the room. Shafts of sunlight come into the room, highlighting the books that fill the bookshelves. She wonders how long it would take to read all those books.

"I have to go," she says. "When Echo writes again, I'll come tell you." With her hand on the doorknob, she pauses. "You remember that book I read? Before Christmas. I'm reading everything that lady wrote. I've got as far as *Emma*. It seems like every book tells the same story. But the people are different. I feel like I know them."

With a wave of her hand she is on her way. She will stop by the paint store and pick out the paint for Echo's room. A soft color, maybe yellow, to match Echo's bedspread. With her job and all, she'll be real busy getting ready for Echo.

2

On the last day of February Mary Lou stops by Anne's office with a second card:

Dear Mama,

All night I heard the snow fall. This morning the pine trees outside my window looked like the Three Wise Men. I miss you. How is Gran Gran?

Echo

The card is postmarked Washington. Together Mary Lou and Anne look at the picture on the card, wondering at the beauty of the snow, at its depth. Mary Lou seems able to glean enormous reassurance from the few words on the card. "I think she sounds great," she says, her eyes green as lettuce under the green and blue wool cap she wears. "Don't you? Just imagine hearing the snow fall. 'Course Echo's hearing is above average, but all the same it must have been a heavy snowfall. Imagine how Echo felt waking up and seeing everything covered and changed, you know, changed the way snow changes everything, and Echo there, all nice and warm, looking out at the pine trees."

After that the cards come faster and faster, and each time Mary Lou receives a card she appears in Anne's office, swooping in like some exotic bird on the hard-edged days of a heavy frost to perch for a minute on a chair or move quickly about Anne's office as they ponder together the meaning of place and the implication of the few words scrawled on the most recent card.

Together they ponder Echo's latest postcard from a town in Oregon called Mist.

When Mary Lou moves to the map Anne has thumbtacked on her bulletin board so they might trace Echo's journey, Anne sees that her feet, encased in worn boots laced up to her knees, look combat ready, while her brightly colored skirt, of some gauzy material that floats this way and that, makes that part of her seem airborne.

"Just think what Echo has to come home to," Mary Lou says, tilting her head so that the small bell hanging from her right ear chimes faintly. "Echo will love Stitch," she adds, her finger on the black dot that is Mist.

"And she'll have the blue-and-white bedspread," Anne ventures.

"And Sugar's babies might come in March. Echo loves kittens and they are so pretty when their eyes open. We never have a bit of trouble giving them away. We just put this sign in the yard: KITTENS FREE TO A GOOD HOME, and people run through the house, grabbing up Sugar's kittens. Later they stop by to tell us how smart their kitten is and how pretty, you know, bragging on it. We make a lot of friends that way."

She sounds fine, but she's not, Anne thinks. *The thin face. Cheeks without color. It's as if the intensity of her longing for Echo's return is burning away a healthy body.*

Still she enjoys Mary Lou's visits. She soon feels as if she has known Gundren, a man apparently able to live happily in two different cultures. And Mary Lou's stories about her Dairy Queen friends make them seem at once exotic and cozy, their lives filled with surprise and possibility.

"There's this man comes in the Dairy Queen," Mary Lou says one day, her earrings dripping sparkling blue and green stones that fall to her shoulders. "He's a lawyer, a real nice man. Henry. That's his name. Henry tells me about his cases and his new baby girl, and I tell him about Echo and about Gundren's family. Then he buys a hamburger and a coke. And there's Mr. Trollop, who we're trying to get into housing."

"Who's Mr. Trollop?"

"He lives right next to the Dairy Queen. Under the viaduct. He's homeless. Maudie and Chester, they see about Mr. Trollop. But they can't figure out how to get him into housing. But Henry's got him on a list now so you never know," raising her right shoulder, rummaging in her purse, asking with a grin, "Gum? It's Juicy Fruit."

Bemused, Anne listens, swept away by Mary Lou's idiosyncratic acquaintances. And always at some point, "Tell me about your week," Mary Lou will say, and Anne, in an attempt to dredge up something that will approach the irrepressible life Mary Lou leads, despite her dead husband and runaway daughter, mentally skims over events that seem matter-of-fact to her in order to be able to offer up one or two shards of information she is willing to share.

"You mean you have a club that talks about books? Just about that?" Mary Lou asks when Anne mentions her book club. "After you say you liked the book or you didn't like it, what else is there?"

And Anne carefully explains. "We bring to a book all that we are," she says slowly. "And because we are so different, one from the other, we each find different ideas, different treasures in it. These conversations about the book enrich our enjoyment of it."

"That is really cool," Mary Lou says, and pointing to a book on Anne's desk, *Wuthering Heights*. "What's this about? Does it mean *Weathering*?"

"It's an archaic form of the word with the connotation of turbulence, of storm, in it. Take it," Anne says, carelessly breaking a cardinal rule about never loaning books. "Read it and we can talk about it."

The memory of Mary Lou's expression, clearly that of a woman on a mission, as she carefully wraps the book in her bright pink mohair sweater and sallies forth, makes Anne smile, and she finds herself smiling still when she walks into her ten o'clock class.

Only rarely does Mary Lou stop by Anne's office unless she has heard from Echo. On one such day, "I brought you this present," she says, handing Anne a brown paper bag tied with red ribbon. "I got it at the student craft show," smiling proudly as Anne unties the ribbon and takes a tissue-wrapped package from the bag. "This old lady (she looks just like Mrs. Santa Claus) makes them. It's a birdhouse. See? It has these tiny blue shutters and white columns and this little blue door, just like a real house."

Anne is pleased. "I can't think why I've never had a birdhouse," she says. "Thank you. It's a wonderful present." Mary Lou sits down for a minute, gets up to look again at the map tracing Echo's journey, sits down. *She needs to eat more and she needs more sleep,* Anne thinks. She leans forward. "Mary Lou, you must take better care of yourself. Are you eating properly?"

Ignoring her question, "I'm glad you like the birdhouse," Mary Lou says.

On the way home Anne stops at Birds Unlimited for birdseed and a book identifying Texas birds. That evening she hangs it from the young maple tree just outside her study.

On April 7 Echo writes that she had seen the Pacific ocean. A week later she sees the gray whales off the coast of California. "Can you believe it?" Mary Lou says, shaking her head, setting her dolphin earrings into brisk leaps and dives. "Now that's one thing I want to see more than anything. Can you imagine a whale? Can you? I can imagine some part of it. But not in the ocean. And not its size. I can't imagine how big it is. A football field? Oh, how I'd love to see a whale!"

And when on a soft day in May Mary Lou hurries into Anne's office waving a card, the radiance on her face broadcasts the card's message. "Guess what!" she says, "Echo's coming home." Tracing Echo's journey across the country and down the coast, she says, "See! Don't you see! She's getting closer and closer. She will be home by fall!"

"Mary Lou, that's wonderful. Does she say that?"

"No, but look at the map. Straight down the coast, and now she's headed this way. She's coming home."

3

By late September the leaves of the sweet gums and scrub oaks, shocked by a record-breaking cold spell, fall into pools of gold and yellow beneath the trees. All summer Echo's cards have come, and now they come faster and faster. Sometimes it seems to Mary Lou that they drift into her mailbox, are swirled into it by a chance breeze, waiting to be read by anybody, everybody.

On the fifteenth of October Mary Lou drops by Anne's office with Echo's latest message—a picture of Kit Carson, postmarked Trinidad, Colorado.

"Here she is, right here," Anne says, getting up from her desk to show Mary Lou the dot on the map. Anne is as excited as Mary Lou.

And a week later Mary Lou comes with three postcards received in one week. The first from Albuquerque. Then Clovis. Then Muleshoe.

"Muleshoe!" Anne says. "Mary Lou, Echo's in Texas! Can you believe it? Can you? Here she is," she says, putting her finger on the dot just inside the Texas border. "Muleshoe. Such a name!"

The way she says it makes Mary Lou giggle. Anne smiles a big smile. Then Mary Lou has to laugh out loud and Anne throws back her head and laughs. Then they laugh so hard that Anne has to get a tissue and wipe her eyes.

It isn't just the name, *Muleshoe*. It's having Echo no more than a couple of inches away on the map that makes Mary Lou happy. Now that she is so close, Mary Lou sets her alarm, gets up before good daylight and waxes the floors and washes the windows, rubbing them with old newspapers. When she gets the card from Lubbock she rakes up all the leaves and sweeps the porch. After Abilene, she cleans the stove and refrigerator, thinking Echo will be here any day. When she sees the card from Weatherford she goes to the grocery store. Afraid to leave the house after that (It would be too awful if Echo came while she was out!), she cooks. All of Echo's favorite things. Cinnamon rolls and fried chicken and black-eyed peas and potato salad and chocolate cake.

But now here she is in Anne's office plucking one tissue after another from the box Anne holds out to her. "It's been over a week," she sobs, "and Echo's not here. And Weatherford. Well, you can see where it is. It's just on the other side of Fort Worth. I could walk to Weatherford. Well, I just don't know. Ordinarily I'm not a worrywart but now, well, I waxed the floors and I baked a chocolate cake that is Echo's favorite. Watching out the front window for her, I left it in too long. When I took it out I looked at it, and with it almost burnt, I said to heck with the icing and went out and sat on the steps with Stitch until the moon was up and it got cold. Mama came over this morning. 'Take heart,' she said, 'take heart. Our Echo will be home any day now,' and she started to cry and I guess that's what got me started."

Reaching for another tissue she sees the box is empty. "Well, I guess I'd better quit crying," she says. "I've cried through a whole box."

"Mary Lou, I'm so sorry. I wish I could help. Look, what

about seeing one of our counselors? We have such good ones. I have one in mind. Dianne could help you. I'll call her right now."

"No, you're my counselor. And Echo's all right," Mary Lou says, consoling herself. Consoling Anne. "I don't know what got into me. Oh, I almost forgot. I got this surprise for you. Tony and I will drop it off at your house this afternoon."

"I'll be home about four," Anne says briskly.

"You don't even need to be there. We'll leave it outside, by the back door."

"Echo may be at home right now, waiting," Mary Lou tells her. "There is one thing though. If I have to leave for something besides work (Echo knows to look for me first at the Dairy Queen), I'll leave your phone number and address on her pillow. That way you can tell her not to leave, to wait right there for me. Is that OK?"

Anne is glad to say yes to that. Mary Lou can tell. "You'll find the surprise when you get home," she tells her. "It'll be there, by your back door."

On her way out to the pickup, she thinks how glad Anne will be to see the wood, at least half a cord, by her back door.

4

Mary Lou spends the next few days in limbo not knowing when Echo will come. One minute she feels like Echo will be on the porch the next time she looks up, and the next minute she'll turn right around and feel like she might never see her again. In the middle of the night she wakes up and tries to keep from thinking about what could happen. And then looking at her nails she's bitten to the quick, *Mary Lou, get hold of yourself,* she thinks.

By Saturday afternoon she is so restless she goes to work at three even though she isn't supposed to be there until six. About ten o'clock that night Maudie pours herself a cup of coffee and cleans off a booth. She sits down and takes a sip so hot it makes her Adam's apple bounce a couple of times. "Come over here, Lou," she tells Mary Lou. "Let's take a break. Chester can manage by himself for a few minutes."

Maudie is wearing a long black sweater that reaches just below her behind and black tights over legs as skinny as pencils. The latest fashion doesn't always look right on Maudie, but you can count on her to wear it. Maudie doesn't think she's too tall or too thin to wear anything they have in Dallas. This is what she says. Maudie loves clothes.

When Mary Lou takes a seat across from her in the booth, she says, "Mary Lou, you're worrying yourself sick over Echo. I don't know where everybody is tonight. Well, the usual crowd will come in after the game, but you go on home. Me and Chester can handle it. And you got some time coming."

Mary Lou is relieved. It's not like she's been holding her breath waiting for Echo, but she might be coming up the driveway this minute.

"Maudie, thanks. But before it gets too late, I'd better call Anne. She worries."

"Sure thing," Maudie says.

When Anne says hello, "I haven't heard another word," Mary Lou tells her, "but as soon as I hear something I'll call you."

"Mary Lou, I know it's hard, but someone, I don't remember who, once said that the three hardest things in the world are 'to try to please and please not, to bed to sleep not, and to wait for one who comes not.' "

Mary Lou says it over to herself. It is something to think about later.

"Try not to worry."

"I'll call you just as soon as I hear."

Tossing and turning in bed that night Anne's words come back to her. The first two, sleeping and pleasing, have never been a problem. But the last, waiting, that is hard. Plumping up her pillow she decides it *is* the worst thing in the world. And besides the waiting the house is too hot. She kicks off the covers, gets up, and turns down the heat. Then she goes into the kitchen to get a glass of milk, but when she opens the icebox door she forgets why she is standing there. Crossing her arms she stands in front of the open icebox and thinks about Weatherford, a little old town no bigger than a minute. And so close. Echo so close. Suddenly she knows exactly what she has to do. It just comes to her out of the blue. Relieved she goes back to bed and sleeps the rest of the night like a baby.

By two o'clock Sunday afternoon, the truck all packed and Sugar in the cab, she stops by Anne's to say good-bye. Anne makes a pot of tea and while they drink it, they talk. Really it is Mary Lou herself doing the talking.

"The thing is," she says, "everybody comes in the Dairy Queen sooner or later. Everybody. People passing through town. People moving into town. It might be a lady who's just not in the mood to cook. Or it might be her little boy's crying for the free cowboy glasses they're giving away with the ninety-nine-cent Belt Buster. But sooner or later everybody comes in, and when Echo comes in, I'll be there."

Anne's teachery look has appeared. "Mary Lou, I don't . . ."

Mary Lou thrusts out her hand, a traffic cop's signal. "My mind's made up. Maudie called up her friend Josie (Josie manages the Dairy Queen in Weatherford), and she'll put me on for a couple of weeks."

"What if Echo comes home while you're in Weatherford?"

"If she does, your address is on the front door and the back door and her bed. And if she goes to the Dairy Queen Maudie will know where I am."

Anne holds out her hand. "Good luck. And when you're settled, let me know." She bites her lip and frowns. "Are you sure you want to do this?"

"I have to go. You don't know how good it feels to be doing something, not to be waiting. Just waiting."

"For one who comes not?" Anne says.

She nods. "Waiting's not for me. I'm going to Weatherford." Saying it lets her know it's right. "Oh, and there's one more thing. Tom Davis, my neighbor, has Stitch, and Tony says he will keep Sugar, but he's out of town this week and won't be home until Monday. Would you keep Sugar for a week?"

"Mary Lou, I don't know a thing about cats. What if she ran away?"

"Oh, she would. You'd have to keep her locked up in the house."

Mary Lou can tell Anne wants to say no, but with her mama's allergies and her neighbor keeping Stitch and Ed still treating her like she is poison ivy, she just sits still and hopes that Anne will do it. After all, keeping a cat a week. What's that? She isn't asking for the moon.

Finally, Anne nods. "A week," she says.

Relieved, Mary Lou steps outside and brings in the litter box and cat food. Then she hurries out to the pickup to get Sugar.

Chapter Nine

1

CHRISTOPHER is driving Anne to his house for dinner. He is driving an '87 Volvo, a modest car for a former navy lieutenant. Or so Anne thinks. He calls it his pickup. It is mid-August and hot. She feels wrinkled and sweaty in her white linen pants and sleeveless black tee shirt. She will be glad to get inside. Either the car's air-conditioning is not working well or it is not working at all.

When she had opened the door and seen him, seen his really great smile, his lively brown eyes, she was immediately, surprisingly glad to see him, and she had given him a quick hug. But now she feels discontented. Almost irritable. She has spent the summer teaching and Christopher has been traveling, *perhaps* traveling. She's unsure of this. And the long hot drive to his house has given her time to reflect that, in the five weeks of his absence, he has not been in touch with her. Not by e-mail, telephone, or letter.

One reason she had been so glad to see him was that she has so much to tell him. But by the time he turns into his driveway, somewhat overgrown by grass, and hurries around to open her door, she is beginning to feel quite resentful, although she coldly observes that his house, set back on the property, is beautifully kept. When they reach the door, he unlocks it, pushes it open, and steps back to allow her to enter. Immediately she is charmed by the room. By its old, darkly stained wooden floors. And the long down-filled sofa and, opposite it, two armchairs, the three pieces orderly and comfortable around a small cherry table, all in front of a fireplace. Off to her right is a desk and on the walls two, no three, paintings. A primitive catches her eye. It is the figure of a young girl with her hands demurely folded. Its subdued colors fit the simplicity of the room. And just off this room, a smaller room, "My book room," Christopher says. She walks around the room reading the titles of the shelved books—books on physics, of course. And history. Biography. The arts. Astronomy and architecture. She touches a telescope that rests on a stand.

"I just finished assembling it," he says. "If you like we'll take a look at Orion later."

Already she is feeling soothed by his presence (and by his house that is refreshingly cool), so that when he brings her a tall ice-filled glass of gin and tonic, she follows him into his kitchen. He takes a copper pan from a rack above the stove and sets it on a burner. "Tell me," he says. "What about your summer?"

"I've applied for a sabbatical. I'm pretty sure to get it."

He turns the burner off and comes around the island where she stands. "That is wonderful." He throws back his head and laughs. "It's terrific. Now where will you go? What will you be doing?"

"If I could get on an airplane I'd go to Europe. But now I

suppose it will have to be Boston. By train. I'll read and do some research and write while I'm there."

Christopher has forgotten how tall she is, although while he was away he had tried to remember her eyes. But how could anybody remember eyes like that? Really extraordinary. He lifts his glass, touches hers. "Maybe you can find a way to slay that dragon," he says seriously.

After a supper of roasted red bell peppers, an onion tart, smoked salmon (all of which he has made), and a bottle of good merlot, they sit in the living room, she in an armchair, he on the floor by his stereo. "This is a great album," he says. "Frank Sinatra."

"What is it?"

"It's *The Wee Small Hours*. I think it's his best album. Listen."

Watching as he bends forward and slips the CD into the player, she is very aware of his very broad, straight shoulders. Sinatra's voice drifts out. "In the wee, small hours of the morning," he sings, "you lie awake and think about the girl."

If this is a seduction scene, Anne tells herself, it's working. When he stands to pour another glass of wine (she's had three and she feels lightly, happily tipsy) she gets up and walks over to him. "Christopher," she says.

"Yes?"

"Christopher, I need to go home. You see I've got this cat. Mary Lou asked me to keep her for a week and I forgot to feed her before I left." She picks up her purse. "And I don't want a relationship. I've had two. Relationships make me unhappy." And now she's at the door. She turns to look at him. "I'm going to live alone now. OK?"

His expression is unfathomable. A slight frown. Surprise? A shrug. "Well, OK," he says.

At home she feeds Sugar and falls asleep listening to Sugar's purring only to wake up an hour later. *Did he intend a seduction?* she wonders. *Or did I? Well, whatever,* she tells herself and immediately falls into a deep and dreamless sleep.

Opening her eyes the next morning, she remembers. And she has a headache from the wine. Still, she remembers all too clearly the attraction of his lean body, the soft expression in his eyes, her blood gathering in all the right places. When she had walked to stand close to him, he had not moved away. But neither had he kissed her. Thank God! And then she had blurted out something about not wanting a relationship and had seen his face. Whatever his expression meant, surprise was clearly a part of it. Thank God for that, too. A relationship is the last thing she wants! She has spent the past year reaching out to friends and finding new interests. She enjoys confiding in Joan. When she told her about her addiction to *All My Children,* Joan had laughed and laughed even harder when Anne made her promise not to tell the book club about it. She has become close to the members of her book club. And she's involved with her students, although trying not to be. But she cares about them. And peculiarly (even as a psychologist she finds it peculiar), she is in a good relationship with her lost family, with their *memories.* Looking at her album (she keeps it on her bedside table) she now finds reassurance in it, remembering their voices, their words, their laughter.

Adjusting her pillow she is reminded of her headache. The pain is on the left side of her temple. Remembering last night makes her more conscious of the pain. She feels slightly embarrassed about what she said to Christopher last night. And what must he be thinking? Irritably she turns over and, seeing the time, forces herself out of bed. She takes a long shower and dresses, pulling a yellow sweater over her head and stepping into a tweed skirt. Their first meeting must be casual, she decides. At her dressing table she brushes her hair and braids it. She notices that a green-leafed branch on a live oak tree outside her window is reflected in the mirror alongside her face. A touch of spring. Leaning toward the mirror she examines her face. Leaning still closer she imagines a new serenity there. From Sister Alicia? From climbing a tree? The notion makes her smile. But nevertheless she believes it is there. Eminently satisfied that her first meeting with Christopher will not be awkward, she leaves the house early.

But that day passes and then another. A whole week goes by. And then two. She sees him almost every day. Walking across the campus. Eating lunch with a colleague. Lecturing to a class. When the third week begins, *This has gone on long enough,* she thinks. He was probably made uncomfortable by her honesty. It probably scared him.

Well, this is ridiculous, she tells herself. Hastily closing her desk drawer, she walks to his office. A long walk across the creek that divides the campus. Up the stairs. Down a long hall. By the time she arrives she's out of breath. His door is closed. She knocks briskly.

He opens the door, raises his eyebrows. "Anne, Anne come in. Please."

"I wanted to tell you that when I had dinner with you, I didn't mean . . ."

"I was just thinking about what you evidently . . ."

"To scare you," she finishes.

"What? Scare me?" He takes her arm, draws her into the room. Chuckling, he says, "Anne you didn't scare me." He frowns. "But the only reason I invited you over for dinner was to . . ."

His neck is becoming flushed. The color slowly rises to his face.

"Christopher, I know. It's all right. It's silly to mention the wine, the music. But you see . . ."

He unwinds from his chair, stands, and closes the door against a line of students (mostly females, she notes) gathered there. Then he says, "Look, what are you doing after class? Let's take a walk."

"Yes. All right. But Christopher, what I need is friendship."

"Friendship is perfect." He puts his hands in his pockets and smiles down at her. His smile fades; a frown appears. "You see, right now I don't even know where my wife is."

2

Watching the plumber work to unstop her sink Anne is bemused by the memory of the evening when her book club's discussion of Camus's *The Last Man* had careened into a discussion of the attraction women feel toward blue-collar workers. There had been a broad variety of opinions about whether it was true, and if so, then why. It was true, they said. This was immediately decided. But their ideas about why blue-collar workers were so very attractive ranged all the way from the idea that they were more masculine to the notion that they might be more inclined to put women on a pedestal. "And that's exactly where we need to be!" Samantha had said to a burst of good-natured laughter.

But when the plumber leaves an hour and a half later, taking with him a check for $165, she decides to tell the book club that this plumber was not only attractive but probably very tall when he stood on his billfold.

She's becoming more at ease with living alone, although it is an art she has not yet mastered. As she goes about the most ordinary day-to-day tasks, bittersweet memories of Donald often occur. Unbidden. Then she turns to her work and finds it satisfying.

In just these few weeks Christopher has become her mentor and friend. They have an easy friendship. She knows now that he was a navy lieutenant and that he was invalided out of the navy. He has told her this. Despite his being separated from his wife he seems to enjoy his solitude.

In late November as Anne walks to her car after class, she sees that the bare limbs of the trees etch themselves against clear skies. She hears the soft call of a dove and, above this, the trill of a mockingbird. She takes a deep breath and the moisture-laden air brings to her the heady scent of the Gulf. All at once she senses possibility: Her lectures will be met with wide-eyed wonder; every student will complete every course; she will not be asked to serve on a single committee. And one day Echo will walk into the Weatherford Dairy Queen.

Full of good humor and optimism she stops by Christopher's office after her last class. "Anne!" he exclaims. Swinging his chair away from the desk, he rises and gestures to her to sit in it. When she shakes her head he sits on his desk, clearly pleased to see her. With his angular features, his straight firm chin, he has the face of a warrior but the demeanor of a priest.

"Tea? Would you like a cup?"

Again she shakes her head. "No, it's too nice to be inside. It's a nice day for a walk."

"Let's go," Christopher says.

And almost immediately, surprisingly, she finds herself walking with Christopher along the three-mile jogging path that encircles the campus. They walk in silence, he matching his stride to hers. They could be miles away from the campus, from Lone Oak. The path before and after them is empty of humanity. Mesquites outline the trail they follow, walking along the sturdy hardness of gravel and rock. The leaves of the mesquite cast a delicate green against the delicate blue of the sky.

"Wait," he whispers, his hand on her arm. Far ahead something disappears across the path in front of them. A brush of yellow.

"A coyote," he says.

She feels no need to talk. So easy is he walking by her side, dropping back when the path narrows, skipping over the small creek, allowing her to cross however she chooses. She steps across using the flat rocks as stepping stones. The sun beats through the cold, heating the rocky path; mesquites break the wind so that soon she has unbuttoned her jacket.

"Christopher, do you find it easy to live alone?" she asks, her words finding the thought that had danced around her subconscious mind all day. "You seem so perfectly contented."

Now she knows why she stopped by his office. When she had stopped seeing Donald and sent Allen away, she had evidently chosen to live by herself. She is determined to do this. To live fully. Richly. As Christopher does.

Waiting for his answer she sees that his gray sweater is stretched unevenly below his hips and his blue jeans are worn so thin they are white at the knees. Noticing, she smiles.

"Absolutely," he says now. "It's the life I've chosen. I enjoy the freedom of it, the independence. I've been through a long and difficult marriage and so, for now, living alone suits me."

"Any advice for me?"

He laughs. "No. No advice."

"None?"

"Give yourself time."

"I just don't want to be neurotic. Any more than I am now." She grins. "You know I'm afraid to fly."

"You've made no secret of it," he chuckles. And she hadn't. Her openness is beguiling. That first meeting on campus. With her flashing silver needle and thread, she sat, weaving a ribbon of white lace. All of it—her hair falling over her face as she tatted and the work itself—had had a hypnotic effect so that the president had to say his name twice before Christopher realized he was being introduced to the faculty.

Now she says, "I've been counseled, tried imaging, been hypnotized. Nothing works. I can't fly."

"Do you need to fly?'

"Sometimes it's inconvenient not to."

Stopping, he takes her arm, gestures to the college. "Wait a minute. Is this what you want to be doing?" he says.

"I love to teach but I'd like to study and write for a year. I'd like to do some research. Maybe in England."

"And you can't fly."

"That's about it," she says. Then, "Want to jog? These shoes are OK for a mile or so."

She leads the way jogging comfortably at first then increasing her stride until she's running. When they reach the campus Christopher jogs ahead to swing open the heavy door of the library building where, inside, the two of them bend to drink deeply from the water fountains.

That afternoon Anne stops at the nursery for pansies. She has always liked gardening, and she has time for it now. Exploring her garage she finds a trowel and a bag of fertilizer. The bed just to the side of the front door needs color, and here she trowels out twelve small holes for the dozen yellow pansies she's bought.

Halfway through her task a shadow falls over her. She looks up to see that Joan, carrying Nikki on her hip, is walking up the drive. Nikki, his nose running (Nikki's nose is always running), is in a blue sweater and mittens. Joan is snuggled into a red woolen jacket, gloves, hood, and warm black pants. But her jacket is unzipped, and Nikki clutches her white blouse so that her black lacy bra is revealed.

Feeling more and more comfortable with abrupt questions (is it because she lives alone?), she asks, "Joan, do you think I'm a lesbian? Becoming one?"

"Well, you've no history of it," Joan laughs. "What made you ask that?"

"I noticed your breasts."

"Women always notice breasts. Men notice legs."

"Really? Well, I guess I'm not then. Come on in. I'll make a pot of tea." She holds out her arms, takes Nikki on her hip. "Come here, Nikki," she says. "I have a flower for you. See. Joan, pick up one of those pansy plants. Nikki can take it home and plant it."

And with Nikki comfortably on Anne's hip the two women, still giggling about their conversation, go inside for tea.

Comfortably settled in bed that night it occurs to Anne that the astonishing events of this past year have made her past unworthy of notice and her future endlessly monotonous. Was Mary Lou a lifeline to another kind of existence, one richer and more compelling than that which she has previously known? A lifeline that she failed to grasp? In her mind it had begun a year ago with the sighting of Echo (she thinks of it as a sighting, a glimpse of something rare, to be recorded, set down), and it had ended with Mary Lou's departure. And in between there were all those flash points, a Roman candle of them, each more vivid, more dramatic even, than the others. There was Mary Lou and her runaway daughter. And Anne's own visit to a psychic. There were the reawakened memories of her dear family. And that moonlit night of the Gypsy music and the women dancing. And the bloody goat making its desperate run. And the image, perfect and whole, of Sister Alicia stepping out of the woods. Waking in the middle of the long autumn nights she sometimes tells herself, *Well, I climbed the tree,* and finds this strangely comforting.

Chapter Ten

1

THERE is not much traffic. But even with the sun visor down there is a harsh glare bouncing off the steely gray of the divided highway. Turning from the glare Mary Lou sees the Herefords, some grazing, some lying down, strung out across the pasture that runs alongside the highway. Shades of soft gold. They are real pretty. She can't see the windmill, but there would have to be a windmill nearby. When she was little, Echo loved to draw windmills. Miss Timberlake, her second-grade teacher, had taught her how. Mary Lou had framed the best one. Darn! She left it behind.

She has left everything behind. Mama and Anne. The class. Stitch and Sugar. Her house. Hers and Gundren's house. His clothes still in his closet, except for his boots. Right after Gundren died she moved his boots to her closet, where they had stayed, except for that one night with Ed. Thinking about Ed stumbling out of the door that night makes her laugh at herself. She isn't sure why. Poor Ed. But there was Gundren. Always Gundren, electric with energy. Walking toward her, tipping his hat and grinning. Her heart gives a sudden lurch, reels toward the black despair she felt for months after his death. Threatened, she pulls over to the side of the highway and stops. Lowering the window she draws the cold air deep into her chest.

A car passes and slows. She waves it on, grateful for the diversion.

Raising the window she eases back onto the highway. She forces herself to think about the day ahead. First she has to find the right Dairy Queen. There are two of them in Weatherford. Then a place to stay. Wondering about that she pops open a Coke. Water would taste better but she is in too big a hurry to stop.

But when she drives into the Dairy Queen parking lot, it is early still, the sun not halfway down even in late October. She gets out, locks the pickup (her bags being right there on the front seat in plain sight), and goes inside. Just two tables, one by an older couple and the other by a man reading a newspaper, are occupied.

She helps herself to a glass of ice water and sits in a booth. Red imitation leather. Cracked. But everything looks clean. All the empty tables cleared. The floor damp-mopped. Maudie was right. Josie is a good manager.

From the kitchen the clatter of dishes and voices promise warmth and ease. Two men come in. Truckers. One a big man and the other just as tall, but skinny. The couple is leaving. After the waitress rings them up she walks toward Mary Lou, but when Mary Lou shakes her head and points to her water, she backtracks to get water for the men. Setting the water on their table, "Hey, Chet. Doug," she says.

They hold the glasses in their hands and drink. They do not

look up. "Well, I know he did it," the big man says. "He's guilty as hell."

Holding her order pad the waitress frowns. "Will y'all stop ragging on Coach Meyers long enough to tell me what you want?"

She has the tiniest waist Mary Lou has about ever seen. And the biggest bosoms. A Dolly Parton shape. Poor thing! Standing on your feet all day is hard enough, but with a shape like that! Well, her back must just about kill her.

The waitress shifts. "I don't have all day. What do y'all want?" Sounding impatient.

"Josie, you know the answer to that," the big man says. His face is broad. Sunburned. Shoulders beefy. Thick neck. "You got what I want." Leaning forward so that his nose almost touches the waitress's chest, "Josie, you know what I want," he says. "But for now, I'll take a cheeseburger. Cut the onions."

Josie raises her eyebrows and rolls her eyes toward the ceiling. She takes the pencil from behind her ear and begins to write. Then the big man, Chet, drops his napkin. Reaching for it he stands halfway up and puts his hand on Josie's bottom. "Excuse me, Josie," he says like it's accidental. But his hand stays right where he put it.

Such nerve! Mary Lou can't believe her eyes. "That's enough!" she says and is on her feet and, with her hands on her hips, leaning over their table. "Sexual harassment," she says firmly. "It's against the law."

The men stare up at her, openmouthed. Chet scowls. Then he grins. And laughs. And keeps on laughing. She thinks he might choke and die right before her eyes, he laughs so hard. But after a minute he wipes his eyes with a paper napkin, sticks a toothpick in his mouth, and pushes it to an angle with his tongue.

"Sexual harassment my foot," he says. "Where do you think you are? In Washington, D.C.?" Wiggling the toothpick with his tongue, grinning, he glues his eyes to her chest.

Holding her ground Mary Lou processes the situation. *Don't lose your temper,* she cautions herself. *Be calm.* Slowly she picks up the two glasses of ice water and carefully pours one over Chet's head and, for good measure, pours the second one over the "gimme" cap worn by the other.

Jumping up, grabbing napkins, mopping his face, "Who in hell are you?" Chet gasps.

"I told you, Chet," the other one says, taking off his "gimme" cap and shaking it. "I said you better watch your mouth. All the women, they all watch that woman on TV. My wife, all her sisters, they all watch her."

Giving his cap a final shake he settles it on his head and nods to Mary Lou. "Ma'am," he says.

She reads the words on his cap: *My take-home pay won't take me home.*

Still sputtering, Chet says, "Josie, there ain't no call for stuff such as this. Now you got to remember there's more than one place to eat in Weatherford." Fretting. Almost whining.

"Chet Matthews, you feel free to take your business right on down the road!" Josie says.

"Well, there was a lady at one of these places, maybe it was Jack-in-the-Box, sued for hot coffee," Chet says, still wiping water and brushing ice from the red leather seat.

"Ice water's not hot coffee," Josie says, settling it. She turns to Mary Lou. "You're Mary Lou. In here from Dallas. I'm Josie." Her smile is warm.

In his seat again, Chet growls, "Dallas. Well, why don't she go on back to Dallas."

Josie whirls on him. Putting her face close to his, "Hush," she hisses. "You just hush, Chet Matthews. This here is Mary Lou, and she's lost her daughter."

Chet slumps in his seat. "Sorry," he mumbles. Lowering his eyes, Doug takes off his cap and settles it again on his head.

Josie touches her shoulder. "Sit down anywhere, honey. I'll get us some coffee."

Mary Lou starts toward a booth, hesitates. "Which is non-smoking?"

"Smoking's about all we got. People want nonsmoking they go somewhere else," Josie says, wheeling off toward the coffeemaker. Returning with mugs of steaming coffee, she takes packets of sugar and thimble-sized containers of cream from her pockets and sits down, smiling broadly.

"You caused a stir anyway. Things were a little too quiet before that." Glancing over her shoulder toward Chet, she says, "He don't mean nothing by anything. He's my ex-husband. You know like the song: 'All My Exes Live in Texas.' "

"Oh, Josie. Golly, I didn't know it."

"Don't worry about it," Josie says. "He just can't get it in his head we're not still married." Shaking her head she empties cream in her coffee, adds three packages of sugar, and stirs.

"I don't know what got into me, why I got so mad. One day we talked about sexual harassment in a class I took."

"Maudie told me you'd been to college, but I'd have known it anyhow." Tilting her head, she says, "Honey, you look real tired."

"I didn't sleep much last night. Journey proud, I guess."

Josie's face fills with understanding. "If you need a place to stay, I've got you one."

Tiredness sweeps over her. She hugs the warm mug in her hands. "Oh, Josie," she says, relieved. "Where?"

"It's with Miss Weems. She's got an old house here on Weems Street. Named after her family. The Weemses. She can't sell it and she can't keep it up so she takes in roomers. I talked to Miss Weems this morning. All she wants is fifty a week and somebody clean. You'll see the For Sale sign in the yard, but don't worry. It's been up for sale over a year."

"A year," Mary Lou says. "A year," she says again.

"Go on over there. I'll draw you a little map. You get a night's rest. Check in tomorrow. Around two." Josie leans forward, her gray eyes intense. "Before you go, could you tell me what your girl looks like?"

"Well, it's been a year since. . . ." Dismayed, she feels the sudden tears. Impatiently she wipes them away. "I don't know what gets into me sometimes." Fumbling in her purse she finds a tissue and blows her nose. "Well, Echo has black hair, black as coal. And she's dark. Her eyes, they're just beautiful, like sapphires. She's about the prettiest . . ." She bites her lip, straightens her shoulders, smiles. "You'd know her. If she came in that door, you'd know her. Anyone would know Echo."

2

Miss Weems's house sprawls across the lot. It is painted gray, but the paint is peeling and patches of white show through.

Mary Lou climbs the steps to a big wraparound porch. Off to her left a white wicker swing, stirred by the wind, moves a little. Along the porch railing stand pots of straggly plants not likely to make it through the winter.

She rings the doorbell and waits. She rings it again, listening to be sure it works. She can't hear a thing so she knocks and right away hears the yipping of a little dog and footsteps coming to the door.

The door opens. An old lady stands just inside the screen door, peering out. "Yes?" she says.

The lady is wearing a dark dress and black shoes that lace. Her thin white hair is pulled back in a bun so tight that her pink scalp shows through. Her eyes are blue and faded. She is not wearing a speck of powder or lipstick or rouge. No makeup whatsoever. Her complexion is pure white and thin as tissue paper.

"My name's Mary Lou Burgandy. Josie said you . . ."

The woman pushes the screen door outward. "Josie called just yesterday about you, Mrs. Burgandy. Now don't they make the best hamburgers?"

She looks Mary Lou over, starting with her shoes.

Mary Lou's shoes are white as snow. Jeans starched. Shirt a little wrinkled but freshly ironed. Miss Weems is really clean. Mary Lou has never seen anybody who looks so clean.

"Come in. I'm Wilamina Morris Weems. We'll go right into the parlor."

The parlor is filled with books: in shelves, stacked on tables, on the floor. Leather-bound and cloth-bound books. Bindings deep red and faded to pink. Brown and black and dark-blue bindings. Big books and thin books. Mary Lou has never seen so many books outside a library.

The furniture is carved, its upholstery black. Mary Lou runs her fingers over the carving on the back of the sofa. "It's real pretty," she says.

"Yes," Miss Weems says, patting the back of a tall chair so that the diamond ring on her finger sparkles. "These are American antiques. Most of the antiques in this country are European. But you probably knew that."

"No, ma'am. I hadn't heard it."

Miss Weems takes a seat in a high-backed chair, motioning Mary Lou to the sofa. Mary Lou runs her hand over the upholstery. It looks like satin but it feels hard.

Noticing, "It's horsehair and original to the piece," Wilamina Morris Weems says.

"Oh." She folds her hands in her lap. The lady's name sounds like an antique, too.

"Albert!" Miss Weems calls. "Oh, Albert!"

A little dog trots into the room. Black with a white face. His fur looks like the horsehair on the furniture.

"I want you to meet my little guest. This is poor Albert. He'll be visiting with us for a while."

Mary Lou pats Albert's head. "Visiting?"

"Yes. A few days." Miss Weems presses a handkerchief to her lips. "Egg money."

Mary Lou thinks maybe Miss Weems's mind is failing. Her mama says that everybody in her family went to their grave with a good mind.

Mary Lou picks Albert up and holds him in her lap to stop him trembling.

"I see you like dogs," Miss Weems says approvingly. She stands. "Would you like to see the room?"

Mary Lou follows her across the hall. Albert plods along

behind her, his head down. Miss Weems opens the door and stands just inside.

"It's a front room," she says. "Fifty dollars a week. In advance."

Mary Lou walks into the room. She looks at the bed. "Mahogany," Miss Weems says when Mary Lou touches it. It has a high headboard carved with flowers. A rocking chair with a footstool ("Needlepointed by my own dear mother," Miss Weems says) sits by the window. There is a round table by the bed with a lamp on it. The base of the lamp is a girl holding out her dress. The dress has lace on it.

"It's nice," Mary Lou says. She walks to the window and sees a giant sycamore tree growing just outside.

"I had curtains at the window but I took them down. They're washed but they haven't been stretched. Leroy was supposed to come yesterday and put the stretchers up. He takes care of the yard. Leroy is right undependable. But he's been with us long as I can remember."

"I don't mind not having curtains."

"We'll get them up this week sometime. Now I don't have central air, but you have the use of the kitchen. The bathroom's next door."

"Thank you."

She puts her hand on the doorknob. "Come on, Albert. Let's go so Mrs. Burgandy can get settled. Oh! Tonight's my card night but I put a casserole in the oven for you. Tomorrow's soon enough for you to think about grocery shopping."

After Miss Weems leaves, Mary Lou sits in the rocking chair and puts her feet up on the footstool. It is almost like staying in a hotel. She has never slept away from home before. Well, that isn't true. She and Gundren had spent their honeymoon in Hot Springs, Arkansas. Stayed four days.

After a while she hears Miss Weems leave. She bathes and puts on her gown and robe. In the oven she finds a chicken casserole and a baked sweet potato. The kitchen feels lonesome so she takes a plate to her room and sits in the chair by the window and eats. Afterward, she washes and dries the dishes and puts them away.

Then she sits in the rocking chair again and watches the night come on. The trunk of the sycamore tree gets darker and darker until it seems like a kind of soldier on guard. Pretty soon she can't see the furniture in her room or the room itself or even the house across the street, but she feels the strangeness of it all. Maybe it was a mistake uprooting herself to come here. A wild goose chase, Mama called it. But here she is. Nobody's daughter. Nobody's mother. Nobody's friend or neighbor. Nobody. She has never been that before.

Chapter Eleven

1

YELLOW leaves cling to the elms in Anne's front yard. In her garden a handful of straggling blooms hang from tattered bushes. Everything around her is dormant, quietly gathering strength.

Beneath the day-after-day monotony of the pewter sky, Anne has firmly settled into the changes she has made. Straight teeth no longer matter. She has taken off the rubber bands for comfort. She enthusiastically teaches the single parenting class, which is so successful that two other campuses have initiated their own. Invited to share her expertise, she says, "The class teaches itself. It teaches me."

Most of the time she enjoys living alone.

Like tonight. She is with Christopher, who has become a regular at Uncle Calvin's Coffee House, a place she had never been in all her years with Allen.

It was once a small Catholic chapel, now the scattered tables covered with blue-and-white-checked cloths, together with the informality of the musicians and the leisurely air of the patrons, give the place a cozy air. The music is both acoustic and eclectic. Tonight Tish Hinojosa, one of Christopher's favorites, will sing Spanish and English folk songs and an occasional country-western folk song.

"No cigarette smoke. No alcohol. It's different. Coming here with you is one of the advantages of living alone," Anne says.

She is wearing what she calls a costume. It is a very long, full black skirt and a soft, white cotton blouse. A very relaxed blouse. Her thick black hair hangs straight. When she bends her head it falls forward over her face. In candlelight her eyes are a darker, almost navy, blue. Her only makeup is lip gloss, applied medicinally to her mildly chapped lips.

Christopher's features are strong in this light, almost sculpted. A firm chin with a deep cleft in it, a nice mouth, glittering brown eyes. He is wearing the same clothes he wore at school today. Anne admires his total disregard for clothing. In these few weeks he has become a friend. She can say anything to Christopher. Now he leans forward, touches her arm.

"But haven't you always lived alone?" he is asking. They have returned to her favorite subject.

She says, "When my family died, I was in school, and at the university there were roommates and boyfriends and, afterward, so-called *serious* relationships, although most were not serious."

"No poets? No philosophers?"

She looks quickly at his face, searching for a raised eyebrow, a gossipy smile. *Oh, please,* she reprimands herself. *Christopher asking a question through innuendo? Not this man. Not ever.*

"Once I thought I needed someone, a man, for companionship and sex, but I don't feel that way now. I feel sure. Centered. I may even try to fly again. Christopher, I yearn to be able to get on a plane and fly to England, to Venice, to the south of France."

A young girl brings lemon pie for the two of them, herbal tea for Anne, and for Christopher, hazelnut coffee. She sets yellow plates and cups and saucers on the blue-and-white-checked tablecloths.

Christopher smiles. "So you tried flying once? What happened?"

"I went out to Love Field, stood in line at Southwest to buy a round-trip ticket to Houston. My heart beat faster and faster. My mouth got dry; I couldn't speak. The man in front of me said, 'Are you all right?' I wasn't. I was dizzy. I stumbled to a chair and put my head down. They brought a wheelchair and checked my vital signs. Isn't that crazy?"

"No. Not crazy."

"Well, I may try flying again. I climbed a tree recently."

Christopher laughs. Smiling, never taking his eyes off her face, he makes her feel eminently fascinating.

"Tell me about *that*," he says.

And she does. She tells him about Echo (who, in her mind, has become a kind of wood sprite, more illusion than real) and about climbing up to the tree house before falling dizzily into its center when she reached it. "I felt so brave when I climbed down. Looking up, I couldn't believe I had climbed up that high. Echo said I was cool."

He reaches for her hand and squeezes it. Now Tish Hinojosa comes and, leaning back in their chairs, the two of them relax into the songs she sings. And every word, every phrase Tish sings reminds Anne of Donald. For a few minutes she sits quite still, her eyes lowered, but when she feels Christopher's eyes on her, she looks up and smiles. When the set ends, he says, "Come on. Let's get out of here."

In the car he turns on the ignition. "Wait a minute," she says. "It was the music. It was stupid, really. All that relationship did was make me unhappy ninety percent of the time. He is married. He has wonderful children. But even if there had been no family, it was not a good thing. For either of us."

She unfastens her seat belt and turns toward him "Now. Tell me. What about you? I'm interested. Not just curious."

He hesitates. "It's an old story. It's happened over and over again."

In the pale light cast by a streetlight her eyes look black. She's leaning forward slightly. "Well, it hasn't happened to you over and over again," she says.

And then he tells her. He tells her about his failed marriage. He had loved his wife, he says, but she resented the impersonal challenges of the navy, its constant demands. She grew more and more dissatisfied and discontented. And then one day he came home on leave and she was gone. She had fallen in love with, she said, a nine-to-five man. A month later he was wounded by "friendly" fire in a training exercise. Four surgeries were followed by three months of rehabilitation, and then he was discharged from the navy. "Teaching was a damn good decision," he says. "I'm enjoying it."

After a minute he touches her shoulder. "Come on. Let's slip back in and catch the last set?"

"Let's go."

He opens his door, hesitates. "There's one more thing. That's where I was all summer. I was trying to find her."

2

The weather turns brisk. Anne's energy is boundless. She walks, sometimes alone, sometimes with Christopher. She pops into an aerobics class in the afternoon and later sits in on a conversational French class. There's not enough time to do all she wants to do.

When Tony and Dylan—two entrepreneurs wearing caps and grinning—stop by her office with flyers, she's happy to see them. Dylan is in complete remission. The circles under his eyes have faded to an old bruise. He has gained weight. "Seven pounds," he tells her. Dylan believes he will live until Lennon is sixteen. After that? New drugs. A vaccine.

The flyers they bring—red, yellow, blue, and green—are attractive, offering Small Repairs: House and Garden, and are sprinkled with skillfully drawn cartoons of house and gardening tools. The two of them will come that very afternoon and give her an estimate. And Tony will pick up Sugar, Mary Lou's cat.

They arrive early and walk with her around the property to see what repairs are needed. Wearing jeans and old sweaters, they carry clipboards, dutifully taking notes on each task. Their interest in her place is, it seems to her, faintly paternal.

Suger's interest in them is frankly curious. She follows them from room to room, leaping into her favorite napping places and running up trees when they are outside. And purring.

Tony carefully examines the house. He opens windows to check facings and trim, turns on lights to peer at the hardware of French doors. He finds a hole just under her roof and a screen that needs replacing. He bends, stretches, makes notes, and talks.

"My specialty is windows," he says. "In this part of Dallas most of these old houses need their windows replaced. Look at this bay window in your study. See. It's not airtight. And part of the seal has rotted away."

He stops writing, turns, and frowns at Anne. "Dr. Hamilton, do you think Mary Lou could ever love anybody else? I'd make a good husband. And if Echo comes home, I'd be a good father, too."

"It's been over a year, fifteen months since her husband's death, but that's not long. She needs the tincture of time."

"Well, I've got twenty thousand dollars saved. When the time is right, I'll tell her about that. What was that word you said? The what of time?"

"Tincture. It's a naturally occurring substance, a healing that takes place through time."

"Tincture. The tincture of time." he says. "And it occurs naturally. I like it."

"Drive over to Weatherford. Take her out. She's probably tired of hamburgers." Opening a closet door, she points to the ceiling. "Tony, isn't that a leak? Is it a roof leak?"

He pulls down the stairs, goes up into the attic, and comes down. "It's from the air-conditioner. I'll take care of it first." He brightens and, whistling, puts the stairs back up. He whacks his thigh with his clipboard. "We'll do a good job, Dr. Hamilton."

Dylan is the gardening expert. Walking slowly through the grounds, admiring this tree, fingering the leaves on that bush, kneeling to check the soil, he is clearly a man who has all that he wants. He has time.

"Dylan, I lost three azaleas last winter. Don't you think we should replace them?"

"Maybe. But this isn't the time. We'll do it in early spring. For now let's bring in a little mulch and fertilizer and see if these other bushes won't fill up those spaces. I'll bring a ladder next week and do some trimming, and I'll clean the gutters. Won't cost much."

When they finish their inspections they stand in Anne's utility room and watch Sugar leisurely bathing her face. Dylan picks up her food and litter box. Anne picks up the ball of softness and hands her to Tony.

"Meow," Sugar says. Draped like a rag over Tony's arm, she looks reproachfully at Anne.

"Tony, I'll keep her a while longer. I've grown accustomed to her face, her purr, her claws," she says, laughing.

The next day they bring estimates. Dylan's is less than Tony's. Both are reasonable. The work is to begin on Saturday.

When they arrive it is sixty-five degrees and the wind has freshened. The energy of the young men is contagious. The three of them work all morning. Anne opens her windows to let the house breathe. *Mother used to say that,* she remembers. She waxes furniture; Tony repairs window trim; Dylan makes a bed of rosemary, thyme, and mint beneath a kitchen window. Then he begins a butterfly bed, having researched the shrubs and flowers that attract them. She likes his ideas.

That afternoon Anne waters the begonias on the deck that have bloomed out of season. Tony replaces a rotten board in her deck. Squinting, he sights along the board, tries to fit it in, shakes his head. "A little more has to come off. About a half an inch." He puts a knee on the board and shaves a little more off the corner. "I'm thinking of driving over to Weatherford this weekend. I'd like to see her. What do you think?

"I think she'd enjoy that. But call before ten. Miss Weems turns the phone off at ten."

The following week she polishes silver, cleans out closets, and, thinking of *84 Charing Cross Road*, she steels herself and culls books from her shelves to be taken to the library.

One day Tony brings sandwiches and Dylan brings cookies. The three of them, made ravenous by work, eat almost silently. Now that she has decided to live alone, her house is filled with Dylan's whistling and Tony's talk about Mary Lou and Sugar's purring. Her house. Communal. Solitary. Both. *I live with ambiguity,* she tells herself.

She sends a couch out to be recovered. When it returns it reminds her of the faded, flowered down-filled couches that she imagines fill the country homes in England, a place she will one day visit. Her spirits soar.

3

Even as it unfolds Anne knows she will always remember this day, this Sunday morning in November. The leaves have fallen and it is quite chilly. It is dark outside when she turns on the coffee and puts a croissant in the small oven. She grabs her red cashmere robe (she loves it because it's moth-eaten and repaired and because it's old) and pads barefooted out to get the paper. By the time she returns her house smells of baking bread, though it's only a croissant in the warming oven. She puts her breakfast on a tray and takes it back to bed. She is becoming a hedonist. She will say this to Christopher.

A bite of the croissant, a sip of orange juice, and she

plunges into the *Dallas Morning News.* First the book pages. Favorite writers. Favorite reviewers. Favorite part of the paper. She drinks the orange juice, dutifully takes her vitamins, and opens the book pages. *The Dominions of Spring* by Donald Lewis. The words leap out at her. She turns to the review, her eyes gulping it down: "Confident voice. . . . Restrained. . . . Lush, yet a certain withholding. . . . Entwining the erotic and comic. . . . Sense of loss. . . . Missed opportunity for grace. . . . Transcendent voice."

Thirty minutes later, having abandoned the blue breakfast tray, she is at the bookstore, at one of their tables, the book of poems, *his* poems in her hands. The first poem, "First Meeting," is so wholly sensual, she feels Donald's hand on her thigh. Reading the phrase, "scent of rosemary," she remembers *his* scent, tart and fresh, like grapefruit, and his mouth moving from mouth to neck to breast, her hand caressing his head, his shoulders, his mouth touching her then, and now, touching her again through sound and image. She remembers the logistics of meeting him, each day sweeter than the one before because each day's drive brought her closer. She remembers the formality of their public selves, the careful greetings, in sharp contrast to the joy they took in each other when, laughing, discarding clothes, they closed the door and were alone together.

Then, Donald never mentioned his wife. His joy at being with her told her all she needed to know. Told her all.

He will call, and I will fly to Manhattan, she tells herself now. He will call because it is all there. The places they have loved each other. The forest in Oregon that first spring. Before a fireplace in a bed-and-breakfast in Nachez. The sweet biscuits and meadow honey they had at breakfast. The giant dogs that were at home on the place overlooking the Mississippi. And that first time. In her hotel room. All of it here. In the book she holds in her hand.

He calls at ten that night. "Did you see the review?" he asks without preamble. He sounds sleepy.

"I read the poems."

"Dearest Anne. They're for you. Come to New York on Friday. Be there by three. Can you? Will you?"

"Yes. Oh yes, I'll come! What hotel?"

"The Stanhope. Anne, you can drive if you leave tomorrow."

"No. I can fly. And I'll come. I'll fly."

"My darling Anne. Dear, dear love."

"We've wasted all these years."

"No. Not wasted. Never wasted."

"I'm packing," she told him. "I'll be there on Wednesday, by noon."

"Wait. Anne, nothing's changed. My family. Nothing's changed."

"I'll be there. I'm flying. Good night, my love."

When Tony and Dylan, with the now seven-year-old Lennon (whose grandmother has a doctor's appointment), come on Tuesday afternoon to present her with a final bill, including supplies, she cannot keep from smiling.

"You look mighty happy today," Tony says.

"Oh, I am, Tony. I'm flying," she swallows and says the word again, "flying to New York on Friday."

Dylan gazes at her. Tony blinks. "Sounds nice," Dylan says.

"Oh, it will be," she says. "I'm happy about it."

They look at her, waiting. When she says nothing more, "It's nice to be happy," Tony says politely.

After they leave she chooses the clothes she will wear to

New York. Her warmest coat. Black skirt and white silk blouse. Heels. Donald likes women to wear heels.

Although she has not yet packed, everything is out and ready when the phone rings. It's Christopher. She has to tell somebody. She tells Christopher.

"So you're leaving to meet this man? When?"

"Day after tomorrow. And I pray I can make myself get on that plane. And stay on it." Now she's giggling. "After we're airborne, I'll have to stay on it."

"What are you doing tomorrow?"

"Teaching. Getting everything ready to take a personal leave day."

"I can help with the flying thing."

"No, you can't."

"Maybe I can. I'll pick you up tomorrow at four."

"All right," she says doubtfully.

Donald calls at eleven that night, twelve his time. He wakes her up. "Tell me what you thought about the poems."

"Loss is there." She is yawning. Gathering her thoughts, she says, "I like what the reviewer said. I like the tenderness of voice, without sentimentality. I remember those magnificent dogs."

"In Nachez? I'd forgotten that we . . . I'd forgotten we saw them together."

"How could you forget that?"

He laughs. "I was looking at you," he says.

She resists the urge to probe. "Until Friday," she says.

But she cannot go back to sleep. *I'd forgotten we saw them together,* he had said. But they *were* her poems. They were *her* love letters. She opens the book again. "First Meeting." Their first night. She reads it again. It could have been any hotel room. But it was *their* room. In the bar they had sat at a table in the corner. Her dress was black. But maybe the poem needed a woman in white. And a couple at the bar. She will ask him.

After lunch the next day she slips into black slacks and pulls on a black-and-white cashmere sweater. Her lipstick is bright red because the day is overcast.

Christopher comes at four. "Where are we going?" she asks.

"To the fairgrounds." Arms crossed, he leans against the doorjamb, waiting for her to get a raincoat. He follows her to the car, opens the door.

"Do you think the fair can help me?"

"Yup."

"You're a man of few words."

"Yup."

"You've been watching too many old movies."

"Maybe," he says. And they laugh.

At the fairgrounds they buy cotton candy for him. "Real men don't eat pink cotton candy," she says. They buy popcorn for her. They throw balls to win a teddy bear.

They pass a booth with guns. "What about shooting?"

"I've had enough of that," he says grimly.

"Sorry."

He reaches for her hand, squeezes it. They walk on. They see prize pigs, a horse show, a bird show. Acrobats from China. They eat corn dogs and watch the people. They stroll, ride the merry-go-round. It's almost dark when Christopher says, "Here we are."

"Here?"

"We're going to ride the Ferris wheel."

"Oh, Christopher, I don't know. I don't think I can."

"You climbed the tree."

She nods and swallows. Now they are in line, moving closer and closer to the ticket booth. She feels her heart beating. Her mouth is dry. *I climbed the tree,* she sternly reminds herself. She thinks of the bloody goat making its desperate run for survival. *She* could turn and run. Now her mouth is so dry she cannot swallow.

Without looking toward her he says, "Two tickets. Adults." He turns to walk to the Ferris wheel. "Coming?" he says over his shoulder.

She steels herself and follows. The gray-headed man who takes the tickets makes her think of Charon rowing people across the river Styx. But the Ferris wheel goes up, not across a river. She can do this.

Now they are stepping onto the Ferris wheel. She can turn now and walk away. Run away. But Christopher is stepping into a seat. She follows. The man secures the safety bar.

She closes her eyes. "I'm scared," she says. "I can't do it!"

"Wait! Wait," she cries, but the man has pushed them off, setting the seat into a gentle swing, and already they are rising, rising. She opens her eyes and looks straight ahead at the blue of the sky. She closes them again and grips the safety bar.

The wheel stops. He leans over to see why it has stopped, sending them into a dangerous swing. "Christopher!" she says sharply. Her mouth is dry. Her heart is beating its way out of her chest.

"Look up," he tells her. "Look at the clouds."

They lean backward, setting the seat into a gentle swing. "We are very, very safe," he tells her. "You're all right."

She grips the safety bar with one hand and holds his arm close with the other. Now they are at the very top. The wheel stops. "We're on top of the world," she says, shakily.

Now they are sinking, stopping, sinking. "Do you want to get off?" he asks.

She shakes her head. Now they are rising, rising, stopping. She takes deep breaths. Ferris wheel yoga. Leaning back she looks down on the world. They go around four, five times, ten times. She loses count. She looks at the clouds tumbling around them. She looks at Christopher's face, alive with pleasure. The wheel stops; the attendant dislodges the safety bar.

"Again," he urges. "Let's ride again."

"Why not," she says. After the third ride he says, "Why don't you try it alone?"

She nods. He secures the safety bar and leaves. She can do this. Closing her eyes, she breathes deeply. Her heart slows. She opens her eyes and looks at the sky. The Ferris wheel rises and sinks. She sees Christopher throw back his head, laughing. He gives her a thumbs up. She rides again by herself. Then with Christopher. "I did it," she says.

Driving home she is triumphant. "I can fly," she says. "To New York tomorrow. I can fly anywhere. To Paris and London and Venice."

Christopher walks her to the door. She says, "So what if my heart beats, my mouth goes dry. I can fly," she tells him. "Good night, Christopher. And thank you. Thank you."

After taking a shower she wraps herself in a towel. Coming from the bath she sees her clothes, not yet packed, sees the black lace of panties and bras and a nightgown. Clothes for a tryst. Donald had said, "Nothing's changed." *I have my children. I love them. And I am still married,* he was telling her. But none of this has anything to do with her. She loves him, loves his voice, the poetry he writes. They will walk together in New York, she matching her stride to his. He will read his poems to her. She will tell him she loves them, these love letters to her.

She has made her reservation. Perhaps he can meet her at the airport. She picks up the phone and dials the Stanhope.

"Oh, Anne, darling," he says. "I'm happy. There's been no one since you."

Questions gather in her throat. Tomorrow is beginning to seem like a dream. An illusion. The poems, a lyrical reverie. Not hers. Not *just* hers. There are too many hotel rooms in the poems. And picnics. Donald likes picnics. She hears his voice again, the surprise in it, saying, *I'd forgotten we saw them together.* And a minute ago, saying, *There's been no one since you.* She takes the receiver from her ear and looks at it. Donald is still talking. She holds it to her ear again. His voice is full of passion and poetry. While he talks she sees him again, almost always with a swarm of admirers. She remembers the sadness that had settled on his wife's face when she looked at her husband.

She interrupts him. "Donald, I'm not coming."

"What? You're not coming! You can't mean that," he says. "You said you could fly."

"It's not that. I can fly."

"What is it? I've made plans. I'm meeting with my publisher in the afternoon but after that we'll have dinner at the Algonquin. And champagne. It will be like it used to be."

"No, it won't. It can't be. Your life is the same. I've changed mine. I like my life now. It's better." Laughing she says, "Now I can fly."

"There's someone else, isn't there," he accuses.

Still laughing, "There's lots of someone elses," she says.

Chapter Twelve

1

FATHER D'ACOSTA is a solitary priest, but not in the way of most priests. In this great old Dallas church his solitude, although at times a hairshirt, is often simply scratchy, slightly heavy. It is a shirt woven of a simple yet fervent need, a single passionate longing. He yearns to be able, in the manner of other priests, to be given God's grace in order to bestow God's grace. For is not this the office, the deepest office of a priest? And yet he cannot do this. For all the years of his priesthood he has lived with this failure, has become accustomed to the weight of it. Sadly it is a burden that grows with each passing hour of each day. Yet how simple to others is the bestowal of this gift. From the moment Father Keeney enters a grief-filled room, those in his presence feel that he loves them above all others. His tenderness promises God's healing; his compassion offers a future of brighter days. And the joy Father Morris takes in sunsets and birdsong and rain, in good food and brandy, in the religious and the secular, that very joy promises God's grace. Father O'Brien bestows this gift through the easy benevolence of his hearty laughter, his quick wit. The warmth of his embrace. But he himself? How clumsy, how ineffective is his offering. To the deepest needs of his parishioners he is able to offer only a frozen formality. "God moves in mysterious ways. . . . ," this to a man who had lost his job, or "His wisdom ordains. . . . ," to a woman unable to bear a child. In joy and in sorrow his parishioners turn away from him. And is it any wonder? At times his whole being is slack with regret. But always after the hardness of the day there came the perfection of the evening Mass. This Mass, at once curative and elegiac, is his saving grace.

This evening's prayers begin the long preparation for the season of the Nativity. The clear precise Spanish of his parishioners rises, floats in liquid syllables into the soft air of the church, while from outside comes the cooing and fluttering of pigeons returning to their nesting places.

In the stained-glass window high above his head the sainted Margaret Mary Alacoque of France prays before the Sacred Heart. Just below this window Father Endes's painting of the Virgin of Guadeloupe, gorgeously arrayed in a gown of blue like no other, and with golden stars too numerous to count, is hung. Beneath the window and the painting Father d'Acosta kneels and urgently prays, demanding rather than supplicating. He suspects it is the newly hung cross at the back of the church that has engendered this sense of urgency. Primitive, passionate, a Corpus of the eighteenth century from Guatemala, the crucifix reminds him of the sweet promise of his boyhood. As he gazes over the heads of his parishioners toward the crucifix at the back of the church, the plaza, and the Alameda of San Miguel de Allende, its sienna-colored streets and houses, its hungry dogs and laughing children—the entire village of his birth rises before his eyes.

Surrounded by these memories of his childhood and by the perfection of the evening Mass, he fervently prays for all children, for the mendicants who come to the cathedral for its warmth and light, for the old and the young, for the sick in body and mind, for those in despair. And finally, turning again to the altar, he prays fervently for Dolores O'Malley, a woman from his own village; prays that she, who has been given everything, might also be given the grace of God. Then her face would reflect her contentment, her mouth would speak the sweetest of words, and her hands, never still (even at the altar as she waits for the Body and the Blood), would rest quietly in an angle of repose. Thus filled with the contentment that God's grace brings, she would be able to conceive. And blessed with a child, her Irish husband would become the true benefactor of the cathedral for, speaking to Father d'Acosta both as a friend and as his wife's priest, he has promised as much.

"You would bargain with God?" Father d'Acosta had said to him sternly.

"Only if it be His will," John O'Malley had responded soberly and, putting on his hard hat, had hurried off to supervise his crews.

Now the Sanctus bell sounds, heralding that most sacred moment, the elevation of the Host, and Father d'Acosta rises and, turning to the people, lifts his arms. At that moment he sees the face of the girl. In the single shaft of light diffused by the stained-glass windows into a rosy glow, he sees her face framed by hair as black as night, sees her eyes blaze forth like stars. And throughout the service while he kneels and stands and kneels again, he sees the light touch her face again and again. Caught by the innocence and beauty of it, he sees her rise and hold out her hands as if in supplication before she falls, falls softly as a leaf might fall, onto the faded kneeling bench.

After the last worshipers leave Father d'Acosta hurries to his study. There he watches as Sister Mary Celeste holds a glass to the girl's lips. When she has drunk, he asks "Child, are you ill? Hungry?"

"No," she says so softly that he only sees the word on her lips.

"What is it you need?" he asks, hating the useless questioning, for the need is there, welling up from her eyes, overflowing the room. When she does not answer, "Dear child, I will pray for you," he says, hearing the cold formality of his words.

But she does not turn away from him as others have done. Instead, looking intently at his face, she nods, her gaze steady. The thought comes that in just such a way did the deer that grazed near the monastery in the Colorado mountains look at friendly intruders.

"What is it you want?" he asks again.

"The sanctuary of your church," she whispers.

Disbelieving, he asks, "What? What did you say?"

"Sanctuary. I need this."

Sister Celeste bustles about. "Girl, you need some food," she says. "Hot tea. That'll fix you up. Now, you come with me and I'll see to it."

Taking the girl's hand, she urges her to her feet and it is then that he sees she carries a child. "Wait! Sister, the girl's . . . *embarazada*," he says softly, finding the Spanish easier.

"I know, Father. I see that," she says, ushering the girl from his office toward the small room where she takes her meals. "When she's had a bite we'll come back. Then you can decide what's best to do. Doubtless, Saint Mary Margarets will take her."

When they have gone he sits at his desk hearing again the whispered plea. Opening his dictionary he finds the word: *sanctuary: a consecrated place, shelter, a refuge for wildlife, protected from predators.* Sister Celeste is probably right. Saint Mary Margarets would be the best place for the girl. He has been there on numerous occasions. To baptize. To give communion. And always he is surprised at how young these girls are, giggling and whispering through the services, reading paperback romances, weeping over soap operas, as they await the birth of their babies. Sighing, he looks at the definitions once more, reading the last again: *a refuge for wildlife, protected from predators.*

A half hour later, still at his desk, he receives the two of them. Sister Celeste takes the chair on his left while Echo, her face without expression, sits quietly on the black leather sofa. Waiting for him to speak, Sister Celeste seems focused on her hands folded calmly in her lap. He clears his throat. "My name is Father d'Acosta. You know Sister Celeste. What is your name?"

"Echo."

The word startles him. Who would choose such a name for a child? Unusual, and yet, having heard it, it seems no other would have done.

"Echo, where is the baby's father?"

"I don't know. He had to leave."

Looking at her face he knows she speaks the truth. A social service worker might well have asked more about the father but he'd be damned if he would.

"Do you have a home?"

She shakes her head.

He tries again. "Echo, with whom do you live?"

"Jamie and I were together. Then he left. I don't know where he is. I want to live here until the baby comes. Here. In the church."

Sister Celeste opens her mouth, closes it, opens it again. "Why child, what an idea! That's out of the question. You can't stay here. But we'll find—"

Interrupting, his voice is firm. "Sister Celeste, we'll decide all that in the morning. Tonight Echo will sleep in the bishop's room."

"But Father . . ."

"Until morning."

"But Father," again.

"Open up the room. Tomorrow morning the child can walk in the garden, feed the birds, rest. Tomorrow morning's soon enough for decisions."

2

Never before has Father d'Acosta appeared before his bishop with a request of this kind, but three days later here he is, sitting across from him. Nervously, hesitantly, he has put the matter forward with as much clarity and detail as his English allows, although he doubts that any language would have done.

When he has finished, Bishop Moore puts his elbows on the desk and makes a pyramid with his fingers. Shaking his head he says, "You know the problems this will create. I can only imagine a small part of them. There will certainly be talk about the strange girl in the priest's lodgings, even though she will share the lodgings and be chaperoned by Sister Celeste. And the logistics. To say it will be awkward and awkwardly expensive would be saying the least."

"If you saw Echo. She's so unlike the girls at Saint Margarets. She could never stay there. Why, to put her there . . . it would be like caging a deer."

Bishop Moore taps the side of his head with his forefinger. "Do you mean that she's not . . . ?"

"No. She's quite bright. Brighter than most. But in a different way. She notices things. She likes to be outdoors. She reads.

"What does she read?"

"She enjoys reading hymnals. Or seems to."

"Hymnals," Bishop Moore says, and after a minute: "Unusual, but," a quick thin smile, "wholesome." He settles his eyeglasses more comfortably on his nose and pushes the desk chair back so that he might cross his legs. "When is the baby expected?"

"She is not sure. Sometime this winter."

Bishop Moore stands and walks over to the window. He turns, comes to the desk again, and sits, leaning forward, in his chair.

"Has it occurred to you that this might be a hoax?" he asks. "A young girl, pretty, with the face that is often mistaken for innocence, she may not be what she seems. She could be manipulating you. Me. The church. And I will not have it."

"Come see for yourself. A few hours. You be the judge."

"Next week. I'll come on Monday," and standing, allowing his ring to be kissed, the bishop signals that the meeting is over.

Bishop Moore's visit on Monday is brief. He sits beside Echo in the garden and watches as she tosses bread crumbs to the sparrows that tumble from the wild pear tree. After no more than twenty minutes he rejoins Father d'Acosta in his study, stirs cream into his coffee, and butters the slice of warm banana bread served by Sister Celeste, who has worn a bright smile all day, presumably in the belief that the bishop's visit will serve, as she has repeatedly said, "to set things right."

When he has finished the bishop delicately wipes his fingers on the worn linen napkin in his lap and carefully places the napkin on the table beside his plate. Then he stands and runs his fingers over the worn fabric of the sofa, the scarred mahogany of the desk, and finally, the badly repaired molding into which the window overlooking the garden is set. Father d'Acosta joins him at the window. Silently they watch the young girl, still graceful under the weight of her pregnancy, attach a hose to a water faucet, turn on the faucet, and add water to the birdbath beneath the small statue, made headless by vandals, of Our Lady of Guadeloupe.

Bishop Moore turns to Father d'Acosta, motioning him to his own chair behind his desk. He draws the smaller chair back and carefully settles his long angular frame into it. Pushing the wire frames of his eyeglasses higher on his nose, he leans forward.

"The girl would not fit into Saint Mary Margarets," he says. "We are in agreement. But there is much to consider: Our most affluent parishioners, some with quite generous hearts, have moved to the suburbs. The present worshipers are, for the most part, without certain employment; where once we saw men in suits and women in silk dresses, we now see men, those lucky enough to have a job, wearing work shirts and hard hats. If the church is to serve the needs of these people; that is, if the hungry are to be fed, the naked clothed, the homeless sheltered, we must have the munificence of one or two men who, having been given much, can give much in return. One such man spoke to me recently, promised that . . ."

"John O'Malley."

"Yes. And Dolores, his wife. Might not this child be the answer to their prayers?"

"But to ask that the girl give up her baby . . ."

"You yourself said she is not like the others. Talk to her. See what her plans are for the baby's future. If she agrees that her baby needs a good home and loving parents, parents who would give her baby everything a child might need, she can stay here. Of course you will not tell her this is the condition upon which our permission that she stay rests. I want no coercion in this matter. And it might be that the O'Malleys will want to meet her before it's decided. If all should agree, our lawyers will prepare the documents. Father, in a situation so delicate, all needs must be considered: the church's, the parishioners', the O'Malleys', the girl's. A priest's duty is to balance these needs. Appropriate balance. That's the key."

He rises from his chair, places his hands on the small of his back. He smiles briefly, raises his eyebrows. "This interest of yours in the girl," he says. "What occasioned it?"

After a while Father d'Acosta speaks into the silence. "I have asked that question of myself," he says. "I do not know the answer."

As he leaves the room, the bishop turns his head again to

glance once more at the girl in the garden below. Father d'Acosta feels curiously cheated by the ray of sun that, reflecting off his gold wire eyeglasses, obscures the expression in his bishop's eyes.

The papers signifying intent had been drawn up in triplicate and signed early in the morning by Echo. Handing her the document, Father d'Acosta had carefully explained: "The agreement is not binding. But it is a solemn promise that you intend to allow the O'Malleys to take your baby from the hospital, to adopt him or her when the required waiting period is over, and to raise him or her as their own beloved child. Echo, it would be a cruel thing to allow them to believe the baby will be theirs if such is not the case. Do you understand?"

"Yes," she answered, and had carefully written her name on each copy, frowning as she read and explained to him the meaning of each paragraph, so that he might know her understanding was complete.

Then they are signed by the O'Malleys, who have met Echo, spoken with her, and are sure that a child from such a mother, no more than a child herself, would indeed be blessed by the home they could provide. "The child will have our love and all the material advantages he will need," John O'Malley says proudly. When he has finished with the document he turns his wife's face toward the window. "Father, do you not see the resemblance? Dolores could be the girl's older sister. Look at her coloring, the shape of her face."

"Why, that's so," Sister Celeste says sturdily, just as the champagne cork pops from the bottle.

And indeed the resemblance is pronounced.

When the document has been witnessed the party toasts the

baby-to-come and the parents-to-be. That Echo was not present, that none found their way to the window to see Echo in the garden, leaves a somewhat bitter taste in Father d'Acosta's mouth. Or, he thinks later, it might only have been the champagne.

3

Not since he was a boy has Father d'Acosta felt what it was to be a family. Now day by day his sense of family grows; ill-assorted, oddly shaped, but still, three, almost four generations of a family. By the end of the first week Sister Celeste has taken the girl under her wing: "Child, better get off your feet, rest a little while." Thus clucking over her, remonstrating with her, in her very old age Sister Celeste has become a grandmother. And although he keeps to his usual routines, Father d'Acosta never enters or leaves his study without pausing at the window that overlooks the garden where Echo, more often than not, can be found.

Presided over by Our Lady's headless statue the garden has been long abandoned. Here Echo, with a set of gardening tools (provided by the O'Malleys), digs and weeds and waters. She keeps the water in the birdbath fresh, seeds (also provided by the O'Malleys) in the birdfeeder plentiful, and the beds richly cultivated.

"Weeds or flowers, it's all the same to her," Sister Celeste tells him. "She works as hard with one as the other."

On an early November day, having finished his sermon, Father d'Acosta walks with Echo through the garden. In answer to Echo's request he names those plants he knows.

"This is Queen Anne's lace," he says, holding the feathery leafed plant in his hand. "When it blooms, it does look like a queen's lace. This is sage and this, I think, this is a kind of thistle. I'm not sure."

But his ignorance about most of the plants Echo tends drives him to a bookstore for a field guide, and after supper, as Sister Celeste sits with her handwork, he roams its pages finding himself interested, not so much in the cultivation, but rather more in the identification of aptly named plants, plants such as Shepherd's Purse and Lizard's Tail and Beggar's Ticks.

When Echo retires to her bed (moved beneath windows that are always open, no matter the weather or cost of air-conditioning) he and Sister Celeste talk with amusement and pride about Echo's garden. In a few days the variety of birds that come there sends him again to the bookstore for a guide to Texas birds.

"Echo is taking some interest in her appearance," Sister Celeste says one evening. "She asked me for stockings, the kind young girls wear." Leaving him at a loss to know she means pantyhose, she goes on embroidering the pillowcase she is making for the bishop. "And I believe that she's taking up handwork. This morning she asked for embroidery thread," she continues, adding somewhat immodestly, "I suppose she's noticed the fineness of my stitchery."

A week later he looks out the window and sees that, overnight, a head has appeared on the shoulders of Our Lady of Guadeloupe. Calling Sister Celeste from the kitchen, he hurries out into the garden and sees that the head, like the heads of rag dolls his sisters had played with as children, is skin-colored, the mouth and eyes clumsily embroidered.

"Why, Father, this isn't right!" Sister Celeste exclaims. "Echo made this head with pantyhose!"

"Wait," he says. Taking her arm he leads her to the bench in the garden. "Sit down. Let's sit here a minute. I don't know that it isn't exactly right. Look at her. Look at Our Lady. She's smiling. And she does seem quite at peace."

It is that very next day, in the early afternoon, that he looks into the garden and sees a thing he will remember the rest of his life. He has made the last of his telephone calls and has written a letter asking for further details about the Guatemalan crucifix when he looks out the window and sees the possum. Surprised by its daytime appearance he watches it making its way heavily across the garden. When it reaches the magnolia tree he sees the babies clinging to her back—five, no, six of them. It is a full minute before he notices Echo sitting on the bench before Our Lady and sees that she, too, watches as the possum makes her laboriously maternal journey across the garden. All at once Father d'Acosta aches to know the girl's thoughts, to be able to read her mind. Since she has signed the letter of intent she has not mentioned the baby. Most of the money the O'Malleys have sent (the last from California, where John O'Malley is playing the Pebble Beach course) has been spent by Echo on garden supplies. What connections does Echo make, he wonders now, between herself and that curious animal? Does she feel regret? Longing? Curiosity? He is powerless to know. But looking into the garden he feels that the slow progress of the possum, the fabricated head of Our Lady, the motionless girl—feels all three have come together for a purpose, and that it is a message, indecipherable, but still a message for him.

Chapter Thirteen

1

MISS WEEMS says Mr. Sam Witherspoon will be coming to pick up Albert, the Boston bull. "Sam will be right for Albert," she says. "They're both getting on in years. And Sam's bound to be lonesome living in that big house all by himself without Martha."

When Mr. Witherspoon arrives Mary Lou sees the match right away. Mr. Witherspoon plods stiffly along with his head down just like Albert. And they both have round brown eyes that bulge a little.

The three of them stand in the parlor looking down at Albert. "Albert, you'll like Mr. Witherspoon," Miss Weems promises. Albert looks up at Mr. Witherspoon, turns his back on him, and trots out of the room.

Miss Weems says, "He's a little shy at first, but he'll be just fine. Now Sam, Miss Barbara's cousin has already paid the fees. Albert's had all his shots and, as far as we know, he's healthy. But he's mighty lonesome right now."

Albert sticks his head back around the door. Mr. Witherspoon plods over, stoops, and pats his head. "Well, little feller, you reckon we can get along?"

"Sam, Dr. Read said a walk twice a day would help him more than anything."

"Yes, ma'am. We'll see what we can do about it."

"A constitutional walk would do you a world of good, too, Sam Witherspoon."

He nods, bends to fasten a leash to Albert's collar. "Well, come on little feller. I think we can hit it off together."

"Sam, you try him out a week, and if it don't work out, bring him back. I've got somebody else looking for a small dog."

After Sam and Albert leave, Miss Weems is all smiles. "Sam's been right lonesome since Martha died, and there's nothing like a little dog to lift a person's spirits," she says. Then, "Well, let's get to our reading, if that suits you."

And it usually did.

Mary Lou will not let herself think about a second Christmas almost upon her and still no word from Echo. But reading about Jane Eyre so far away and in trouble helps. *What does she have to worry about?* she asks herself. It gets dark early and a lot of times they have an early supper together, and afterward, they read in the parlor. It's cozy. Miss Weems doesn't have a television because she subscribes to two papers and that's more news than she can digest. That first week, her eyes bothering her, she asks Mary Lou to read to her. Reading to somebody slows Mary Lou down, but it gives her time to think about Charlotte Brontë, the lady who wrote the book. Is the book really about her life? Mary Lou thinks it must be. How could anybody make all that up?

Pretty soon it is like the two of them have their own book

club. "Mary Lou, put that little stick of wood on the fire and we'll read until it burns up," she says. The book, named *Jane Eyre*, is about a girl named Jane Eyre who takes chances. Reading it makes Miss Weems wish she had taken some. "My life could have been so different," she says one night, getting up to poke up the fire, "but every time a boy took a shine to me, 'Who is he?' Daddy would say. One time Kenneth Thompson came to the house and, sitting in the parlor with Daddy and me, he broke out in hives right before our eyes."

Miss Weems laughs when she tells it, but then she says sadly, " 'Course he never came back."

Christine Jessup from New York City comes one evening bringing Ginger, a little black cocker spaniel. Christine is the prettiest girl Mary Lou has even seen, with skin like a china cup and the biggest eyes and black hair.

"Miss Weems, I'm so relieved you provide this service," Christine says. "My husband is allergic to dogs, and Mother loved her little dog. These last few years Ginger was a good companion, just about Mother's only companion."

"Christine, you know my fee. If it's satisfactory, leave her here a few days. When I know Ginger's personality and temperament, I'll find a good home for her. Now don't you worry."

And sure enough in a few days Robert Ellis Wentworth shows up. "Robert Ellis," Miss Weems says. "I've decided to let you have the Jessup dog, Ginger, if you hit it off." Right away they seem to, him throwing the ball and saying, "Good dog, good Ginger!" when she brings it back.

"Miss Weems, I don't believe I know Ms. Jessup," Robert Ellis says, gently picking up Ginger, holding her on his lap.

"Robert Ellis, you do know Christine Jessup. Her mother was

an early member of the Delphian Club and her grandmother was a charter member of the Twentieth-Century Club."

Ginger hops down and, with the ball in her mouth, sits at Robert Ellis's feet and wags her tail.

"Who was she?" Robert says, bouncing the ball into the library.

Mary Lou notices that everybody in Weatherford asks, "Who was she?" They'd go way back. "Who was his grandmother before she married Judge so-and-so?" they'd ask. Things like that.

"Why, Robert. Christine Carter is who she was," Miss Weems says firmly. "Your mother and Christine's mother played cards the first Wednesday of every month until Mrs. Carter got too sick to hold the cards."

"I believe I do remember her now. When Christine was little her nose used to bleed when it snowed. Sometimes it'd bleed so bad they'd have to stop the game in the middle of a rubber."

Satisfied, Miss Weems scoops Ginger up in her arms. "Well, here she is. Now Robert, Ginger's frisky. What she needs is exercise. When you come in from work you get a Frisbee and take her to the park. You hear? She's a nice little dog and we don't want Mrs. Carter coming back around to haunt us now, do we?"

"No ma'am!" Robert Ellis says.

In a few days Mary Lou looks forward to coming home to Miss Weems's house. She likes her room. Almost nothing in it but her clothes. She likes the sheltering feeling of the house with its wide porch and all the trees.

Sometimes in bed at night she feels like a kite cut loose and drifting. In a way she is. Nobody to see about. Nobody to see about her. It isn't a good feeling but it isn't a bad one either.

And each night she hopes that tomorrow will be the day when the Dairy Queen door will open and Echo will walk in.

2

Mary Lou thinks up the idea one day while she is waiting at the courthouse square for Miss Weems. They are going to the Austins' that evening to get Hannah, a yellow lab. It is a shame, really. Mrs. Austin dead and not a one of her children who wanted Hannah.

Sitting on the bench that day, Mary Lou notices the bumper-to-bumper traffic. *Why this is better than the Dairy Queen,* she thinks. Two highways intersecting. If she's anywhere in Texas, Echo is bound to pass this corner.

When she tells Miss Weems about her plan, Miss Weems says, "There's no sense to it, Mary Lou. It's the month of December. You'll catch your death of cold sitting on that bench in all this weather." Impatiently Miss Weems floorboards the gas pedal. "Children stay up nights thinking up ways to worry their parents," she mutters to herself, braking the car, making a U-turn when the sign says No U-turn. "I'm glad my life took the turn it did. We'd all be better off without children."

Miss Weems is talking to herself but Mary Lou knows she means her to hear every word. When they are almost to the Austins', Mary Lou has listened long enough.

"Miss Weems, when you get to know Echo, you'll be glad I had her. In most every way she's a wonderful girl."

Miss Weems looks at Mary Lou so long that Mary Lou has to reach over and steer. "Well, if you're going to sit on that courthouse bench in the middle of winter, you better bundle up," was all Miss Weems said after that.

When Mary Lou gets off work the next day, she walks over and sits on the bench. And the next day. And the next. Every day from four o'clock until dark, rain or shine, she sits on the bench waiting for Echo. *Miss Weems is right,* she tells herself sometimes. There is no sense to it. But then she'll see a pickup or an SUV, and she'll let herself hope.

Today the sun is out so that even at fifty degrees Mary Lou feels warm. The courthouse looks especially nice against the blue sky. She does admire the Weatherford courthouse. There isn't one prettier in Texas, she is sure.

That first week, Mr. Swanson, the courthouse custodian, said, "Miz Burgandy, since you're a widow, how'd you like to go up on the Widow's Walk? I don't take many folks up there, but I'll take you." *Widow.* She had to think about that. She had never thought of herself by that name. She just thought about Gundren leaving her. Then she said, "Well, Mr. Swanson, since I am one, I'd like to see it."

And up they went, climbing, climbing, Mr. Swanson huffing and puffing and stopping to get his breath, and on the way telling her about the women in New England who climbed up to get a good view of the sea, waiting for their husbands to sail home. He said, "I guess as many women out here on the high plains needed a place to watch for their husbands, hoping they'd be coming back from the war, just like those ladies in New England."

She looked down, saw the little midget trees below, and then her eyes followed the highway toward Lone Oak. She could see a long way, maybe fifteen or twenty miles. "We're above the clouds," she exclaimed.

"We are. We're up over ten stories."

"I'm looking for Echo," she said.

"And don't I know it," he said, and after that was quiet while she looked out over the town and the fields and the creek beds, some of them with water.

It is something to remember. She plans to take a trip someday and visit all the courthouses in Texas.

She is a little early today. She hasn't seen many of the regulars. Mr. Swanson has stopped by but, with the pigeons and all, he couldn't tarry. And Mrs. Carroll from the drugstore has brought out a big cup of hot coffee. She's been doing that every day since the story was in the newspaper with a picture of Mary Lou sitting on the bench. The picture was on the front page. ECHO, CALL YOUR MOTHER! the Weatherford paper said. Mary Lou has had better pictures taken, but with the rain and all, her hair had been a mess and she hadn't been wearing earrings.

Now, what surprises her is that, not even knowing Echo, everybody in town wants to help. Trucks and cars slow down and the drivers roll down their windows when they pass. "Any luck yet?" they holler. Or, "Has she called?" If they don't stop they give her a "V for victory" or a "thumbs up" or a "hook 'em horns" sign. Everybody on foot stops to ask, and the church ladies bring food and tell her they're praying.

She almost always has some company. Today it is Fred Pierce. Fred lost track of his mother when he was eighteen and joined the army. Now he is fifty-two and bald. But who'd know it? He always wears his Rangers cap. Today she and Fred sit on the bench and when the light changes they take turns standing up to look into every vehicle. A black Pathfinder is passing now.

"Nope," Fred says.

"Why, it's Josie!" Mary Lou cries as Josie screeches to a stop.

"Hurry!" Josie says. "Echo's just ordered a cheeseburger to go." Taking off before Mary Lou gets the door closed, "We're sure it's Echo!" Josie says breathlessly.

By the time they pull into the parking lot the news has spread. Waitresses from the other Dairy Queen and a leather-jacketed biker and two "gimme"-capped truckers and Mr. Grant from the newspaper and Sam Witherspoon with Albert are all there, grinning and nodding and giving "V for victory" and "hook 'em horns" and "thumbs up" signs, everybody excited, but quiet like in church.

They step back, making a path for her when she gets out of the truck, and Chet, Josie's ex, holds the door open for her. And then Mary Lou sees her, this dark-headed girl at the cashier's and before she turns around Mary Lou lets herself believe for a minute it is Echo, although in her bones she knows it isn't. Then the girl turns, surprised, scared a little when she sees everybody looking at her. Mary Lou shakes her head and then, suddenly dizzy, she has to sit down.

After a while Mr. Grant takes her home and neither one of them says a word the whole way. When he lets her out, "What a story. What a story," he says, but she is just worn out with the whole thing.

3

After that it is like she has crossed over a bridge, but she doesn't see it until she calls up Anne. At first she just feels like sleeping. But she doesn't. She asks for longer hours at the Dairy Queen and works so hard that sometimes she is too tired by nightfall to read to Miss Weems. But she begins to save money. When she has three hundred dollars she opens a savings account at the bank.

Then one night with full tables and everybody in a hurry, Mary Lou looks at all the people eating and going about their business and not keeping anybody awake at night and, *Echo, what's wrong with you!* she says to herself. *Worrying all these people in Weatherford and your grandmother and Anne and Miss Weems and me, Echo, me! Worrying all of us just about to death.* And that is when she gets mad at Echo. She never has before, but thinking about it that night she does. And the idea comes to her that, since Gundren died and Echo ran away, she has just drifted with Echo always on her mind. Not even drifted—staggered—from one thing to another, not even noticing Thanksgiving, missing Christmas (and about to miss it again), jumping into Lone Oak college (she is glad about that), and then almost into Ed's arms (she is glad she didn't). *And now,* she tells herself, *Here I am in Weatherford, Texas, with everybody in town worrying about Echo.*

After three days of being mad she calls up Anne. She tells her all of it, how sweet everybody has been about Echo, and how when she saw their faces at the Dairy Queen she got mad at Echo, and she can't get over it. As she talks she can almost see Anne leaning forward, frowning a little, listening. "I still love her, but I'm just so mad," she finishes.

She thinks Anne will have to process it, but right away she says, "Mary Lou, I almost feel relieved. You have been in denial so long."

"Denial?"

"Yes. You remember how you used to go to sleep at night imagining you could swim across the ocean to Gundren. And then you kept on hearing his voice."

"And telling myself he was in his truck, driving around somewhere."

"Yes. In a way you've done the same thing about Echo. She left almost fifteen months ago, and until now, you believed that any minute you might look up and see her."

"Well, I might."

"But you might not. This anger that you feel is natural. The wonderful thing about it is that it frees you to go on to the next passage."

Mary Lou holds on to the phone. It is beginning to seem like a lifeline.

"Mary Lou?"

"I'm here. I'm thinking."

"I'll send you some information to read. It might help."

"About being mad?"

"About the stages of grief."

"Oh."

"Mary Lou, Tony Orchard called yesterday. He asked all about you. I told him everything I knew. Tony's moved to Lone Oak."

"Mama will be glad. She likes Tony."

"I do, too. Mary Lou, I'll call you in a few days. And see how you're doing."

"I don't go to the courthouse square anymore. I'm coming back to school pretty soon."

"Good."

"How are things in Dallas? Your classes and all."

"We're finishing up a semester. Oh, I've got a sabbatical. Next year I'll be going to Europe to study." She laughs, "But this weekend I'm doing some Christmas shopping."

Mary Lou thinks about the money she has saved. "Me, too," she says. "Anne, thanks. Thanks a lot."

"Mary Lou, you're going to be just fine," Anne says. "You might remember that Echo did not run away to hurt you. Remember the note she wrote? And the cards. She loves you."

Even after Anne says good-bye, Mary Lou holds on to the phone, holds on until a recorded voice reminds her to hang up. *Echo loves me,* she tells herself. *She wasn't running away from me.*

4

Mary Lou hates to tell her. She waits until after supper when they are settled in the parlor. "Miss Weems, I'll be going home pretty soon."

"I knew you couldn't stay forever. But it will be right lonesome around here. When will you be leaving?"

"I can't leave until we finish the book. We have to find out if Mr. Rochester finds Jane. We know he's looking for her," she says, trying to get a smile out of Miss Weems.

"Well, now, why don't you just stay until spring?"

"I've got plans. I'm going back to school. And Mama worries about me the way I worry about Echo. The way I *used* to worry," she amends.

"You don't worry anymore?"

"Lately I've been too busy."

Miss Weems sighs. "Mary Lou, put a stick on the fire and we'll read until the fire goes out."

Miss Weems's voice sounds just the same, but Mary Lou sees her trembling hands when she takes down the book, removes its cover, finds the place, and hands it to her.

What she told Miss Weems. It is true. She doesn't worry so much. The truth is she has gotten so busy she hardly has time to turn around. On Wednesdays she goes to the movies with Josie and on Sundays to church with Miss Weems. She walks Hannah every day, Hannah being too big for Miss Weems.

She and Josie make a date to go Christmas shopping the first Saturday they can both take off. It is a day early in December. The weather is unusually warm and a little rainy. But when she steps outside the rain has stopped, so she drops her keys in her purse and walks downtown. Turning the corner at the courthouse she sees Josie waiting for her on the courthouse bench.

"Mary Lou, a truck and two cars stopped to ask about Echo."

"It beats all how everybody wants to help."

"Well, one of these days . . . ," Josie says.

"I know. Josie, you look great today!"

Josie wears a red plaid skirt and a blue denim jacket, with her red hair, curly from the rain, tied behind her neck. She reaches back and reties the plaid ribbon in her hair. "My hair. It always gets like this when it's damp."

"Josie, big hair is in again. Now how much did you save this week?"

Josie is saving to have her breasts reduced. Mary Lou doesn't blame her.

"I've saved another hundred. I've got enough for one."

At this they both break into peals of laughter, bending over, holding their sides, leaning against the wall of the post office.

Catching her breath, "Oh, Josie! You'll have enough in no time," Mary Lou says, not even sure why they are laughing.

Josie grins. "I know. I'm excited about it," she says as they cross the street.

Right away Mary Lou finds a red sweater for Albert at the Knit Two, Purl One shop. It matches the one Mr. Witherspoon always wears. In the same shop she finds an embroidery kit for Miss Weems. A little house in the top left-hand corner matches one in the lower right-hand corner. There is a path from one house to the other with flowers alongside the path. "The way to a friend's house is never long," runs in black letters along the path.

"Perfect," Josie says.

At Western Rodeo, a nice jewelry store, Josie pays eighty dollars for a silver belt buckle shaped like a bucking horse, for Chet. "Neither one of us can get over being married to each other," she tells Mary Lou.

"Josie, you're in denial. I've got a book about it. There's a whole chapter on denial and divorce."

"I've heard about denial," Josie says vaguely. But she doesn't ask to read about it. Instead, "Let's eat somewhere special," she says.

Josie has to go to work after lunch but Mary Lou stays and buys a Greg Brown tape for Josie. Then she piddles around downtown looking at Christmas decorations and buying a tiny dog basket with a brown-and-white terrier in it for Miss Weems's Christmas tree. She likes everything she's bought.

Then, still in no hurry, she starts home. In five minutes she is out of town and walking past the nice old Weatherford houses. Except for a magnolia here and there and a live oak or two, the trees are bare. But in two or three months they'll be leafing out. A warm mist has begun to fall and she lifts her face to the promise of spring. As she walks past, lights begin to come on in the kitchens and bedrooms and dens of the houses. She thinks about the people coming in from work and wonders what they are looking forward to. Then, thinking about Miss Weems and taking Hannah for a walk and reading *Jane Eyre* in the parlor, she walks faster. Enjoying the mist on her face the thought comes that not since Gundren's death has she been made happy by a thing as simple as this.

Chapter Fourteen

1

As the time for Echo's delivery draws near she no longer appears at breakfast and no longer works in the garden, although she still walks there and, wearing Sister Celeste's heavy cape against the cold, sits on the bench before Our Lady of Guadeloupe for long periods of time. Seeing her there Father d'Acosta is reminded of a plant in the garden that, when touched, curls its slender leaves in upon itself as if seeking its own beginning. Her pregnancy has transformed the once slender girl into a woman so enormous that delivery seems impossible. Except for her eyes no traces of girlhood remain.

Time seems suspended as they wait for the birth. Whenever he has to leave the household he hurries back, recognizing his own need to be there and sensing Sister Celeste's deep anxiety for the girl. Still, when Sister Celeste taps gently on his door at three o'clock in the morning, saying, "It's time, Father," he feels dismay.

"It's too soon," he tells himself. "She's not ready for this."

Instantly awake he dresses quickly and hurries downstairs,

turning on all the outside lights as he goes so that Echo may not stumble and fall coming across the patio from her quarters. He makes coffee for himself and tea for Sister Celeste. When Sister Celeste and Echo come in, Echo's face taut, her eyes enormous, the brown paper sack she carries hurts his heart.

"I have a small case," he says, but she shakes her head. "This is fine."

"Do you have everything you need?" he asks then, hopelessly ignorant of what might be needed. When she nods he puts his heavy coat over her shoulders and opens the door that leads to the garage. Then he remembers the present, a gown, yellow and ridiculously small ("For a boy or a girl," the salesperson had told him), he had bought the week before.

"Wait a minute," he says, closing the door against the cold. Running up the stairs and down again, he puts the blue-and-pink ribbon-wrapped package in Echo's hands. But when he sees the faint wash of tears in her eyes, he takes the package from her and tucks it into the paper sack.

When they reach the hospital, Sister Celeste, armed by temperament for its bureaucracy, hurries ahead. He sits by Echo's side in the waiting room and together they watch Sister Celeste hand over previously signed documents, fill out others, answer questions. When this is finished Echo is led away by a nurse, Sister Celeste following close on their heels. Just before the little troop disappears around the corner, Echo stops and, turning toward him, solemnly lifts her hand in a half-wave.

He stands a minute looking down the empty hall. When he turns to leave the hospital, he hears Sister Celeste call his name.

Breathlessly she hurries up to him. "Father, you can go home now."

"Sister, I was on my way."

"Pray for Echo. Pray for the baby. I'll call you as soon as the baby comes."

"Sister, calm yourself. Echo's in God's hands."

"I know Father, but I'm helping Him," she calls over her shoulder, trotting off.

Reaching the church he goes into his office, sits at his desk and lists calls to be made, tasks to be done. Then, exhausted, he simply sits, watching the frozen hands of the tall clock, begrudging it its slow ticking. Even the time it takes to leave a message on the O'Malley's answering machine to say the baby is on its way seems an intrusion. And John O'Malley's answering call to say they would pick up the baby in a few days, and would so advise the hospital, seems another. Two or three times during the long afternoon he looks down into the garden, and each time is struck by how deserted it is without Echo.

At six he drives to the hospital to wait. In less than an hour Sister Celeste appears, wiping perspiration and tears from her face. "The baby's here," she says. "It's a boy. A wee thing. And Echo's fine. She's tired, but she's fine." Sighing, she rubs her back. "Let's go home. I'm too tired to breathe."

But as they drive back to the church Sister Celeste harnesses enough energy to plan Echo's future. Echo will finish high school. She will then go on to college. She will become a horticulturist. He could, she told Father d'Acosta, arrange all of this on a scholarship. Echo would come frequently to the garden, the place where she had first become interested in the science of horticulture. They would spend long afternoons with her, drink tall glasses of iced tea. She would marry, have other children.

Sadly, Father d'Acosta remembers the yellow dress in the paper sack, a dress Echo will never use. "Oh, God," he says.

2

The rain is a sheet of water against the windows. A vaporizer spits moisture into the room, but the girl in the other bed, Martha, her name is, keeps on coughing.

The nurses are mad. They stand outside the door and talk about how mad they are. "You know Debra," the one who had brought Martha's baby to her says, "if she has a hangnail, she calls in sick."

"Sue Ellen might as well not be here. Slow as Christmas until a doctor turns the corner."

"I know, honey. Well, let me see can I get things going in here," the tall one says and comes on into the room.

Martha is nursing her baby and the nurse helps and forgets to be mad. "Honey, they ain't nothing here yet, but the baby wants practice."

"Ouch," Martha says.

But the nurse gets the pillow adjusted and the baby adjusted and Martha adjusted, and now the baby sucks noisily. On what, Echo doesn't know, but hearing the liquid sounds, Echo feels a small surge of menstrual blood. She shifts to her side to see Martha's baby. It is red and bald like it needs feathers or something. Then the same nurse comes with another baby and looks down at her, frowning.

"Here's your boy and here's a bottle," she says. "I suppose you've talked to your doctor about the immunity system of an infant. Well, it's none of my business."

She lays the bundle down by Echo. Echo turns back a corner of the blanket and sees two thin eyes. Thin and blue with tiny wrinkles going along the tops and bottoms. The baby stares at her. Hard. If he blinked she didn't see it. Then he frowns. He yawns. Without teeth he looks like Mr. Roseborough.

"Well, hello Roseborough," she murmurs. "Your name is Roseborough."

She puts the bottle into his mouth. He swallows three times and is asleep, a milky rivulet at the corner of his mouth. Pulling her gown away from her chest she sees that her nipples leak cloudy drops of moisture. She puts his mouth on her nipple. He sucks a minute and falls back asleep. The rain picks up, comes down in torrents; its wetness seeps into the room, mixes with the vaporizer and the milky smell of the baby. She sleeps and dreams they live beneath the sea, and all of them—her baby and Martha's and the nurses and everybody in the hospital—are swimming in sunlit waters. Roseborough, like a little dolphin, swims close beside her, turning when she turns, staying close and playing beside her. The nurses in their starched white uniforms and the doctors with their starched coats circle cozily around, all of them happy and swimming free in the gleaming sunlit waters.

Voices outside her door wake her. Loud and excited. A real commotion.

"I did read the orders. The girl's not nursing."

Something to do with her.

Then, "You didn't read far enough. He's going to be adopted. The paperwork's done. She's checking out."

"Oh, Lord." A new voice, deep.

"It wasn't on the orders. I'd have seen it."

"Shorthanded as we are, something like this, bound to happen."

"The computers are down." The deep voice again. "You two straighten it out with the girl. Everything's crazy in records. I'm going down there now."

The door flies open. The tall thin nurse and a dark-headed one with a wide mouth and thick glasses stand in the doorway.

The thin one goes over to Martha's bed. "You doing all right, honey? You need any help with the baby?"

The dark-headed one comes and stands by her bed. "We're sorry about the mix-up. You can get dressed when you feel like it. The paperwork's all done. Somebody picking you up?" Without waiting for an answer she leans forward, folds the baby blanket around Roseborough, and picks him up.

"No," Echo whispers, and again, "No," as the nurse hurries from the room with the baby in her arms.

Echo listens to the rain. Her nipples leak milk from breasts so swollen they don't seem like hers. Martha's baby nurses again. Echo turns away to watch the rain spatter on the darkening windows. Steam from the vaporizer pours into the room. She sleeps again.

When she opens her eyes the rain has stopped and it is night outside. Then the room fills up with Martha's husband and her mama and daddy and her grandmother and two sisters, all wearing blue jeans, even the grandmother, and all of them saying whose nose Martha's baby has and whose eyes and where did its chin come from.

In the middle of it all Martha pulls her husband down and whispers in his ear. "Aw," he says and snaps his head around to look at Echo. Then she whispers to her mama, who comes right over to Echo's side of the room. "We're bothering you. I know it and what you need is your privacy. Want me to draw the curtain?" Whisking the curtain across the middle of the room, "No sooner said than done," she tells Echo.

Now, Echo tells herself and gets up and goes into the bathroom. She puts her hand into the brown paper sack and feels down past a hairbrush and cotton pajamas and sanitary pads and three pairs of cotton panties and, *there!* she feels the three hundred dollars held together by a rubber band. She takes it out. The note she found when Jamie took her home is there, too. Mama has written: "Echo, call Professor Anne Hamilton: 214-363-6081. Address: 4907 Merryview Drive, Dallas. She will know where I am. I love you. Mama."

She slips into the blue dress she wore to the hospital, puts on her white tennis shoes, and tucks the paper sack under her arm. Then she walks down the hall and stands at the nursery window. Roseborough is asleep. She watches the nurses hurry in and out. The thin one isn't there. And the one who took Roseborough away isn't there either. And the computers are out. She had heard the nurses say it. When only one nurse is there, leaning over a crying baby, she walks into the nursery, picks up Roseborough and, following all the doors marked Exit, she finds her way out into the safety of the dark night.

Chapter Fifteen

1

TONY has come to gather up ladders and gardening tools. He walks around the house examining repaired window frames and a water faucet. Anne writes a check for the last of the repairs. Satisfied with his work, Tony says, "Dr. Hamilton, have you thought about painting your kitchen, maybe just one wall?"

"No," she says.

"Maybe a soft red."

"Well, Tony, I've never thought of red as being soft."

"I've got some paint in my truck. It's called, 'Soft Red.' I'll get it."

She stands looking at the almost-white wall, considering. A color would be nice in here, but red? Allen never liked red. When Tony returns with the paint, she says, "I'll try it. Leave it and I'll paint a test board."

Tony finds a newspaper and sets the paint on it. Prying the lid off, he grins at her. "I'm thinking about running over to Weatherford next weekend and taking her out. What do you think?"

"I think it's a great idea. But remember. Miss Weems turns her phone off early."

The next evening Dylan comes, ringing her doorbell. "Well, Dylan," she says.

"Brought you something," he says. "And hey, you've painted that wall. That's a great color. I like it." Then, walking quickly to his truck, he pulls a Christmas tree from the back of it.

"The nursery gave it to me. Lennon and I have already put up our tree. Well here, here's a good place," he says, setting it in her living room in front of the windows. "What do you think? Do you want it?"

"Yes. This is nice. I'm having my book club over next week. It's the first time I've ever had them."

"The ladies will enjoy the tree," he says. Screwing the tree into the stand while Anne holds it straight, he says, "I'd be glad to help you get the lights on."

From the attic Anne hands down dusty boxes labeled: *Lights, Ornaments, Manger Scene*. "Dylan, you look wonderful. How do you feel?"

Stringing the lights, he says, "I'm feeling really good now. The doctor says I'm in complete remission. And Lennon's doing great, too."

"I'm sorry you didn't bring him with you."

"His grandmother took him to the Science Place. If I'd known about the tree, I'd have brought him."

He is silent as he puts the last string of lights on the tree. They stand together admiring it.

"It's lovely," she says. "Dylan, thank you."

"I guess you know that the class, most of us anyway, we still get together."

"I know it. I'm glad."

"We keep up with each other."

"Friends."

"You bet. Betty and I are taking in a movie tonight. So I guess I'd better take off."

Whistling, he walks down the drive to his truck. *Mother Mary comes to me. Whispering words of wisdom, let it be.*

Picking up the tune and humming along with Dylan, Anne smiles. Her brother loved this song.

2

Anne is returning each piece of flatware to its place in the silver chest. Her house smells of bread making and burning candles and flowers. Since Allen is out of her life her house looks more like a place where a friend might drop in. She sees herself taking her hands out of soapy water and drying them on a cup towel on her way to answer the door. "Come on in the kitchen," she could say to Joan or Tony or Christopher.

Smiling ruefully she glances at the clock. Since it is almost eleven a visit is unlikely. And, besides, she is too tired for whimsical thought. The book club members have talked lightheartedly—a play recommended; a movie, in spite of its critical acclaim, disparaged; a neighbor's move regretted—and she has enjoyed it. Joan was the last to leave.

"Thanks for having us," she said. "Your house looks lovely. The beautiful rugs. Your books everywhere and the Christmas tree. Isn't this the first time you've had a tree?"

"Yes, a student brought it. I don't know why I haven't had one. This is the first one I've put up since my family died."

Getting ready for the party had made her look at her house with new eyes. The red wall was so cheerful she brought the love seat from her bedroom and put it in the window alcove. Then she brought the small rug from her study and placed it in front of the love seat.

Looking at the arrangement now she can't imagine why she hasn't done these things earlier. The kitchen looks cozy. All it needs is a rocking chair, and she has one stored over the garage.

When Anne has restored the kitchen to its usual order, she goes through the house checking the locks on the doors, turning off the lights, the stereo, looking in on the brightly colored Dufy sailboats in the study. She takes a warm shower, goes through a brief exercise routine, and is slipping into bed when the doorbell rings. Instantly alert she puts on her robe and hurries down the hall. She turns on the outside lights and looks through the small glass aperture. Seeing the face, the sapphire eyes, "Echo!" she says, flinging open the door. "Come in. Oh, Echo, where have you been? Your mother's been frantic!"

Echo, as if unsure that the opening will accommodate the bulk that moves beneath the heavy overcoat she wears, pushes the door open wider. Her eyes shine against her dark skin; the black hair framing her face falls far below her shoulders. But except for her face, no trace of the young girl remains.

"They're looking for us," she says, thrusting a bundle into Anne's arms. "Tell Mama not to let them have him." Wheeling around, hurrying awkwardly, she calls, "Tell Mama not to let them have Roseborough." A taxi is waiting; she steps into it.

Immobilized by the surprise of it Anne watches the taillights disappear around the corner. Echo in a taxi. It seems so incongruous. She stands there looking down the street until the weight in her arms causes her to turn back a corner of the blanket and see that she holds a baby in her arms. "My God!" she whispers. "Oh, my Lord!"

Looking at the baby's small nose and tiny mouth, she struggles to think. Now, the first thing to do is . . . but what is the first thing to do? She closes the door and, with the baby in her arms, walks to her bedroom and eases it onto the middle of her bed. "Tell Mama," Echo had said. Of course. She will call Mary Lou. But it is after eleven. Miss Weems's phone would be off. But the Dairy Queen will be open.

She dials information and gets the number of the Dairy Queen in Weatherford. After the eighth ring she hears, "Hello."

"Is Mary Lou Burgandy there?"

"No, ma'am."

"When will she be in? I must speak with her. It's important."

"Three! I said three fries! Freddy, write it down!"

"What?"

"You ordering something?"

"No, I need to speak with Mary Lou Burgandy."

"She ain't here."

"Could I speak with the manager? With Josie?"

"Ain't here either."

"Does she have a telephone?"

"I'm new here. Started Monday."

"What's Josie's last name?"

"Everybody just says 'Josie.' "

"When will Josie be back?"

"Pretty soon, I reckon."

"Would you ask her to call to call— Never mind. I'll call back."

She turns to the sleeping baby. Roseborough. Echo had

said, "Don't let them have Roseborough." He is lying on his back, his arms alongside his head. Lying in the middle of her bed, he looks so little! *They,* Echo had said. They were looking for the baby. And for Echo. She turns on the television. The Attorney General is speaking, explaining that even though a young man has been found innocent by the military tribunal he will not be released. *That's crazy,* she thinks. *And here I am sitting on my bed with a newborn baby.* This is crazy, too. But now here's the local news. A woman is speaking. ". . . has been kidnapped from the hospital by a young woman. No. Let me correct this. The baby, a boy, weighing eight pounds and three ounces, may have been taken from the hospital by the mother. The police do not believe that the motive is ransom. Both the mother and baby have disappeared. Dr. Stewart, a pediatrician on the staff of St. James Hospital, advises that the infant's formula can be purchased from any grocery or drugstore. The police are asking that the mother get in touch with them immediately. If you have any information about the whereabouts of this baby or the mother of the baby, you are asked to call the police immediately."

Anne lifts the receiver. Replaces it. *Am I aiding and abetting a crime?* she wonders. But "Tell Mama," Echo said. She will call Weatherford one more time.

The baby opens its mouth and begins to cry. The cry is full-bodied. Angry. Not to be denied. Anne runs to the kitchen. Tony has written his number on a message pad. She dials the number.

"Hello," he says sleepily.

"Tony, Echo's left a baby here. I answered the door and she put a baby in my arms and left in a taxi. The baby is crying."

"What? A crying baby, did you say? What?"

"Echo rang my doorbell, put a baby (I think it's hers) in my arms, and said 'Tell Mama not to let them have Roseborough.' I think Echo has kidnapped a baby."

"Her own baby!" Now he is wide awake.

"I know. It sounds crazy."

"I'm on my way."

"Here?"

"No. To Weatherford to tell Mary Lou. It's almost twelve o'clock, and their phone's turned off."

"Tony, the baby's crying. I need the formula. No, here's a bottle in its blanket. But the police . . ."

"We'll be back by good daylight. I'm out of here now."

"Tony," she begins, but the line is dead. At daybreak she will call the hospital, and they can call the police. But Mary Lou will be here before daybreak. She will wait for Mary Lou.

Soon after daybreak, Anne, propped against pillows piled high against the headboard, is giving the baby the remnants of a bottle. She has left a message on Christopher's phone telling him she cannot run with him this morning.

The telephone's ringing wakes Roseborough. He squirms, opens his eyes, and stares at her. She grabs the phone. "Hello," she says.

The baby's lip trembles. He begins to cry.

"Anne, that sounds like a baby."

"Christopher, it is a baby. It's Echo's baby, I think. She put it in my arms and left in a taxi." She picks up the baby. "Shush now, you're all right." She gently bounces the baby on her shoulder. "Now. Now," she tells it.

"Woman, what a life you lead! All undercover, too." He is

smiling. She can hear it in his voice. "Wait a minute! Do you need anything?"

"Formula. I don't know. Mary Lou will be here soon."

"I'll go by the drugstore. Maybe they can tell me what a baby needs."

The baby takes three swallows of milk and falls asleep. She should probably burp him but she's not sure how to go about it. And he might not like it. She eases him onto the bed. Roseborough, sleeping, opens his mouth and reshapes it into a V. Then he opens his eyes and stares. Still staring, he stretches. He yawns. Then he hiccups. "You're a busy baby," she tells him. He yawns again and is instantly asleep. His eyelids are thin. The tiny veins that run through them cast a faint shade of blue. Now his eyes tremble beneath them. Anne looks at the clock. It is after seven. Mary Lou will be here soon. Thankfully, she stretches out on the bed beside Roseborough and watches him sleep.

3

They are in the parlor, Miss Weems going "Tsk, tsk, tsk," and Mary Lou saying, "a baby" over and over and then, "But where's Echo? Where is she?" and saying that over and over until Tony eases her into a chair.

While Miss Weems makes hot tea Tony tells Mary Lou that Echo put the baby in Anne's arms and said, "Call Mama. Tell her not to let them have Roseborough."

"Oh, my dear," Miss Weems says, handing Mary Lou a cup of tea.

Mary Lou looks up at her. "Miss Weems," she says, "I have to go. I know I promised to stay until we finished the book, but . . ."

"Of course, child, of course you must go. Now you get dressed and I'll help you pack." She turns toward Tony. "Mr. Peach . . ."

"Orchard," he says. "Tony Orchard."

"Yes. Well, why don't you go in the kitchen and make Mary Lou a sandwich and a pot of coffee? There's a thermos in the bottom drawer to the left of the stove."

Mary Lou slips on her jeans and pulls a sweater over her head. Then she strips the closet bare and empties the chest of drawers, piling her things on the bed. The careful way Miss Weems separates and smooths and folds her clothes makes Mary Lou feel calm. While she brushes her hair and packs her makeup, she collects her thoughts. She will need her truck in Lone Oak. She will drive herself home.

"Miss Weems, would you call Josie? Tell her what happened? Tell her I'll call her."

"I've already thought of that. Of course, I will."

When she is packed, Miss Weems touches her arm. "Mary Lou, come in here a minute," she says, and leads the way into the parlor, where she carefully takes the novel, *Jane Eyre,* from the shelf. "I want you to have this," she says, wrapping it in tissue paper. "We'll finish it together someday. It's a very early edition."

"Oh, Miss Weems, thank you. You know that I'll miss you every day."

"Lone Oak isn't that far. We'll see each other," Miss Weems says.

When they are ready to leave Miss Weems stands on her

front porch wrapped in a bedraggled shawl. "Mary Lou, you be careful, driving. Mr., uh, Mr. . . . You stay right behind her."

"I will," Tony says, and under his breath, "It's Orchard!"

As Mary Lou backs out of the driveway, the sight of Miss Weems looking so fragile, so old, but standing ramrod straight and not shedding a tear, sets the tears to rolling down her cheeks.

Chapter Sixteen

1

MARY LOU stands in the bedroom doorway of Anne's house. Tony stands behind her, his hand on her shoulder. Arms folded, her forehead creased by a deep frown, she gazes at the blue bundle in the middle of Anne's bed. Only the baby's head is visible. The head is covered with a light brown fuzz. *Is this Echo's baby?* she wonders. *But how could it be?* His face is haughtily, disdainfully turned away from the side of the bed where she stands. *I can't believe this. Echo, hardly more than a child herself, a mother?*

And not in a million years has she ever thought about being a grandmother. Her eyes narrow, her lips tighten. She straightens her shoulders and walks into the room. Slowly she eases herself onto the bed and, propping one hand on the side of the bundle, leans forward to see his face. Shaking her head in wonder, in disbelief, she puts her hand into the blanket that swaddles him tightly as a sausage. Feeling his warm body she carefully unwraps him. He opens his eyes and stares at her. He yawns and carelessly waves one tiny hand in the air.

"Well, hello there," she says.

His eyes are navy blue and slanted at the outside corners. *Like Gundren's,* she thinks. Picking him up, Mary Lou holds his head in the palm of her hand, his body resting on her forearm. His eyes swivel toward Anne.

"Well, now," Anne says. "I think you know me, Roseborough. You're looking right at me."

He sighs deeply. Again the tiny hand waves in the air. Now both hands wave, churning the air. He kicks one strong kick with both feet.

Mary Lou smiles. "He's strong," she says. She sits him up, supporting his head that falls forward into her hand. "Look," Mary Lou says, her little finger inside a tiny curl at the base of his neck. "He has my hair."

Roseborough takes a deep breath and opens his mouth crookedly, then closes it. The baby, in this position a little fat Buddha, rolls his eyes upward as if trying to find the source of the voice he hears.

"There now," Mary Lou says, cradling him in her arms. "*There* now," she says.

The baby gazes intensely at her face. His hands are trustingly folded on his chest. "You are cute," she tells him. "I'll give you that!"

"Mary Lou?" Tony says.

"Well, you're here now," Mary Lou whispers. "And we can't take you back." She runs her hand over the soft down on his head and traces the deep crease at the base of his neck.

"Mary Lou?" Tony says again.

The baby opens his mouth in a smile. He opens it wider and wider. He turns pink; he turns lobster red.

"My goodness," Anne says.

He lets out a cry, a full-bodied cry of rage and indignation.

"He's hungry," Mary Lou says. "I'll get his bottle." She wraps the baby again and picks him up. "Now, now, it's all *right*, you're all right," she croons.

Tony turns to Anne. "I'm gonna take off for a while. I've got some things to do. But I'll come back around noon. Mary Lou, will you be here? Mary Lou?"

"Tony, I don't know," and now Mary Lou is hurrying from the room, holding the crying baby.

"I think she will be home by noon," Anne says gently. "And Tony, at this minute, right before our eyes, Mary Lou is becoming a grandmother."

"Yeah, well," he says. He stands a minute, frowning down at the empty bed, before striding determinedly out of the room.

When Mary Lou returns, the baby is sucking noisily from the bottle she holds. "Has Tony left?" she says. She sits on the bed again and feels a rush of pleasure when his small hand closes around her finger.

The two women sit, one on either side of the bed, watching the baby. He opens his squinty eyes and gazes at Mary Lou. She chuckles. "I think he knows I'm family," she says.

The sun moves, a cloud shifts, golden light fills the room. Mary Lou's hair is red in the light. Her face is rapt. One blue-jeaned leg is crossed over the other, making a nest for Roseborough.

The baby opens his mouth, closes it, purses his lips together, smiles. "Look at that!" Mary Lou exclaims. "*Look* at that!"

Sated, he falls into a deep, impervious sleep. "He's sweet," Anne says.

Later in the kitchen, "How could she?" Mary Lou asks.

"How could she leave this baby? I don't understand Echo. I never have. I never will," she says sadly.

I'd rather love a porcupine than Echo, Anne tells herself. And after a minute, "Mary Lou, we need to call the police. Would you like for me to do that?"

"Well, I am his grandmother. I'd better call. Will you hold him? I'll just let them know he's all right."

Mary Lou straightens her white sweater around her hips and pulls her mass of thick hair up into a ponytail. Then she takes a deep breath, picks up the telephone, and dials 911.

Watching Mary Lou as she prepares to call, *She has completely accepted Roseborough,* Anne thinks. And then, *Weatherford was good for her.*

"This is Mary Lou Burgandy," she is saying. "You know that baby that was kidnapped from the hospital? Well, he's here. I'm his grandmother, and he's all right."

But it's not a simple message. By the time Mary Lou talks to one officer and then another and another, telling each of them who she is and who Echo is, and giving her address, phone number, and social security number (Echo doesn't have one)—a faint wrinkle appears on her forehead. With every word she lifts her chin a little higher.

"They sounded mad," she says when she finishes the call. "The last one I talked to, the chief of police, sounded *real* mad."

Despairing, she again wraps the baby in his blanket and sits on the love seat in Anne's kitchen while Anne squeezes fresh oranges and makes toast. Looking at the baby's features, so like Echo's when she was a baby, Mary Lou feels a surge of . . . distaste. For Echo. Wild horses couldn't have drug, no, *dragged* her away when Echo was a baby. But not loving Echo makes her feel uneasy, like she doesn't know her own self anymore. Her mind wheels toward the tree house. And Echo in it. Echo's postcards. *Stop! Stop thinking about Echo,* she commands. But then, *How could she?* she asks herself again.

Turning her chair toward the kitchen she watches Anne slice and butter dark bread for toast. Wearing a blue sweater and black pants, and with her hair tied back with a brightly colored scarf, Anne looks like somebody in an old movie. Katharine Hepburn, maybe.

Anne turns to her and puts her hands on her hips. "Mary Lou, I've missed you," she says, smiling. "My life has been a little dull lately."

"But I bet you didn't need all this. My goodness."

"It's fine. We'll get it straightened out. Look! I've got mango chutney for breakfast," Anne says, holding up a jar.

"I've never tasted it. What is it?"

"It's mangoes and nuts and pineapple. Some lemon juice. It's good with fresh bread."

Before they finish the breakfast (that Anne serves on a small table beside Mary Lou), Christopher arrives. Taking his hand, Mary Lou sees a gaunt, tall, faded man. *None of them care how they look,* she thinks. *But his smile is nice.*

After he has been introduced to Mary Lou and, proudly, to Roseborough, Christopher perches on a bar stool in Anne's kitchen and displays the bottles, diapers, and formula he has brought. When they tell him all that has happened he says, "Mary Lou, I think you may need a lawyer."

Before Mary Lou can ask why, the telephone rings. Anne picks up the receiver.

"My name's John O'Malley," a voice, hoarse with anger, says. "My wife and I are the adoptive parents of that baby you kidnapped. We're filing charges—kidnapping, abandonment—against you and the whole kit and caboodle out there."

"How did you get my number?" Anne asks. "Do you even know my name?"

As if she hasn't spoken, he rasps out the words: "An officer and a man from the child protective services in Dallas are on their way there now to take custody of our baby and, let me warn you, I intend to file charges." A click signals the call is over.

"Mary Lou, he says someone is on the way here now to take custody of Roseborough."

"Well, they can't have him. That's ridiculous. I'm going home right now. As soon as I get home I'll call the Lone Oak sheriff. The sheriff is a friend of Gundren's. He's got no truck with Dallas," Mary Lou says, furiously putting bottles and formula and diapers into paper sacks.

"Here, I'll take these out for you," Christopher says.

Turning to pick up Roseborough, Mary Lou says, "Anne, don't worry. The sheriff and Gundren rodeoed together. When they get here, send them on out." She smiles. "His name is Dallas. How's that for irony?"

"Irony?"

"A sheriff named Dallas who doesn't like Dallas. Miss Weems taught me irony," Mary Lou says.

"Maybe you ought to think about majoring in English."

"I might," she says seriously.

"Well anyway," Anne says, "they have no reason to take Roseborough from the arms of his grandmother." And looking at Christopher, "Do they?"

"I think *you* need a lawyer, too" he says.

Immediately after Mary Lou's departure, Father d'Acosta

calls. An ally, Anne decides, listening to the gentle voice. But before she can explain, Father d'Acosta is urging baptism. "It's what Echo wants," he tells her. "She wants the baby to be baptized just as Echo and Echo's father were baptized."

"But Father, a man, a John O'Malley, says he has adopted the baby. He is bringing charges. He can't do that, can he?"

"John's a good man." Father d'Acosta says, *maddeningly* gentle now. "I don't think he will actually bring charges. Dr. Hamilton, with the O'Malleys the baby will have a good home, a fine education, Catholic parents. Again, this is what Echo wants."

Completing the conversation, Anne turns away from the phone. "Mary Lou will get no support from that priest," Anne tells Christopher. The next call is from the hospital. "At the very least there will be charges of malfeasance," one of the administrators, whose voice has turned to ice, reports.

Hanging up before the woman is finished, Anne staggers to the bar to sit by Christopher. She drops her head into her hands. She rubs her forehead. "I'm at a loss," she says.

"Are you sorry you didn't fly off to New York?" he asks.

"Not one bit," she says firmly. "He's married. And a relationship with a married man is not what I need." She gets up and takes cups and glasses into the kitchen and puts them in the dishwasher.

She moves like a dancer, he thinks, watching her bend and straighten and reach.

"I don't know what I'm going to do about my marriage," he says. "Any advice?" he asks, echoing a question she once asked him.

"No. No advice."

She brings more coffee and together they ponder the mystery of Echo. *Where is she? Why did she leave her baby?* They shake their heads, unable to imagine answers to these questions.

Finally Christopher says, "Anne, it's not a simple matter. The judge may not allow Mary Lou custody of Roseborough. A strong case could be made that the child was abandoned. Unless Echo returns it's possible that Roseborough *will* be placed in a foster home until the judge decides. This could take weeks, even months."

Anne opens her mouth to speak but no words come. Slack with fatigue and sympathy she allows herself to be drawn into the comfortable, reassuring arms of Christopher.

2

Sheriff Dallas had come as soon as Mary Lou called. She has to smile when he steps out of his car because he is so big, and, with a pistol on each hip, looks even bigger. He is wearing a white hat. The white hat tickles her. "I declare Joe, you could be a movie sheriff," she tells him. He grins and takes a seat on her front steps to wait for the Dallas police.

With Sheriff Dallas on duty she can put her mind on Roseborough. She changes him, puts a clean sheet on Echo's bed for him, and makes up four bottles of formula.

After that she comes out and sits on the steps beside Joe, holding Roseborough in her arms. Looking at his broad shoulders she knows that anyone could tell he used to be a linebacker for Lone Oak. He could have played football at the university, too, but he decided to come on home and help his daddy farm. Gundren said he was almost too big to rodeo, but Joe always liked the sport.

When the Dallas policeman comes, he jumps out of the police car like he's after a terrorist. Sheriff Dallas gets slowly to his feet. He nods. "Officer," he says.

In case there's a dustup, Mary Lou moves away from the steps to hold the baby in the rocking chair.

The Dallas policeman has black hair that grows low on his forehead. His ears are small and tight against his head. His eyes dart around like he's looking for some backup. "Lady, we're here to take custody of the baby," he says. His voice going up at the end makes it a question.

"Well, you've come a long way for nothing," Joe says, sounding real friendly and sorry, too, that the officer has made the trip.

Then the woman from the child protective services gets out of the police car and smiles at everybody. She's an African-American and taller than the policeman and sounds pleasant. "Mrs. Burgandy, we have to take custody of the baby. We're under orders to do so."

"No." Mary Lou says, gently rocking the baby in the big white rocking chair that Gundren had traded a saw for.

"Mrs. Burgandy, let's make this easy," the Dallas policeman says. "Now you don't want any—"

"No," she says again, feeling real calm with Joe there. She remembers Joe throwing down a bull. The policeman looks like a bull calf compared to Joe.

Then Mama drives up, screeching her tires she's in such a hurry, and Mary Lou can see right away that she takes to Roseborough. She takes him out of Mary Lou's arms and shows him off to Joe.

Joe says, "You know, he looks a lot like Gundren. That's his grandfather," he tells the Dallas people.

"I don't see any resemblance there at all," Mama says stiffly.

"Mama, where is your Christianity? Gundren's dead," Mary Lou says.

"That don't matter. He looks like our people. What do you think?" she asks the Dallas officer.

"I think we'd better radio headquarters," he tells her.

Well, headquarters must have said to come on back because the officer says, "Lady, we'll take custody of that baby in court. On January 4."

"I wouldn't worry about it a minute," Joe tells Mary Lou, watching them walk fast out to the car.

"I'm not worried," she says, adding, "well, maybe a little."

The next day it seems to Mary Lou that her house begins to mend itself. Mr. Davis turns Stitch into her yard and Tony shows up again to drop off Sugar and mow the lawn. Roseborough likes Tony, but then Roseborough likes everybody. Unless he's hungry. Sugar looks at Mary Lou reproachfully, swishes her tail back and forth, jumps up into the easy chair, and disdainfully turns her back. Mary Lou has to laugh.

Tony stays on looking around for things to fix (Lord knows, there's plenty around that needs fixing), and all over the house there's the scent of horses running and clover blooming until finally she says sternly, "Tony, I'm not looking for a grandfather for Roseborough right now," and hands him a BLT sandwich for lunch.

Tony opens his eyes wide, eyes as clear and as blue as the sky on its best day. "I hadn't ever thought about being a grandfather," he says and stays to fix the screen door.

When he's getting ready to leave she says she'll be back in school for the spring semester. "What classes will you be taking?" he asks.

"English and Automotive," she says, adding, "Tony, that blue shirt looks good on you." Well, it does. *Real* good.

Tony grins and tips his hat (Gundren again), "Save me a seat in that automotive class," he says.

A while later she bathes the baby while Mama fixes iced tea, "Mama, I do think this baby looks like Gundren," she says.

"Why, he doesn't look a thing like Gundren."

"Mama!"

"Gundren was a handsome man. Not steady, but handsome." Putting the baby on her shoulder she whispers, "You are your grandmother's very own beautiful boy."

"Great-grandmother, Mama. I'm his grandmother."

Mama lifts her chin and squints at Mary Lou. "You don't tell it, nobody'll know it."

"Good Lord."

"It's the truth. You could pass for twenty-five. Thirty at the most."

"Mama, I'm proud to be a grandmother. And I'll bet you're about the youngest great-grandmother in Lone Oak."

That perks Mama up and she says she'll keep Roseborough while Mary Lou goes to Wal-Mart to get what's needed. Wandering up and down the aisles she picks up diapers and bottles and formula and gowns with drawstrings so his feet won't get cold, and blue receiving blankets, all the time feeling sad about not loving Echo. They have all kinds of seats for babies now. Car seats and swing seats. A Mickey Mouse seat. All in all she counts twenty-three different kinds. And thermometers: rectal, oral, and an ear thermometer that costs a hundred and fifty dollars. She'd raised Echo by just resting the back of her hand on her forehead to see if she had a fever.

When she gets home Mama is singing Roseborough a song about what his daddy will buy him. "Mary Lou, with a baby, you don't need all this menagerie," Mama says, shooing Sugar out of the rocking chair so she can burp Roseborough over her knees.

"I know it, Mama, but Sugar's no trouble. And I can't put Stitch out on the street. Besides he's out in the backyard right now eating weeds."

Late that afternoon Mama gets ready to leave. The lines on her face are deep. When she stands she puts a hand on her back before straightening up. She lifts her chin and puts her hands on her hips. "If you need anything from the grocery store tomorrow, call me," she says. Bending over, she gives Roseborough's foot a kiss.

She opens the front door and stands in it, looking sad.

"Mama, it'll be OK. I'm just thirty-four. You remember that girl in my class? Betty? She had a baby at forty-three."

"What about your job? You can't just go to work and leave Roseborough."

"Maudie said to bring him next week. Chester will look after him."

"And after next week, what?"

"Mama, don't worry. I'll work it out. There's a nursery at the college."

After Mama leaves and the baby's asleep, she sits in the rocking chair on the front porch. She thinks about Roseborough. She does not let herself think about Echo.

3

On Saturday afternoon Roseborough's court-appointed lawyer shows up. Her name is Claire. She is called an *ad litem* attorney. She is tall, thin, with thin blond hair, a thin cotton jacket hanging off her shoulder, and wearing blue-rimmed glasses that she looks through or over taking notes. She drinks cup after cup of coffee at Mary Lou's kitchen table. The dark circles beneath her eyes look like bruises. She wears loose-fitting, pale yellow pants and a white blouse. She has to keep putting her straight hair behind her ears. She tells them she has stayed up all night reading law. "I don't usually handle child custody cases," she says.

Mary Lou, dressed for her appointment with Father d'Acosta, has turned the appointment with the *ad litem* over to Anne. When the priest called Mary Lou, he was vague about Roseborough's future, saying things like "It's in God's hands," and "The bishop will do what's best for the child." But about the baptism, he was firm.

"This meeting is important," says Mary Lou, frowning at Anne, then at Tony, who has come to drive her to the priest's office. Mary Lou is wearing religious clothes—a black skirt and a black sweater and silver earrings in the shape of crosses.

She crosses her arms, tucks her hands into her armpits, and says, "Father d'Acosta says that after his baptism, Roseborough will be a child of God. Mama says there's no point to it because he already is and what about being saved? Mama says Roseborough will have to be saved. But Father d'Acosta said this is what Echo wants." Her voice, as she speaks, trembles.

"It's a good idea," Anne says.

"It's the right thing to do, Mary Lou."

"It's a lovely ceremony."

"And it's what the priest wants."

Tony and Anne's reassurances bounce, blend, and ultimately satisfy Mary Lou, so that, replacing his blue cap, swaddling Roseborough again, she smiles.

"Claire, whatever you charge is fair. I can pay you. And I do thank you," she says fervently.

"The court pays for *ad litem* attorneys. But how about a pair of earrings?"

"Sure," she says.

Eyes closed, Anne would have known that the earrings Mary Lou wore today would be crosses. They are silver with small stones. The black clothes make her seem wraithlike, like someone recovering from an illness.

After they leave, Mary Lou carrying the baby and Tony the enormous amount of paraphernalia Roseborough seems to require for even this short distance, Claire begins to think in a lawyerly way. "Of course, we're sure that Echo is the baby's mother?" she asks now.

"Yes." Anne sighs, shakes her head. "How could anyone doubt that?"

"Oh, they'll have a good lawyer. The church is taking an interest in this hearing, and the parents who had planned to adopt the child have money. They will want proof that Echo is the mother. We know she is, but they will want records from the hospital and records to show that Echo is Mary Lou's daughter, not just a young woman posing as her daughter. But let's just assume they accept that Echo is the mother right away. As such she has the right to take her child from the hospital. A charge of kidnapping cannot be brought. But other charges can be brought against her. Failure to assume fiscal responsibility. Failure to sign appropriate documents. The only serious charge is abandonment. And we can show she did not abandon the baby. She left the baby in your safekeeping because . . ." Raising pale eyebrows, Claire waits.

"When Mary Lou went to Weatherford to look for Echo, she left my address on her bed in case Echo came home. I'm sure that's the reason. She didn't know where her mother was."

"She was looking for Echo in Weatherford?"

"Echo's last postcard was from Weatherford."

"I see," Claire says, but the tapping of a pencil against her pursed lips clearly indicates that she doesn't see.

"And maybe she was afraid. She had signed those papers and—"

"How old is she?" Claire interrupts.

"Sixteen. Just sixteen," Anne says, and saying that, again she hears Mary Lou's voice, the wonder in it, saying, "Echo's not like us, not like anybody you know. She's like this." And she sees Mary Lou lifting her open hands to the sky.

"Anne, you may be the major, possibly the only, character witness."

Starting at the sound of Claire's voice, she nods, sits straight in her chair.

"I'm trying to foresee possible lines of questioning and lines of defense." Shifting in her chair, Claire runs thin fingers through thin hair and continues: "We need to be ready."

Anne lifts her hands, opens them, in a gesture of acquiescence.

"Now. How long have you known Echo?"

"I don't know her," she answers. "Not really."

"You don't know her? Somehow I assumed you knew Echo."

"I know her only through her mother. But I feel as if I've known her and her family all my life. Even her dead father. Even Gundren. I feel as if I knew him."

"But you have met Echo, haven't you?" At her nod, Claire says, "Tell me about that meeting with her."

"It was in the Roseborough woods and . . ." And now the image, complete and whole, is before her: the slender girl, her long hair flying, running, running, silently disappearing into the ancient woods, vanishing like a deer, leaving behind a path filled with the rustle of leaf and twig and bole, yet a path forever empty, forever haunted by the vision of Echo. Vanishing.

"Anne? The woods?"

Claire is asking her a question. She needs to keep her mind on the questions. "What? What did you ask me?"

"Did you say you met her in the woods?"

"Yes, Echo had left home. Her mother knew where she was but Gundren had always felt that it was better to leave her alone. 'Let her alone,' Gundren always said. That's why Mary Lou had not insisted that she come home."

Christopher stands, runs his finger around the inside of his sweatshirt. Remembering the surprise of conversations she had with Mary Lou about Echo, Anne feels a twinge of amusement.

"Now, who's Gundren?" Christopher asks.

"Her dead husband," Anne says, smiling openly.

"She was listening to her dead husband's advice?" Christopher is interested. "Did she mean this literally?"

"Christopher, it's quite natural to listen to the voice of someone dead, if you've recently lost that someone," Anne says.

Christopher leans back in his chair. "Anne, how in the world did you get involved with all this?" His voice is soft, a gentle probe.

It's too complicated, Anne thinks. How to explain Sister Alicia, the bloody run of the goat, the music of the Gypsies. "It's the single parenting class I taught," she says lamely. "I think it got away from me." Taking a silver comb from her hair, she shakes her hair down around her shoulders, sweeps it up again, and fastens it with the comb.

Watching her, Christopher's brown eyes narrow. He smiles warmly. "I love the way women fool with their hair. Brushing it, pinning it up, braiding it, taking it down. It's nice."

"Almost a fetish," Anne agrees, feeling soothed.

"Let's begin with your meeting with Echo. Tell me about that. Take your time," Claire says.

"Mary Lou asked me to talk with her. She thought I might persuade her to come home." Saying this, the blue-and-white bedspread on Echo's bed swims before her eyes.

Claire nods reassuringly. "Kids do that. Run away. Stay with friends. Where was she living?"

"In a tree house."

"In a tree? Is she a tree hugger or something?"

Christopher laughs. "Anne climbed a tree." His eyes glisten mischievously.

"Yes, she was living in a tree house," Anne continues. "But no, she's not a save-the-trees environmentalist."

"She was living in a tree house? Anne, this makes no sense. I don't think we have a case. Even if Echo shows up, the judge won't give her custody of the child."

Claire is right. It doesn't make sense. None of it makes any sense at all, she thinks.

"Maybe we should allow the adoption to proceed," Claire

says. "Not fight it. Roseborough might be better off with a mother and a father who want him, who would love him."

"Mary Lou loves him now," Anne bristles. "We've got to help for her sake."

"And for the baby's?"

"For the baby's as well."

4

Claire is pleased that the hearing is informal. "It means the O'Malleys are not sure they want to proceed with the adoption," she has told Mary Lou. But Mary Lou is all to pieces. She hasn't slept for two nights. Holding Roseborough in her lap, she carefully leans forward to assess her side. Tony, on the end of the row, looks nice. He's wearing brown pants and a tweed jacket. And boots! She's never seen him wear boots before. Remembering Ed, *Be careful,* she warns herself. As she watches, Tony, leaning forward to take a handkerchief from his hip pocket and wipe his forehead, catches her eye and winks. It's reassuring.

Christopher has his hair tied back with a leather cord. He's wearing blue jeans, a blue sweater, and a jacket with patches on the elbows. Patches! Long hair and patches! Well, the judge probably knows about Lone Oak professors. None of them care much about how they look. Even the *ad litem*, Claire, is wearing a wrinkled suit and scuffed heels. But Mama cares. Mama, wearing a Sunday dress, is sitting next to Claire. Jagged scraps of paper flutter from the Bible she holds firmly between both hands, and with a sinking heart Mary Lou realizes they mark verses Mama is planning to read to the judge. Well, nothing on earth will stop her if she decides to do it. Roseborough hiccups. And hiccups again. Calling attention. Oh Lord. All of it makes her want to get up and leave, just take Roseborough home and call Joe Dallas. Sighing, she looks across at *their* side. An old gray-headed man writes in a brown leather notebook. The man who wants to adopt Roseborough, Mr. O'Malley his name is, sits by the old man. Mr. O'Malley smiles when his eyes meet hers. *Too bad,* the thin smile says.

Straightening her shoulders she tells herself, *Take heart. Take heart. After all, right is right.* She is proud of the way she looks. Wearing a dress and reading glasses and a purse over her arm instead of a backpack, she looks like a grandmother ought to look. But she is so nervous. Trying to keep Roseborough from the sight of curious greedy eyes without smothering him is hard. Now that he has the hiccups, she hopes he won't cry. She doesn't want them to see how cute he is. She had not wanted to bring him. Tom Davis would have kept him, but the judge ordered it. *What if he says I can't keep Roseborough?* At this thought her heart beats faster and faster.

She looks across the room again. Mrs. O'Malley holds a purse in her lap and looks down. Father d'Acosta sits next to her. Seeing him there, she loses heart again. When she had gone to see him about Roseborough's baptism, he had said the O'Malleys would be able to give a baby everything. A nice home. An education. Love. Mr. O'Malley's smile is the smile of a greedy man, she will tell the judge if he asks. Next to Father d'Acosta is a plump nun with blue eyes and pink cheeks and a worried frown.

Roseborough's side has just as many as theirs, and she hopes that counts for something. She leans forward so she can see Anne sitting next to Tony. Anne is going to be Roseborough's godmother even though she isn't a practicing Catholic. She looks beautiful in a blue dress with her dark hair shining and her eyes lively and wise. Seeing her like that, Mary Lou knows that if Anne says the baby should stay with her, with his grandmother, even God would listen. Thinking this, she pats Roseborough and waits for the judge to enter his chambers.

5

First the judge is going around the room trying to sort out who is who. His forehead goes a long way back before his hair begins. A scar in the corner of his lips makes his mouth crooked. He wears little gold-rimmed glasses low on his nose. Looking around the room as he takes a seat, he sticks his nose out, like a hunting dog. He picks up a fountain pen and looks at Mama.

"And you are?"

"Roseborough's great-grandmother," she says. "Echo's always been a strange little thing, but we love her and . . ."

"Just a minute," the judge says. "Let's establish some guidelines. First I want to know who is before the bench. Then, since Mr. and Mrs. O'Malley have agreed to an informal hearing pursuant to their suit to proceed with their adoption of the child, we'll hear from the O'Malleys first. Is that clear to everyone?" He looks carefully all the way around the room to be sure it is clear. Then he says, "The respective lawyers are here to address any questions the O'Malley family has or the Burgandy representatives might raise. Is that clear?"

"We're not representatives. We're family," Mama says.

The judge pauses. "I'm speaking of the *ad litem* attorney," he says.

Then he begins again and Father d'Acosta says who he is and Sister Celeste says who she is. And a nurse with a wide mouth and thick glasses says she is Ms. Keenan. Then the judge nods to the man sitting by the priest. "Mr. McAfee?"

Their lawyer is old, so old they have to wait while he pushes his chair back and pushes himself up. He cannot stand very straight but he tries.

"Your Honor, we're here to decide with whom the baby should be placed while my clients proceed with the adoption process. As you know, the courts have ruled again and again that the so-called 'grandparent factor' is an improper basis for denying termination of parental rights." Mr. McAfee talks on, easy and friendly, for all the world like he is sitting in Mary Lou's kitchen in that old maple rocking chair Gundren traded for a pump. Pushing his glasses back from the tip of his nose where they have drifted, he walks over to the O'Malleys and puts his hand on Mr. O'Malley's shoulder. "Clearly then, the court must focus solely on the parent or parents whose right may be terminated. This child, a child of the court, should be properly cared for in a foster home while the O'Malleys proceed with their plans to adopt the child."

Mary Lou thinks about this while he takes off his glasses and smiles at her. *Something is wrong here.* Then it comes to her. *How can they focus on the parent when she isn't here?*

Claire stands. "Your Honor," she says, "historically and rightly the court has applied a legislative and common-law preference for placement of children in custody of relatives that it found to exist in the state apart from . . ."

Mary Lou loses track of the rest. But that first part is what matters. Anybody would agree. Where else would you put Roseborough but with his own people?

Claire shuffles through her papers, dropping some. She leans over to pick them up, then changes her mind and doesn't. "Your Honor," she says, looking over her blue glasses at the judge, "let me remind the court that this child's grandmother and great-grandmother are present in this courtroom and eager to take care of the child."

"Mr. McAfee?" the judge says.

"Here are the letters of intent that the child's mother signed," Mr. McAfee says. "These letters show what this young mother wants for this child. She wants the baby to have a home with a mother and a father, with parents who will love and cherish her child. Clearly she wants him to grow up with the O'Malleys, or else she would have signaled a change of mind by her presence here."

The judge nods and, without so much as a glance, lays the letters on his desk.

"And here is a list of the expenses the O'Malleys have incurred since they entered into the agreement with the child's mother."

"I believe we have copies of these," the judge says.

Mr. McAfee takes off his glasses and smiles at the judge. "Mr. O'Malley, please tell these folks about your decision to adopt a baby."

"Judge, we've been married for sixteen years, and for all those years my wife has prayed for the blessing of a child. And when this child came along we knew her prayers had been answered."

"Your wife has prayed?" Claire says. "The adoption is your wife's idea?"

"Attorney Morley, now just hold your horses here," the judge tells Claire. He folds his hands and nods toward the O'Malleys. "Can you tell us how you felt when you first saw the child?"

Mr. O'Malley says, "We have never seen the baby. We were in California when the child was born. And my wife was heartsick when the hospital called the next day to say the child had been kidnapped."

His wife again, Mary Lou thinks. Claire is on her feet. "Your Honor, the law specifically exempts parents who abduct their children. A parent cannot abduct a child unless the parent has lost his parental rights. And in this case the mother had not lost hers. She had only said her *intent* was to allow the baby's adoption."

It makes sense. Nobody would call Echo taking her very own baby from the hospital kidnapping! Mary Lou nods her head in agreement.

"Your Honor," Mr. McAfee says, "Mr. O'Malley misspoke. The more accurate term is 'abandoned.' This child was abandoned. Left on a doorstep."

Claire's turn. "He was not abandoned. He was placed in the arms of Dr. Anne Hamilton." She turns and points toward Anne.

Then the next one to talk, the nurse, makes it easy to see why Echo had changed her mind. The nurse, Ms. Keenan, tells how the computers were down and that is why they brought a to-be-adopted baby to his mother and left him there practically all day. When Ms. Keenan finishes she apologizes again for the computers.

But then the judge says, "And does Roseborough's attorney have anything? Ms. Morley? Anything you'd like to ask Ms. Keenan?"

"Yes," Claire says. "The question concerns bonding. Ms. Keenan, in your opinion, when does bonding begin between a mother and her child?"

Well, Mary Lou could have answered that. It begins with that first little butterfly kick. Or with the baby's first cry. And it's a thing that goes on and on.

But the judge says the nurse isn't qualified and tells her not to answer. Then Claire asks the nurse if she knew the O'Malleys. She purses her lips and flicks an invisible speck off her sleeve.

"I don't know them," she says. "But I spoke to Mr. O'Malley when he called the hospital to say it would be three or four days before they could pick up the baby."

Claire looks puzzled. "Ms. Keenan, what was the emergency that kept this couple from rushing home to claim this newborn baby?"

Ms. Keenan uncrosses her legs and crosses them again the other way. "I believe it was a golf tournament."

The judge raises his eyebrows and slowly nods. He leans back in his chair, folding his arms over his stomach. "Seems to me that right now would be a good time to hear from folks who were with the mother shortly before the birth of the child. I think they're right neutral about all this. Sister Celeste, what about it? What about this missing mother? Missing father?"

Sister Celeste stands and folds her hands just below her cross. Her face is as white as flour. Her hands are plump. When she talks her voice is plump.

"I don't know a thing about the father," Sister Celeste says.

"But the mother. Let me think what to say about Echo. I didn't want to take care of her, and I said as much to Father, but after a while, I liked having her there. In just the short time she was with us, the garden came alive. Everything bloomed. Even the weeds. And the birds came." She waits so long to go on that Mary Lou thinks she might be finished. But then she says, "I've never met anyone like her. The phrase that comes to mind is 'endangered species.' "

"A little mystic."

"A mystic, Father d'Acosta?"

"A figure of speech, Ms. Morley."

"Father d'Acosta," the judge said, "could you tell us why you used the word 'mystic' when you spoke of Roseborough's mother?"

Father d'Acosta, tall and thin, stands and, leaning forward, spreads the long fingers of his hands on the railing. "In the garden of which Sister Celeste spoke, a figure of Our Lady of Guadeloupe stands," he says slowly. He straightens so that just the tips of his fingers touch the railing. "Some years ago the figure was vandalized; that is, beheaded. This girl, this young mother-to-be, looking like a young Madonna herself, fashioned a head from stocking material, embroidered a face on the head, and secured it to the figure. One would have thought the effect would have bordered on the grotesque or, at the very least, the comic. But it is, in fact, quite lovely. She is a strange young woman, in some ways still a child." Looking into Mary Lou's face, he says, "She is gentle with all living things." Then he raises his chin and looks hard at the bishop. "I think she would be a very good mother."

"Still," the judge says, "we must consider the wishes of the child's mother. In the interim the child will be placed in a foster home. I'm ordering the Child Protective Services . . ."

"But wait! There's this!" Holding Roseborough, Mary Lou is on her feet and speaking to the judge, to the O'Malleys, to the lawyers, speaking to them all: "There's this about Echo. Echo is not a mystic. And she's not an endangered species. She is my daughter. And sometimes with a mother and a daughter, well, it's like, . . . well, what if a bird looked into its nest and saw a fish swimming there? How could she follow it into the ocean or even understand why it wants to go there? Well, that's how it is with me and Echo. I don't know why Echo's, you might say, migratory, but Your Honor, I'm a homebody and Roseborough belongs with me until Echo comes home."

The judge nods, takes off his glasses, and puts them on the table in front of him. "Mr. O'Malley, Mrs. O'Malley, would you like a few minutes to . . ." But he stops when he sees that Mrs. O'Malley has left the courtroom. Throwing up his hands, Mr. O'Malley says they don't need a few minutes. After the judge and Claire and their lawyer whisper a minute, the judge rises. "It's a nonsuit," he declares briskly.

So it's settled. Roseborough will be exactly where he should be. With his grandmother. But she feels terrible. Her heart has hardened toward Echo. And this is the worst thing, next to losing Gundren, that has ever happened to her.

Chapter Seventeen

1

ALTHOUGH Father d'Acosta is preparing for Roseborough's baptism, his act of defiance before the bishop continues to nip like a little terrier at his sense of well-being. In fact it had kept him awake last night, and the first thing he remembered this morning was the look of displeasure on the bishop's face. Placing the white stole over his alb he is still somewhat amazed, for it had not been his intent to defy the bishop. But then he had said, "I think Echo would be a very good mother," said for all the world to hear, and at that moment he had seen the look of displeasure cross the bishop's face. *It is now in the hands of God,* he tells himself firmly. Determined to focus his thoughts and prayers toward the child and the sacrament of baptism, he enters the sanctuary, reverently kneels and prays:

Dear God, I ask your blessings upon this child. I pray that his grandmother will be strong enough and wise enough to love and cherish the child by following in the path of our Blessed Savior. And I fervently pray for Echo, this child's mother, who seems in some strange way to be almost like a mystic, young but still, somewhat like a mystic. I believe with all my heart that as a true child of God, she will be a good mother. And so I ask your blessing on Echo and on all those who come to witness this sacrament of baptism: the believers and heretics, the saints and blasphemers, all Catholics and Baptists.

As the bells ring to herald the coming baptism, Father d'Acosta stands, then kneels again hastily. *Father, we pray for the soul of Gundren, this child's grandfather. Amen.*

As if summoned by prayer the heavy doors of the church are swung open. Hearing the soft chattering of Gypsies instantly stilled as they enter the church, he turns and sees the women, sees their bright shawls that glow in the soft light of the church, their barbaric jewelry reflecting even the candlelight. The men, trousers low on the hips, two or three with guitars held tenderly, quietly follow the women into the church. Moving past the Guatemalan crucifix the Gypsies come down the aisles to take their places near the Virgin of Guadeloupe, to sit beneath the stained-glass window of the sainted Margaret Mary Alacoque of France.

Seeing them there his heart rises up, catches in his throat. But when he looks at each face and sees that Echo's is not among them, he is filled with dismay. Then solemnly he lifts his arms to the congregation, signaling the procession to begin.

Holding Roseborough in her arms, Anne waits for the music to begin. She looks at the baby's face. Asleep, his dark eyelashes etch the shape of his eyes. Now and then his small mouth flickers into a smile, then moves in perfect mimicry of nursing, and her heart turns over. She loves this baby. This is the surprise of it. She has been with him for only a brief time, and she loves him. She likes all the shapes his mouth can make and the way he smells, and she likes his thin eyelids with their tiny blue veins and his hands. He is very funny to watch. And noisy. Such a presence! She adjusts a soft fold of his long baptismal gown that hangs over her arm. "You're a wonderful baby," she tells him.

They have come early to the church, Anne and Sister Celeste, in order to dress Roseborough in the white batiste dress Sister Celeste has made and embroidered with three small crosses and as many tiny roses. "For Our Lady," Sister Celeste had said, explaining the roses.

The organ swells, the choir bursts into song, the procession begins. When she reaches the cross, Anne bows her head:

> *Dear God, when is the last time I said a prayer? But here in this church, I pray that You will bless my godchild and watch over him. Hold him and Mary Lou safe. And all the single parents. Bless them. And me, as I fly to England or Italy or China. Thankfully I am no longer afraid to fly, but bless the pilots, just in case. And bless Sister Alicia and Christopher and Mary Lou. Bless all those who have come into my life this year. And wherever she is, bless Echo. And for Mary Lou's sake, bring her home safely. Amen.*

Roseborough stirs and a bootie slips from his foot. Tony leans forward to retrieve it and his shoulder brushes Mary

Lou's. Mary Lou takes the bootie from his hand and lifts the tucked folds of the dress to slip it back on.

The organ in full crescendo, the choir sings: "I sing the mighty power of God, that made the mountains rise." Mary Lou lifts her head and, following the cross through colors cast by stained glass, hears the choir singing of seas and skies and the moon and the stars. The thought comes to Mary Lou that here, this, is Echo's song. She prays:

Dear Jesus, I have loved Echo for a long time, all her life, but now I am afraid. The fear is a stone in my heart. When I saw this little baby, I think that's when it happened. Wild horses couldn't have torn me away from Echo when she was little. Now I am afraid I do not love Echo. If I can't love Echo, how can I truly love anyone, even this baby? So please dear Lord, this baby needs your blessing. Amen.

"In lieu of the parents, I ask this grandparent: What name do you give your child?"

"Roseborough."

"What do you ask of God's Church for Roseborough?"

"Baptism."

Tony has never been a godfather before and Roseborough is a cute little baby, even if he does look like a girl in that dress. Tony prays:

Heavenly Father, I think Mary Lou is a mighty special woman. The first time she walked into Dr. Hamilton's class with a worm in one ear and an apple in the other, she caught my eye. I know I can take care of her. But now there's this baby (I'm his godfather), and what if Echo comes home? Well, I just don't know. Thinking about being a husband, a father, and a grandfather overnight, well, it's a tall order. But I know I love her, and I'm thinking about just jumping out there and proposing when the time is right. Oh, and bless Roseborough. Amen.

The priest takes the baby in his arms and says, "Roseborough, this community welcomes you with great joy. In its name I claim you for Christ our Savior by the sign of his cross. I now trace the cross on your forehead and invite your godparents to do the same."

Seeing the priest dip his hand into the oil and touch Roseborough with it, Mama flinches. She talks to God:

Jesus, save us! Don't let the hot oil burn the baby. Mary Lou could have waited until Roseborough was old enough to be saved like any normal person. But she has been dead set on doing what Echo wants, and as she says, baptizing a baby won't hurt it. Thank you, Lord, for the music and the sweet blessings. In some ways Catholic is better. And Roseborough can be saved when he's older. And, dear Lord, help me take care of Mary Lou. Lord, I thought when she was this old she would have a husband taking care of her, but then Gundren got himself killed. Well, this is a happy day. But Lord, I don't know how Mary Lou got herself in with so many Catholics. Mary Lou's neighbor Tom Davis is one; and Tony. I like Tony, and I hoped that maybe someday, when Mary Lou gets over Gundren, she might take an interest in Tony. Or Tom Davis even. Mr. Davis would probably appreciate Mary Lou, his first wife being atheist and all. But now Mary Lou has taken on the job of raising Roseborough, and Mr. Davis might not want a ready-made family. But what else can Mary Lou do? He is, after all, her own little grandson. And he is a darling. Bless Roseborough. Amen.

Father d'Acosta turns to the congregation and, holding Roseborough high in his hands, he says: "God bless you, Roseborough, in the name of the Father and the Son and the Holy Spirit." He places the baby in Anne's arms once more and, holding out his arms to the congregation:

"Go in peace," he says.

"Thanks be to God," they respond.

Pleased with the baptism, eager for lunch, the choir bursts into joyful song as they join the recessional, following the cross down the aisle and out into a surprisingly beneficent January day.

The triumphant sound of the music follows Roseborough's family and friends and the women of the altar guild, who have prepared the celebration, out of the church and into the walled courtyard. Tables with yellow cloths have been placed here and there and on one, wineglasses, crystal plates, and a vase filled with Queen Anne's lace and wood violets and wild lilies, all from Echo's garden. The moss-covered stone walls, the bubbling fountain, and the garden, more wild than not, offer an air of privacy, of sanctuary. Before the east wall the statue of Our Lady of Guadeloupe stands and, adorned with the head made by Echo, smiles calmly and benevolently upon the glittering Gypsies, the shivering Protestants, and the satisfied Catholics. All this awaits the coming of the priest.

The sun is shining enough to take the chill out of the air. Mary Lou is glad about that. Holding Roseborough she sits on a garden bench beside Miss Weems. Tony stands nearby watching Mary Lou as if she might vanish before his eyes.

When Mary Lou looks at the head Echo made for the statue, she has to smile. It looks exactly like the rag dolls Mama used to make for Echo when she was a baby. But Father d'Acosta sees a lot in it. And Sister Celeste does, too.

Everybody has come for Roseborough's baptism. Betty and Maggie from her class. And Dylan and his son. Even Ed has come. And Christopher and Claire. Miss Weems and Josie have come from Weatherford. They left early enough to eat breakfast at the Dairy Queen before coming on to the church with Maudie. And here is Gundren's family, the women with their flashing smiles and glittering jewelry and Aunt Labelle leaning to tell Mary Lou and Miss Weems that Roseborough looks exactly like Gundren. The men stand back, not saying a word, but taking off their hats and nodding to Mary Lou and the baby.

Now Father d'Acosta, his vestments flying, comes hurrying out to join them, and the popping of champagne corks announces the celebration has begun. Mama, touching his arm, says, "Pastor, I thought it was nice, all those things you said over Roseborough's head."

Father d'Acosta gives her a big smile and says what a handsome grandmother she is, and she sees no need to correct him.

Then a Gypsy picks up his guitar and strums it until he finds a tune. "Amazing Grace" is what he plays. Mary Lou has always thought of that as a Baptist song. But the way Father d'Acosta is singing along, maybe it isn't.

"That's Mama's favorite song in all the world," she tells Miss Weems.

"It's a favorite of mine, too," Miss Weems says, folding back the blanket from Roseborough's face so she can see him better. Then she examines his slip, embroidered with his name and date of birth. "That's pretty handwork," she says.

"Thank you. Sister Celeste embroidered it. Oh, Miss Weems, I'm glad you came," Mary Lou says. "When Roseborough is older I'll tell him you came all the way from Weatherford to see him baptized."

"Why, it's no trip at all over here," Miss Weems says, looking carefully at Roseborough. "Honey, this baby looks exactly like you. Never mind what anybody else says. Here now, you let me take him a while. Give your arms a rest."

But when Mary Lou puts Roseborough in Miss Weems's lap, he looks so uncomfortable she wants to take him back.

Roseborough opens his eyes and sighs.

"Miss Weems, holding a baby is just like holding a puppy," Mary Lou says, shifting the baby to Miss Weems's shoulder. "Babies like to nuzzle right up next to your neck."

"I see what you mean," Miss Weems says, patting Roseborough's bottom. "And he even smells like a puppy," she chuckles.

"Miss Weems, I've missed you," Mary Lou says. "And Josie, too."

"Now that I've made the drive once, I'll be coming over more," Miss Weems says comfortably.

Now Josie is laughing at something Christopher has said. Looking at Christopher wearing a black sweater under a black jacket, Mary Lou decides he looks more like a priest than the priest. Roseborough begins to fuss and Sister Celeste takes him on her lap and gets out his bottle. Aunt Labelle leans over and kisses him.

"His name is Roseborough," Mary Lou says, before Aunt Labelle can think about giving him another name.

Then Dylan and Ed are pouring more champagne, and Josie is passing around cookies on a tray, and one of the Gypsies is playing a song that sounds like a dance. And people are talking and laughing and, all at once, it's a party. A party for Roseborough.

Well, Roseborough is baptized, Mary Lou thinks. Just like, just *as* Echo wanted. And here in this place is everybody in the world she loves, everybody but Echo, the one she loves best. *Used* to love. And she should be happy. After all, it's not every day a grandson is baptized.

A breeze stirs, bringing with it the scent of horses running and wild clover blooming. Wondering where it comes from and *knowing* at the same time, she takes a deep breath and walks over to Echo's garden. She leans to smell a tall green plant with milky leaves and blooms of tiny white flowers. Its scent is sharp, bitter, the smell of ragweed. But now the clover scent is stronger. Arousing. She leans to another plant just as Tony hands her a glass of wine. It's Tony. Maybe his new boots. She looks toward him and smiles, but Tony is looking solemnly at the garden Echo made. Now Christopher and Anne, holding Roseborough, come to stand in the garden.

"Christopher, do you want to hold him?" Anne offers and seeing Christopher's startled refusal, she laughs.

Mary Lou smiles, looking at the rag doll head on the garden statue. Tony's face reflects an entire gamut of human emotions—surprise, adoration, something close to shock, as he looks at the baby, then Mary Lou, then the baby again.

Holding the baby on her shoulder, Anne possesses an aura of perfect serenity. *She's amazing,* Christopher thinks. *So beautiful. And she's brave.* He forces himself to look away. He needs to find his wife. And when he sees her again, will he love her? Will she love him? But on this golden day, he's alive. And he's here. With Anne and her entourage. Catching her eye, he winks. And now he hears the lazy tantalizing sound of the guitar and smells the bitter-lemon scents of the garden. When he sees an unlikely flower, bright red, high on the garden wall, he lifts his head to the brisk blue of the sky. *Oh what a day!* he thinks. *It's a day for riding across the Serengeti Plains. Or for swimming the Aegean Sea.*

Anne shifts Roseborough to her shoulder so he can see better. *"There,"* she tells him. "There."

Now Christopher takes the baby, gently cradling him in his arms. Roseborough looks at him sternly. Unblinkingly. After a minute he bursts into loud frantic crying. Anne takes him again. The crying stops.

Christopher laughs a resounding laugh that bounces across the garden. "He likes you," he says. "And I understand that."

Anne smiles. Then she says, "Mary Lou, Tony, I've decided to travel for a while. And study. I have a sabbatical."

"For the summer?"

"For a year. I'll be doing research and writing, but we can e-mail back and forth. But you don't have a computer, do you?"

"I'll get one. I will. And I'll write letters," Mary Lou says.

Anne sees a fleeting frown followed by a quick smile as Mary Lou tucks in a small foot that has slipped from under the baby's blanket. *She looks better,* Anne thinks. "Oh, please. Write me wonderful old-fashioned letters. With pictures of Roseborough."

"I will," Mary Lou says.

"Dr. Hamilton, I learned a whole lot in our class," Tony says.

"Me too," Anne says slowly. "I guess I've learned that no one lives alone. Not really."

They look at her, puzzled. Then they smile fondly, proudly at their teacher.

Watching Roseborough, Mary Lou sees Gundren's wide eyes peeping over Anne's shoulder. She looks at all those who have come for his baptism. Miss Weems, her dress, as always black, her face and hair so clean she looks pink. Josie, finally with enough money for both breasts. And Dylan, strong for now. And Father d'Acosta, his stern look melting away as he throws his head back and laughs again at something Josie has said. And her in-laws. Two of the women, their long hair behind their backs, their golden bracelets glittering in the sun, their fringed shawls—one red and the other black with red roses—swaying as the women move to the music. The guitarist finds a beat. In a minute the women will be dancing.

Christopher and Anne walk over to the Gypsy who is playing.

"Can you play a song called 'Let It Be'?" she asks. The man nods and strums the chorus. *When I find myself in times of trouble,* Dylan is whistling, Anne humming the words. And now Father d'Acosta robustly joins the duet, singing: "Mother Mary comes to me. Whispering words of wisdom, let it be."

When Tony takes Mary Lou home, he stares at her. And stares. A Roseborough stare.

"What is it?" she says.

"I want you to think about me. About me and you together."

"And Roseborough?"

"Of course, Roseborough."

She leans toward him. Holding Roseborough, she puts her head on his shoulder. "You smell so good," she tells him.

"It's Ralph Lauren," he says.

"I thought it was your boots," she laughs.

He kisses her open mouth. "Put the baby down," he says.

"I can't. He needs me."

"I need you. Put the baby down."

"No. Not just yet."

"Will you think about us? About you and me together?"

"I will, Tony," she says solemnly. "Will you come tomorrow?"

He puts his hand on her face, cups her chin. Then he leans and kisses Roseborough. "Good-bye, little fellow," he says. "I'll see you tomorrow."

Walking backward all the way to his truck, he stumbles, catches himself. "Whoops," he says and grinning, touches his hat with his finger before driving away.

By nine o'clock that night Mary Lou is run down and almost too tired to take a bath. Stepping into the warm water she scrunches down to let the soapsuds run over her shoulders. She closes her eyes and relaxes into the comforting warmth of the bath. Then she steps out, dries herself off, and puts on her gown. In the living room she sits down to rest for a minute and then, too tired to get up, she stretches out on the couch.

When she wakes up she remembers the baby. For just a minute she had forgotten about Roseborough. She walks down the hall to check on him, turning out lights as she goes. She tiptoes into his room.

And there is Echo.

Echo curled around the sleeping baby. Her lashes black against her cheeks, her black hair spread against the pillow. Hardly breathing, Mary Lou stands there, watching the two of them sleep. When she had last seen her, Echo was a young girl learning to live without a father. Now she is a woman grown.

From the light in the hall she sees the bulk of her, still with all the baby fat. She wears a dress Mary Lou has never seen. It surprises her. Somehow she'd always thought, when she saw her again, she'd be wearing the same jeans and with the red sweater over her shoulders.

Roseborough stirs and props a tiny foot on the back of Echo's arm. Echo turns and opens her eyes. "Hello, Mama," she says. "Isn't this baby the sweetest thing?" she says and sleeps again.

Then the years fall away and Mary Lou hears her voice. "Isn't this kitten the sweetest thing?" and she sees her, clear as anything, holding a kitten, sitting on the back steps of the house, and looking up at her. Even then a wanderer.

Remembering the past and seeing the present, the stone in her heart begins to dissolve, to melt into tears that roll down her face. She sees the dark circles under Echo's eyes. Or maybe it is the shadow from the hall light. But here, here is Echo in her own bed, and with the baby, and safe, like a dream. Silently the tears continue to fall. She loves Echo. She always has. *Why did you leave? Where have you been?* she will ask tomorrow. Tomorrow is soon enough.

Gradually Echo's breath slows, becomes steady. Roseborough's little chest rises and falls. Quick little breaths.

After a while May Lou puts on her coat and goes outside and sits on the steps. She isn't surprised that Echo has come home. She hadn't even been surprised when she saw her, asleep on the blue-and-white bedspread. She has always believed she would come home.

Echo might be gone tomorrow.

The thought comes. Like the shadow of a bird flying over.

And . . . yet . . . remembering Roseborough's foot propped on Echo's arm like a tether—small, fragile, but still a tether, Echo's home now, she tells herself. But she *will* leave. If not tomorrow, one day soon. And she'll take Roseborough. But Mary Lou will always love her and her baby. Why, loving Echo is breathing.

She looks up at the sky. The night is still and beautiful. The bare limbs of the pecan trees are etched across the stars. She hears the hoot of an owl and the far-off sound of a dog barking and the swish of tires on I-35. She stands and stretches toward the moon. It is full and shining on Lone Oak and on everybody she loves. And it is shining on her, too.

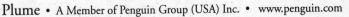

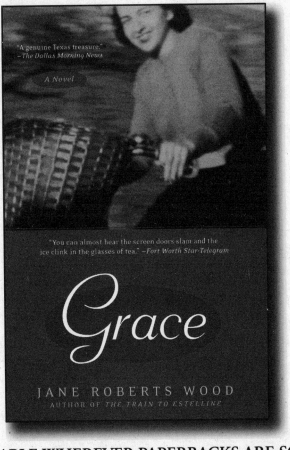